Audacity

Other Walker Adventure novels by Alan Evans

DAUNTLESS
SHIP OF FORCE
SEEK AND DESTROY

Audacity

Alan Evans

Walker and Company
New York

First published in the United States of America in 1987 by the
Walker Publishing Company, Inc.

Library of Congress Cataloging-in-Publication Data

Evans, Alan, 1930–
    Audacity.

    1. World War, 1914–1918—Fiction. I. Title.
PR6055.V13A97 1987   823'.914   87–18956
ISBN 0-8027-0995-8

Printed in the United States of America

10 9 8 7 6 5 4 3 2 1

Acknowledgments

I have received help from many sources while preparing this book and my thanks go to:

The National Maritime Museum and the Imperial War Museum for much information and in particular, from the former, plans of H.M.S. *Hyderabad* (on which *Audacity* is based). The latter also has a fine model of the ship at Duxford.

Chaz Bowyer, author of *Sopwith Camel – King of Combat*, published by Glasney Press of Falmouth.

The Royal Air Force Museum, the Shuttleworth Collection, London University Library, Naval Library and the Bank of England.

Catherine Gavin, Quintin E. K. Merrilees, Mrs. Christina Niven and her son, David.

The staff of the libraries at Walton-on-Thames and Weybridge were kind and helpful, as always.

But, again as always, any errors are mine!

Alan Evans
February 1985

Contents

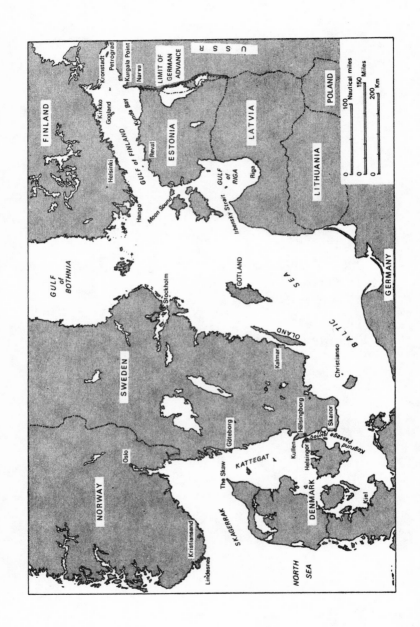

1

A Plot

Commander David Cochrane Smith lay uneasily awake beside the young woman sleeping warm and close. Very faintly, somewhere in the town, a clock struck two. He stared up at the ceiling of the hotel room and wondered just what 'modifications' were being made to his new ship, H.M.S. *Audacity*. This was early April 1918. Although the fourth winter of the war was supposedly behind, a bitter wind still moaned outside and hurled rain to batter at the curtained windows. *Audacity* lay only two miles away at Rosyth in the Firth of Forth but he and her crew, every man-jack, had been ordered on local leave until the work on her was completed. The woman had been waiting, fondly, patiently, for him when he had come ashore. Doubtless there would be whispering behind his back. To hell with them all.

He thought this was a bad time of night for a man to examine his life and it was not conducive to quiet sleep. He would not think of the girl he had loved in Venice.* That wound was healed but the scar was still there. It was not useful, either, to think of the house in Norfolk left to him by his grandfather. He had seen it only once, warm red brick on a cold winter's day and the furniture sheeted like ghosts. There was a photograph of the woman he thought might be his mother. A man should have a place of his own and now he did. But he had yet to spend a night in it.

He did not bear the old man's name, had been brought up by a Reuben Smith and his wife in a village shop, also in Norfolk but a long way from the house. He was still by

* *Seek Out and Destroy!*

right the old admiral's grandson and could take the family name if he wished, but he would not. He had made his way as David Cochrane Smith and so he would remain. He had inherited a mortgage with the house and no money. There was no legal restriction to prevent him selling the house but his grandfather's will held a plea that he would keep it. Although he had only his pay of three hundred pounds a year and some small savings, that was the last wish of a dying man and Smith would honour it. Besides, an empty house and a lack of money need not be problems: the young woman beside him had money enough . . .

A door slammed below like a distant gun and his thoughts went back to *Audacity*. She was a Q-ship, ostensibly an unarmed merchantman, intended to entice a U-boat into making an attack and surfacing, when hidden weapons would be exposed and used to sink the German. It was a dangerous ploy that had worked in the past because the U-boats swallowed the bait, but they knew about Q-ships now. Merchant shipping sailed in convoy these days and any ship steaming alone, inviting attack, would be suspected by a submarine commander. He would not surface, as he probably would have done a year ago, to sink her from close range and economically with gunfire, thus saving his precious torpedoes. Now he would use those fish. Smith had asked for an independent command, said he did not want to go back to the fleet so they gave him *Audacity*. *Lunacy* would have been a better name. Certainly the day of the Q-ship, as a weapon against U-boats, was over.

The coal fire settled in the grate, crunched and flamed. In the quiet that followed he heard the footsteps in the passage outside and then there came a soft knuckling at the door. He slid naked from the bed. The wavering light from the fire cast his shadow on the wall as he crossed the room to stand with his head against the door panel. He was lean, not tall, his fair hair tangled from restless sleep. The firelight made black shadows in the hollows of the thin face. It was not handsome, the pale blue eyes wrinkled at the corners, but still the face of a young man. He asked softly, "Who is it?"

"Buckley, sir." That was the thick, deep, Geordie growl of the big leading-seaman. "We've got orders for sailing. Immediate."

"Wait." Smith dressed quickly in his working clothes, the garb of a merchant skipper as befitted the captain of a Q-ship: old reefer jacket and blue serge trousers. He kept one naval uniform aboard *Audacity*. The others, and his civilian clothing, he left in the wardrobe. The hotel would keep them until – if – he returned to claim them. The woman had promised to see to that.

She slept on as he dressed and he glanced at her but did not wake her. There was nothing now to say but goodbye and he had warned her of that at the start. It had been good while it lasted but now it was finished and she would go back to London where she had found him before he was given *Audacity*. She had followed him here, this was her hotel room. He had a fondness for her but she owned too much already and he would not be added to her list.

He took out his notebook and pencil, tore out a sheet and wrote quickly: 'Sailing orders . . .' He added a few stilted words of endearment and left the paper on the mantelpiece. Then he picked up his cap and the shabby tweed overcoat, his holdall with his razor and toothbrush jammed in one pocket, left the room and closed the door quietly behind him.

Buckley stood massive in sou'-wester, sea-boots and oilskins that dripped into a pool on the carpet. "I've got a cab waiting, sir." He had his back to the solitary gas-jet hissing at the end of the passage so that his face was in shadow, but it was not a face that would show disapproval anyway. They had sailed together many times. Buckley had criticised as 'bloody daft' some of Smith's reckless exploits but never by look or word did he pass moral judgments.

Smith asked, "When did you get word?"

"First lieutenant sent a message a half-hour back, sir."

Smith was supposed to stay in the same hotel as Ross – the first lieutenant – but instead had left his address with him. Ross would have sent messages to all the crew to return to *Audacity*. Some had their homes within a mile or two and the others were aboard a depot ship.

Buckley opened the door of the cab for Smith. The cabbie on his box and the horse between the shafts both slumped miserably under the rain. Smith climbed quickly into the cab.

As it rattled and swayed through the night he wondered where his orders would take him. The Atlantic? North Sea? Possibly even back to the Mediterranean?

He paid off the cab at the dockyard gate, showed his pass to the sentry and walked down to the ship with Buckley a pace behind his left shoulder. *Audacity* lay at the end of a jetty, no other ship near her and without a light save one small lamp at the head of the gangway. Smith looked for any change in her but saw none.

She was built as a replica of a three-island tramp but she was faster than that type of ship, with a full speed of fifteen or sixteen knots. The three 'islands' each carried a hidden gun, a twelve-pounder forward on the fo'c'sle and another aft on the poop, with a four-inch on the superstructure amidships in a housing abaft the funnel. There were four torpedo tubes under the superstructure and four bomb-throwers in the holds forward and aft. She was designed to look like a ship half-laden and low in the sea but in fact most of her hull stood out of the water and she had a remarkably shallow draught – only four or five feet. The theory was that a U-boat's torpedoes would pass under the ship, the submarine's commander would assume they had not run true and so would surface to sink her by gunfire. Smith doubted that any commander would surface and believed that, even if he did, it would not be conveniently close but a mile or more away. The U-boat would then be a very small target in a gun action with all the odds in her favour. The thin-skinned, high-sided *Audacity* would be torn to pieces.

Smith had said all this, forcefully, a month before when he was given command. He was told that his comments were noted and that Their Lordships of the Admiralty knew what they were doing. He came to know his crew – all volunteers – during that month of working up *Audacity*.

He did not know how they would behave in action but he was sure they would do their best for him.

Were those two of his crew now, figures in the darkness fifty yards or so ahead of Buckley and himself? They could only be going to the ship and one seemed to have a kitbag on his shoulder.

His thoughts returned to his orders. It might not be U-boats. There had been a hint that the 'modifications' were to fit *Audacity* for a special mission. That could mean against the German raider operating out of Kiel, a merchantman with hidden weapons like *Audacity*. But hers were four big six-inch guns and she hunted not submarines but British merchant shipping. She had sunk three in one cruise and was expected to sail again. Was *Audacity* supposed to act as both bait and trap? If so, it would be as bad as decoying U-boats. Those big guns would hammer *Audacity* into scrap.

But not if he could help it. Wherever his orders took him he would bring ship and crew safe home again if it was humanly possible. He made that resolution as he splashed through the pools of rainwater on the jetty.

The ship loomed above him. The pair ahead of them had climbed the gangway and now moved beneath the light at the head of it. One paused to look back and Smith caught a glimpse of a white face, chin tilted so that the dark eyes looked down on him, almost arrogantly. Then the figure passed on out of the light and was lost in the darkness.

Smith stopped dead in his tracks, disbelieving, then strode up the gangway. Lieutenant Ross, tall, lantern-jawed, twenty-six years old and newly married, waited close by the light and just aft of the superstructure. He was regular Navy, but like Smith himself he had to conform to *Audacity*'s disguise: his oilskins were not regulation and his old blue cap was that of a mate in the merchant service.

Ross had an awed respect for Smith's reputation at sea but disapproved of his behaviour ashore. Smith knew it and was wryly amused.

But not at all amused now, as he demanded, "That was a woman just come aboard?"

"Yes, sir. The admiral told me to send a man to fetch

13

her and her baggage. He's showing her to the wardroom now. Lieutenant McLeod's there already."

"McLeod?"

"An extra officer. He came with the admiral and he's got charts with him so I suppose he's a navigator but he looks like a gorilla." Ross added quickly, "The admiral's waiting in your cabin, sir. He said he wanted to see you as soon as you came aboard."

That meant now but Smith hesitated. He asked, "What has the yard done to the ship?"

"I only know what I've found since I came aboard a half-hour ago. They've ripped out all the bomb-throwers and torpedo tubes, knocked up a couple of new cabins in what used to be one of the bomb-throwers' messes."

"Any new equipment?"

"None that I know of. I was told not to call the crews of the bomb-throwers so they're still ashore. They don't even know we're sailing."

"The admiral told you?"

The lieutenant nodded. "Came to our hotel himself." Ross had been staying there with his young wife. "He wanted to know why you weren't there so I told him you'd left your address with me and I'd send a man for you. He said he wanted you aboard at once."

Smith started for the ladder leading up to the super-structure and his cabin but paused with one foot on the first tread. "What about this woman? Who is she? Why is she aboard?"

Ross shook his head. "I don't know much, sir. She was staying in our hotel. There were a dozen or so people there who'd been working in our embassy at Petrograd. You'll remember they sent nearly all the staff home through Finland and Sweden, then by ship from Norway, just before the Russians closed their frontier with Finland. She was one of them." He paused as if picking his words.

Smith prompted him impatiently, "Well?"

"The others cold-shouldered her," Ross said unhappily, unable to find a more tactful way. "They called her the 'Russian Whore'."

"*What?*"

14

"It seems she was – well, friendly – with a number of Russian officers and the rest of the people at the embassy thought she'd let the side down."

And now she was in *Audacity*'s wardroom. Smith hid his anger; she was there on the admiral's orders. He turned away, climbed the ladders on the starboard side to the bridge and pushed open the door of the wheelhouse that stood at the centre of it. Before him was the wheel and the compass binnacle. Rain streamed down the windows to his right and through them he had the helmsman's view of *Audacity*'s foredeck, the hatches and the mast, the fo'c'sle. There was no helmsman now, the wheelhouse was empty and the chart table in the far left-hand corner was bare. The door to Smith's cabin was on his left and he tapped on it, took off his cap and entered.

Opening the door had broken the contact and switched off the light but as the door closed behind him the light came on again. The cabin was ten feet square, with a round table at its centre. On the starboard side, to his left now and close by the door were a washstand and beyond it a leather-covered couch. On the port side were his bunk and a wardrobe. Just to his right, an arm's length away, was a small desk. A man was sitting in the chair beside it and turned so he faced the door and Smith. He was a big man in a dark grey civilian suit. His face was square, bushy-browed and big-nosed, the thinning hair on his skull trimmed short and neatly brushed. Rear-Admiral Blackledge had personally given Smith command of *Audacity*. Now he nodded and spoke curtly, "Sit down."

Smith perched on the edge of the couch, hung his cap on the end of the washstand where it dripped, and waited . . .

Blackledge watched him, thinking: This man Smith shows nothing. Whatever he feels is locked up inside him. Odd chap, with those eyes that look right through you. With his record he should go a long way in the service, except he speaks his mind too much and to the wrong people – and now he's getting himself talked about again. Another woman. . . Ross had to send for him. But he's here in very good time, waiting, ready. And he won't ask why.

Smith wondered if they might have installed secret equipment in his ship – some form of listening device for detecting U-boats? And where was he bound this time? But he would be told everything soon enough.

Blackledge took a bulky envelope from his pocket and tossed it on to the table. It slid across the polished wood and stopped within Smith's reach. "Your orders. Open them when you're at sea. I'll tell you as much as you need to know now and answer any questions I can. What do you know of the situation in Russia?"

Russia! The Murmansk run? Around the top of Norway, that was the only way in and out of Russia now her frontier with Finland was closed. Smith said, "I know there's been revolution, the Bolsheviks are in power and now Russia is neutral." He knew a great deal more than that but left it there, suspecting he was going to be told what he didn't know.

Blackledge nodded. "After the Bolsheviks seized power they asked Germany for an armistice and wanted to discuss terms. Germany granted the armistice last December but pressed for peace on *her* terms. While the Bolsheviks argued among themselves the Germans continued to advance, until the end of February this year when the Treaty of Brest-Litovsk was finally signed. By that time they'd over-run the southern shore of the Baltic up to and including Estonia. They're within a hundred miles of Petrograd and they control the Baltic.

"The Russian Fleet lies at Kronstadt, off Petrograd: seven battleships, nine cruisers, seventy destroyers, twenty-six submarines. They are within reach of the Germans. If these were added to their High Seas Fleet it would have near parity with our Grand Fleet in capital ships, and overwhelming numerical superiority in destroyers. The Bolsheviks have promised this will not happen but our government is not certain that they will, or indeed will be able to, keep their word." Blackledge went on quietly, "That Fleet in German hands could mean us losing the war. At best it would be enormously prolonged. With Russia out of it, many German divisions have been transferred to face us on the Western Front, all the Zeppelins have been withdrawn from the Baltic and few aircraft are left there. They are massing for an attack in the west. We know it; they aren't bothering to hide the fact. And we *must* stop them. All could hang on the next few weeks."

Smith sat still, thinking of more years of slaughter, more millions killed or mutilated. What could *he* do? What of his determination to save *Audacity* and the men aboard her? What did the admiral intend for her?

Blackledge went on, "Our embassy in Petrograd has been in touch with a group of Russian naval officers, anti–Bolshevik and loyal to the Tsar. They are prepared to sink some ships of the Fleet at Kronstadt, blocking the rest in harbour. In return they want three hundred thousand pounds in gold, one-third to be paid in advance to meet 'expenses' – probably bribes. You will deliver this gold to them, one hundred thousand pounds' worth, with all despatch."

Smith stared at him, trying to take in the details of this plot and his part in it. The dangers and obstacles crowded into his mind. The Murmansk run was bad enough, but he could not go by way of Murmansk to Petrograd because the two cities were separated by six hundred frozen miles of Russia. He would have to approach by –

Blackledge anticipated him: "You will enter the Baltic through the Sound and proceed to Kirkko, a small port on the south coast of Finland. There you will be contacted by an agent, a Mr. Robertson who has been in business there for a number of years. He is in touch with the Russian officers and will arrange a rendezvous with them. The details of the plot were brought out of Russia by a lady: Mrs. Elizabeth Ramsay. She is aboard now and will accompany the bullion. That is a condition set by the Russians and she knows them and their leader."

Smith asked, "She was a member of the embassy staff?"

"No." Blackledge's answer was abrupt; he obviously did not want to be questioned about the woman.

But Smith persisted: "She has to go with the Russians? That seems dangerous. What purpose could she –"

Blackledge broke in forcefully. "Mrs. Ramsay goes *be-*

cause the Russians insist! I don't know why they should but they do, and that is all you need to know!"

There was silence for a moment. Then Smith asked, "Why *Audacity*, sir? I know I made it plain I thought Q-ships had no chance against U-boats now, but I don't see she's any better fitted for this –"

Blackledge lifted a broad hand. "A conventional warship is out of the question. A Zeppelin patrols the Skagerrak so she would never get near the Sound without being seen and she could never force it. And besides –"

"It seems to me, sir, that a submarine –"

Again the hand. Blackledge said with a trace of irritation, "We aren't bloody fools! A submarine was considered. We passed them through the Sound into the Baltic in 1914. Since then, however, more patrols have been set up and mines laid. The Germans, Swedes and Danes mined the Sound between them. You'll find details in your orders. The real point is that although the submarines sank a lot of ships in the Baltic, once Russia surrendered they didn't have a base. We could see no way of getting them out without taking unacceptable risks so they were scuttled. A submarine *might* still get in, avoiding the mines by running on the surface in the shallows under cover of night and her chances *could* be as good as yours. But once she was in, there would still be the problem of contacting Robertson, the agent. Obviously a British submarine could not enter Kirkko so that would mean a rendezvous with him at sea to arrange the transfer of the gold to the Russians. We know *when* they will be ready, but not *where*. All that would be dangerous for Robertson, perhaps impossible, and if we lose him then the link with the Russians is broken. So it has to be *Audacity*."

He watched Smith's face for a moment, letting this sink in, then continued: "We believe that, posing as a neutral merchantman, *Audacity* will pass through the Skagerrak and Kattegat, and because of her draught of only four or five feet you can skirt the minefields closing the southern end of the Sound by steaming through the coastal shallows. And of course, as a neutral merchantman, you'll be able to enter Kirkko quite openly. We've given you an additional officer, Lieutenant McLeod of the Royal Naval Reserve. He's below in the wardroom now with his charts and kit. He sailed extensively in the merchant service in Scandinavian and Baltic waters before the war. He's a very fine navigator and his knowledge of Swedish is good so he'll be able to do any talking if you are questioned. He also has a smattering of the other Baltic tongues including German, but we hope you won't need that."

Blackledge paused, then looked away from Smith's watchful stare and cleared his throat. He went on, stiffly, "Of course, it won't be as easy as it might sound" – Smith thought, By God, it won't! – "but we believe it can be done. It must be done." That was said with finality.

Smith ran his fingers through his hair, thinking. He said, "The ship came into the dockyard a week ago. Ross tells me they've ripped the torpedo tubes and bomb-throwers out of her. Was that done with this job in mind?"

Blackledge nodded, "You won't need them and it will lighten her, maybe save you just that inch or two of draught that could be vital. You won't be taking the bomb-throwers' crews, either."

Smith thought, Lucky men. Not so the torpedo gunner and his staff who would stay aboard because they were also responsible for the ship's electrics.

Blackledge said, "We knew of the possibility of this plot early in March but we hoped for positive assurances from the Bolshevik government that they would not allow their Fleet to be taken by the Germans. Those assurances did not come but now we have information that German troops and ships are gathering at Riga and Danzig. That may well mean an attempt is to be made to seize the Fleet by force. We dare wait no longer. While we waited, we made what preparations we could, chose the man and the ship. You and *Audacity*. You still have her three guns and you are carrying scuttling charges. There are six of them in the magazines."

Smith broke in, protesting: "Scuttling charges?"

Blackledge replied grimly, "This ship must not be taken. If an enemy patrol tries to stop and board you, then you will fight long enough to be able to jettison the bullion.

Divers can go down to sunken ships and that gold must not fall into enemy hands so you'll ensure it's scattered along the sea-bed. Its intrinsic value apart, if they found it they could well make a shrewd guess what it was intended for and such a suggestion could be very embarrassing, diplomatically."

He waited. Smith sat looking at the fat envelope containing his orders. He could hear outside the cabin the bustle of the ship making ready for sea, men's voices with that of Ross carrying above the rest, the tramp of booted feet. Smith asked, "May I state my objection, sir?"

Blackledge answered coldly, "You may."

"I don't like the scheme, sir –"

Blackledge burst out, exasperated, "You aren't supposed to *like* it! *We* don't like it! But it seems you're full of objections, Smith! You objected to going back to the Fleet and said you wanted an independent command so you were given *Audacity*. Then you immediately complained about her role as Q-ship! We told you to shut up because we knew what we planned for this ship, but now you don't like that either! Well?"

Smith picked up his orders and tapped the envelope on the table. "If this scheme succeeds, sir, and the Russian Fleet is sunk or immobilised, then our involvement could change Russia from being just an unfriendly neutral into a belligerent on the enemy side. If it fails and is uncovered the same applies. And then they might well send their Fleet to fight alongside Germany."

Blackledge said deliberately, "Those risks are known and the decision was taken in the light of them, albeit reluctantly." He stood up and asked, "Any other questions?"

Smith followed suit, sliding the envelope into his pocket. "When does the bullion come aboard?"

"It was embarked tonight, before I told Ross you were sailing." Blackledge spoke quickly now, glancing at his watch as if eager to be away. "The Russian officers will be ready for the night of the fifteenth/sixteenth or soon after. They daren't risk waiting in Kirkko or thereabouts so you must be there by then. Theoretically you should have time in hand, but the weather this early in the year, the minefields, navigational problems, German patrols, are not theoretical. All or any of them could delay you, but you must be at Kirkko on the fifteenth."

Audacity sailed within the hour.

2

"That bloody raider!"

"That's the Norwegian coast in sight to port, sir." The Scottish accent was soft, the voice deep. McLeod turned from the chart table to stand by Smith in the wheelhouse. With justification Ross had said the navigator was like a gorilla: he was so broad his arms hung out from his sides, ending in big, leather-skinned hands. But although those thick seaman's fingers might look clumsy, that was deceptive. They were deft with a pencil and the other instruments of his trade. Indeed, Smith had often seen such hands mending a watch on a ship's mess deck. McLeod stood nearly as tall as Ross but did not seem to be because of his easy slouch.

Smith nodded. Norway was no more than a distant, darker line dividing grey sea from grey sky. The sun had risen an hour before but was still hidden behind cloud. *Audacity* steamed alone, rising and falling in a slow rhythm to a long swell. The escorting destroyers left her before sun-up because a Zeppelin patrolled the Skagerrak from dawn to dusk, and she would be suspect if seen in their presence. But there would be destroyers waiting for her, at a rendezvous outside the Skagerrak, every day for the next ten days. She only had coal for ten days' steaming. She would be out by then – if ever. *Audacity* was pushing into the Skagerrak now, the North Sea astern, ahead of her the Kattegat and then the Sound, the gateway to the Baltic.

Smith asked McLeod drily, "Is this a bit like you're coming home?"

McLeod grinned, big white teeth showing through his beard. "Not really home, but I know it well enough." He was a lieutenant, Royal Naval Reserve, held a merchant master's ticket and before the war had been first mate for a shipping line trading in the Baltic. He spoke Norwegian, Swedish and Finnish well but read them poorly, because he'd learnt them only by ear. He had told Smith at Rosyth, "I can manage some German but I have to think about it, work out first what I want to say." That wouldn't matter because *Audacity* was now supposed to be a Swedish tramp, and McLeod her master.

His grin faded. "The Baltic isn't a pleasure cruise this early in the year, sir. There'll still be some ice about along the northern shores, though nothing to worry us. But we can expect fog, a lot of it."

Smith wished that was all he had to worry about.

Wilberforce, the little steward, showed on the bridge outside then entered the wheelhouse. "Coffee, sir."

"Thank you." Smith took the thick china mug and cupped it in his hands to get the warmth from it, sniffed at the aroma, sipped.

Wilberforce complained indignantly, "'Scuse me, sir, but that chest o' drawers what was fitted under your bunk – the dockyard mateys took them out and screwed on a panel instead."

Smith nodded. "Modification."

"Don't make a lot o' sense, sir. I mean, we never used them drawers, but suppose we wanted to?"

Smith shrugged and said casually, "You know how it is, some designer gets a bee in his bonnet."

Wilberforce shrugged in his turn and went away muttering.

The gold. One hundred thousand pounds of it at nearly four pounds to the troy ounce weighed three-quarters of a ton and the boxes of it just fitted under Smith's bunk. It had been stowed before he or any of *Audacity*'s crew came aboard, but Blackledge had made Smith unscrew the panel and count the boxes. It had taken only a minute or two and then Smith had replaced the panel and signed a receipt. He thought it represented a hell of a lot of money. His own pay was only three hundred pounds a year and a lot of the men aboard drew less than a hundred. *Audacity* herself only cost fifty thousand.

He took his coffee out on to her bridge, stood by the

23

starboard lookout and ran his eyes over the ship. A four-inch gun amidships on the superstructure was hidden by a mock cabin erected around it. The twelve-pounders on fo'c'sle and poop were turned on their swinging mountings and lay on their sides below the deck. She looked innocent enough, just one more three-island tramp among thousands ploughing the oceans of the world. The Swedish ensign flapped from the jack in her stern and big boards painted in the Swedish colours of blue and yellow hung against her sides below the bridge. Other boards bearing her adopted name, *Lulea*, were bolted to her bow and to her stern with her port of registration: *Stockholm*. There was a real *Lulea*, listed in the International Register of Shipping if anyone checked it, but she was thousands of miles away, in the Pacific.

He could find no fault with *Audacity*'s disguise and certainly it should serve here. On this course she could only be a neutral ship headed for a neutral, or German port. Enemy patrols would not stop her. The same would apply once she was in the Baltic. Passing through the Sound and the minefields at the mouth of the Kattegat, however, was another matter: a true neutral would make those passages through the swept channels under escort and that would involve official examination. Smith dared not risk being boarded. A demand to inspect *Audacity*'s cargo would strip away her disguise – her holds were empty except for the bedplates on which the bomb-throwers had been mounted – while a casual question addressed to any of her crew bar McLeod would instantly show they were not Scandinavian. There had been barely time to collect, certainly not to train, even a nucleus of Swedish-speaking men.

Smith told the lookout, "Keep your eyes peeled for that Zeppelin."

"Aye, aye, sir."

The Zeppelin would see nothing suspicious but Smith did not like being observed unawares. Automatically he checked on the appearance of the lookout: modelled on a tramp's crew, every man's dress ranged from oily dungarees to ancient double-breasted suits. This particular sailor wore an old check ulster buttoned to the neck and a trilby crammed down on to his ears. He looked the part.

"Ship! Port bow!" That came from the lookout on the other wing of the bridge and Smith strode across past the front of the wheelhouse to join him. "Tramp by the look of her, sir."

McLeod said at Smith's shoulder, "Probably out of Oslo."

Smith glanced at him, nodded. McLeod, of course, was a tramp's master to the life: reefer jacket over a thick, blue woollen jersey, old blue cap pulled down to his eyebrows. Smith's gaze shifted approvingly to the motor-boat hanging in its davits on the port side. It had replaced the original lifeboat, the twin of that on the starboard side, but was only slightly out of character, no smart launch but simply an open boat with an engine. Only the screw might give things away and the boat's canvas cover had been adjusted to cover that. The motor-boat was there because it might be needed for a rendezvous with the Russians, if that were to be in some tiny cove where *Audacity* could not enter.

"Ship forty on the bow, sir. Another tramp, I think, but mebbe bigger."

McLeod said, "That one'll be out of Kristiansand."

Smith too thought the second ship was bigger and a merchantman. Dismissing both ships from his mind, he leaned in at the door of the wheelhouse to perch his empty cup on the shelf below the screen, then began to pace the bridge; standing was a cold business. He had read and reread his orders during the crossing of the North Sea, pored over the charts with McLeod, asked question after question and listened to his answers. He had to learn all he could very quickly and then make his plan.

He worked at it now. As he paced the bridge, however, other matters intruded on his thoughts. It had turned out McLeod was not additional to complement. Jeavons, the other lieutenant, had not reported to the ship – instead a message had come to the dockyard that he had been taken to the hospital that night in agony, with suspected appendicitis. With one officer fewer to stand watches, that would make life harder for Ross and McLeod, but Smith had expected to spend a lot of time on the bridge anyway. He had told them that *Audacity* was to enter the Baltic simply on a reconnaissance – and if anything happened to him they would find his orders locked in his desk – but he did not believe that they, or anyone else aboard, swallowed that story. After all, there was always Mrs. Ramsay who knew the true objective of this mission, and even though she could be relied upon to keep the secret, everybody would still speculate on her presence in *Audacity*'s wardroom.

But Blackledge had suggested the reconnaissance story before *Audacity* sailed from Rosyth: "It's feasible insofar as it would be desirable to pass a force into the Baltic. It could inflict a lot of damage on enemy shipping, close that sea as a supply route for the enemy."

Blackledge had also said, "If *Audacity*'s disguise is penetrated in the Baltic and you're not immediately brought to action then you get rid of the cargo and afterwards do what damage you can, while you can, because you won't get out. That's in your orders, but how you do it is left to your own initiative."

Or: When the game is up you're on your own. But Smith had thought there was no profit in brooding on that.

He had met Mrs. Ramsay briefly in the wardroom before *Audacity* had sailed. She lounged in a chair, long legs crossed, her silk dress outlining them. Her face was made-up, her full mouth carefully painted. She looked up at Smith out of wide, dark eyes.

He bowed stiffly. "We'll do our best to see you have a comfortable voyage, Mrs. Ramsay."

"Thank you." Her voice was low, husky. "Just get me there, Captain."

"I'll try."

"Try? Those are your orders, Captain."

"And I intend to carry them out. But there are other people between us and the Baltic who also have their orders."

Her lips parted in a smile sufficient to show very white teeth. She spread her arms. "Then I am in your hands."

Their eyes held for a moment then they both looked away. Smith said, "Good night, Mrs. Ramsay."

He had not seen her since. She stayed in her cabin. The North Sea crossing had been rough but she was not seasick. Wilberforce took her meals in to her and reported that she was eating heartily, sitting in her bunk and reading a novel. He smirked. He had never read a novel but he knew the sort of things that went on in them.

Smith thought he could easily have done without Elizabeth Ramsay. She was a distraction, even though unseen, and a complication in that she had to be transferred to the Russians with the gold. *Why?* he wondered. Blackledge said because she was known to the plotters and, more importantly, *because they insisted*. Before they went ahead they wanted the gold – and Elizabeth Ramsay. She was determined to go. Did she have a lover, or lovers, among them? The 'Russian Whore . . .' Did he believe that? Either way, she was another reason for his making haste to the rendezvous with the Russians. The sooner he was rid of this woman with the painted mouth and bold eyes, the better.

He forced his mind back to his planning: How to enter the Kattegat that was barred by minefields, and then on into the Sound . . .?

Some time later he was jerked out of his brooding by McLeod: "That first ship's British and she's going to pass us close."

Smith halted his pacing and looked at her. She would not pass close enough to talk. Her ensign, the Red Duster, flew at her stern. She was old and work-worn, her side showing near as many patches of red rust as of black paint. She would be crammed with a much-needed cargo for Britain, probably making her way around the coast to join a convoy off Bergen for the crossing of the North Sea and meanwhile keeping close to Norwegian waters to be able to run into them for shelter if a German warship appeared. She was still taking a chance on U-boats. Their hunting grounds were the North Sea and Atlantic, but one could well turn up here and the men aboard that ship knew it. Those merchant seamen were brave. Many survived a ship, or ships, sunk under them and yet went back to sea again. Smith mentally lifted his cap to them.

"The other one's Norwegian." McLeod again. "And she's a big 'un."

That was the ship that appeared to be on course from Kristiansand. Not a three-island tramp this one but flush-decked, only the superstructure and masts standing up from the line of the bulwarks that swept from bow to stern of her. She was twice the size of the tramp, showed no sign of rust and she was faster, gradually overtaking the British ship and a half-mile inshore of her. There was something odd about the set of the derricks on her masts . . .

Movement caught at the corner of Smith's eye and he turned and saw the woman, Mrs. Ramsay. Early though it was, she stood at the rail just below the bridge, looking out at the British tramp and waving. Smith realised that as her cabin opened from the wardroom on the port side she must have seen the other ship from the scuttle and now she had hurried out for a better look. She had wrapped a thin dressing-gown over her nightdress – if she was wearing a nightdress. She was worse than naked. Then she looked up at him and he saw that her face, even at this hour, was made-up, her lips painted, smiling. Then her dark eyes met his, and she turned quickly. He watched her walk away, her body sliding under the thin cotton. When she had gone he stood still for a while, eyes now on the tramp receding astern. Then he went back to his pacing.

Elizabeth Ramsay stood in her cabin, her back against the closed door, and shivered. It had been cold out on the deck but that was not why she shivered. That first night in the wardroom he had been formal, distant, shabbily dressed, nondescript except for the palest blue eyes in his thin face. Outside just now, standing wide-legged on the bridge to balance against the motion of the ship, he had looked at her again – and differently.

She thought she read that look. She also knew what she wanted and was determined to get it. She must go her own way. He was captain of the ship that would take her part of that way. Nothing more.

She took a deep breath, relaxing against the cabin door.

Then she snapped upright and away from it, a hand to her mouth, as the rumble of gunfire rolled across the sea.

The noise spun Smith round on his heel and brought McLeod leaping out from the wheelhouse door. They stared aft. "It's that bloody raider!" McLeod grated. "It was her, all the time!"

The British tramp was a mile astern with the raider inshore of her. The ship that had seemed flush-decked was not. The bulwarks had now been struck down to show the teeth their high sides had hidden. There were four guns mounted in the well forward of the bridge, two on either side, and they were all big pieces. There was another in the well aft, able to train to port or starboard. Now Smith saw why the set of the derricks had looked odd: while the false bulwarks were up those derricks had seemed to be seated *below* the apparent flush-deck. The real deck was visible now and it was ten feet lower than the false one.

Smoke wisped from the muzzles of the two guns on the raider's port side. The shells burst on the tramp's fo'c'sle and forward of her bridge. From *Audacity* they saw the flash and smoke, wreckage leaping into the sky then falling to splash into the sea. The tramp stopped.

Smith ordered, "Slow ahead!" The way came off *Audacity*. From her bridge they watched as the tramp's boats were lowered, her crew climbed down into them and began to pull away from the ship. They were hardly clear of her when the raider opened fire again. She had stopped abeam of the tramp and only a quarter-mile away. The old ship shuddered as each big shell exploded inside her.

McLeod ground out, "Target practice!"

Ross was on the bridge now and a harshness in his voice betrayed his anger. "A sledge-hammer to crack a nut! Need they make such a meal of it?"

Smith saw the tramp list slowly to starboard and her head went down. He swung his glasses away, sought and found the two boats filled with men. They were resting on their oars. Watching the end of their ship? He thought he saw faces turned towards *Audacity*, apparently the *Lulea*, a neutral ship. Waiting for her to assist?

The port side lookout said, "I think some o' them fellers in the boats are just in singlets, sir. They're prob'ly firemen come up from the stokehold in a hurry."

Smith had seen them. But, "Keep a lookout on your full arc of search!" he rasped.

"Aye, aye, sir!" But there was resentment, anger in the man's reply.

"Well, *do* something!" The woman's voice skirled the length of the ship. Smith lowered his glasses and saw Elizabeth Ramsay back on the deck below, glaring up at him. "You can't leave them! You can't let those swine treat them like that!"

Smith threw over his shoulder, "Half ahead!"

"Half ahead, sir."

"Revolutions for ten knots."

"Ten knots, sir."

"Yes, sir! No, sir!" She had stepped closer, so that she was almost beneath his feet, head thrown back to shout at him, "This is the Navy, is it? Where's your humanity? Have you forgotten what you're really supposed to be?"

Smith replied harshly, "I told you I had my orders, Mrs. Ramsay, and I would carry them out. Now I have one for you: Get below to your cabin or I'll have you forcibly taken there and locked in."

She stepped back as if he'd lifted a hand to strike her and paused for a moment. Wondering if he was bluffing? He was not, watched her steadily and she saw he meant it. There were tears on her cheeks; she shook her head in anger and frustration then turned and hurried away, clutching her dressing-gown around her.

Smith lifted his eyes again to the ships and the boats. The tramp was awash as far aft as her superstructure, her stern lifting out of the sea. It would not be long before she sank. That was clear to the raider, too. She was under way again and making a lot of smoke, obviously working up to her full speed, hastening away from the scene.

Smith said, "Find out if Sparks picked up any transmissions."

Ross answered, "Aye, aye, sir."

McLeod muttered, "I don't remember if she had any

wireless aerials rigged." He was speaking of the British tramp.

Smith did not remember either, but doubted if she had because wireless was unusual in a ship of that size and type. *Audacity*'s own aerial was a discreet single wire strung between her two masts, difficult to see except from a ship passing close to her and then only with glasses. It was strung now because only supposedly neutral merchantmen had been in sight and at some distance. It would be quickly hauled down if a warship appeared.

Audacity's operator was keeping a listening watch in the wireless office below the bridge, his orders to maintain wireless silence unless capture was inevitable. Privately Smith thought this laughable: it was unlikely they could get a signal off in the chaos and carnage of the last stages of a lost battle, and unlikelier still that it would be heard if they were in the Baltic – the range would be far too great.

Ross reappeared. "Not a cheep, sir."

"Thank you." It was no more than Smith had expected. If the tramp or the raider had sent off a signal, *Audacity*'s Sparks would only have heard it if he had happened to be tuned to the same frequency they were using.

The tramp's boats were moving now, the oars working, and they were headed for the Norwegian coast. McLeod said, "They should be ashore before sunset."

"Good." Ross scowled out at the boats. "The barometer's falling. Not dropping like a stone so there won't be a storm, but falling." He glanced up at the low cloud ceiling. "It'll be a dirty night."

Smith could do nothing for the men in the boats. His orders were clear. *Audacity*'s mission was to deliver the gold 'with all despatch'; no delays nor diversions, no involvement in a fight that was not her own. But he watched the boats intently until they were lost to sight between grey sea and grey sky.

He resumed his pacing, aware of the atmosphere of battened-down rage on the bridge and throughout the ship; he could read it in the hunched shoulders of the group of seamen gathered on the poop and still peering astern.

McLeod voiced it: "I would have liked to have a go at that bastard!"

Ross was silent a moment, then said sardonically, "So would I – then. But thinking about it now, it's a good job we didn't. She'd have blown the hell out of us with those six-inch guns."

That was true and McLeod was obliged to nod gloomy agreement.

Leading-Seaman Buckley stood at the back of the bridge and watched Smith striding rapidly, jerkily back and forth, saw the set face and hard eyes. His captain was in a hell of a temper, he thought.

But an hour later when the Zeppelin cruised overhead at an estimated five thousand feet Smith paused for only a minute to eye the silver cigar shape calmly. Then he turned again. The pacing was still rapid but with a relaxed rhythm to it now. He scowled but the pale blue eyes were abstracted, and behind them a plan was shaping.

Blackledge had said before he went ashore at Rosyth, "You didn't ask why we picked you for the job."

"*Audacity* was chosen and I'm her captain."

"We could have got another captain but we decided on you because of your record. It's far from unblemished but you have a way of pulling things off."

Now Smith wondered if he had. If he could. It was easier said than done. Ahead lay the Sound, patrolling destroyers and mines, but first there were the minefields at the mouth of the Kattegat . . .

3

Night Passage

The mines were laid across the mouth of the Kattegat between the Danish Skaw and Marstrand to the north of Göteborg in Sweden. *Audacity* passed them in that black night of low cloud with drizzling rain driving on the wind and flecked white with snow. Smith took her creeping through the shallow waters close to the Swedish coast, unmined because no ordinary ship could pass there and any minelayer would have taken the ground. *Audacity* drew just over five feet. There was a man in her bow casting the lead and calling the soundings. They had to change the man at that job every fifteen minutes when his hands became too frozen to feel the markers on the line. He had to rely on his sense of touch: *Audacity* showed not a wink of light.

With Göteborg a blurred radiance off the port bow she turned south away from the coast and out into the deeper water of the Kattegat. When the first pale light hardened the horizon she was out of sight of land and she steamed through that day at a lazy five knots. The Sound was less than a hundred miles away and they dared not approach it until the sun was down.

Smith slept through the forenoon then ate lunch alone in his cabin. Rain and snow swirled past the scuttle and the barometer promised no change for the better. If it turned to fog, and McLeod thought that likely, then the passage of the Sound would change from hazardous to downright foolhardy. Smith knew that if he had to wait in the Kattegat for the fog to clear he would lose at least a day. Blackledge had warned of that probability and had allowed for it, giving Smith twenty-four hours in hand. But he could lose no more than that because he had to be at Kirkko on the fifteenth.

He firmly told himself there was no point in worrying about a disaster that might not strike. Then he pushed away his plate and went out to the wheelhouse. Ross and McLeod waited for him there – with Elizabeth Ramsay. She was dressed for the weather in fur boots that came to her knees and a cape with a hood attached to it. In the comparative warmth of the wheelhouse the hood was pushed back. She stared ahead at the oily sea splitting white at *Audacity*'s bow.

Ross said, "Mrs. Ramsay asked if she could have a word with you, sir."

Smith, on the other hand, wanted a word *for* her. Disturbing? Not strong enough. He answered politely, on his guard, "Of course. Mrs. Ramsay?"

Her head turned and she spoke quietly but clearly. "I was angry and upset yesterday but you had your orders and there was nothing you could do. I understand that now. I'm sorry."

She understood it because McLeod had spoken his mind when he met her at breakfast in the wardroom that morning. "He had no choice! And you had the gall to accuse him of cowardice! It's only a year ago, when he was in an old cruiser scraped off the dockyard wall, that he took on two big, new German cruisers.* If there was ever a time for running away, that was it, but did he hell! The things that man's done . . ." And then he went on to tell her.

Smith appreciated the apology and that it was made in front of his officers and bridge-staff. He realised this was deliberate; Elizabeth Ramsay had accused him in public and that was how she would apologise. He was also aware that while the bold dark eyes held his gaze, their message was clear: This is just an apology. No more than that. Accept it, don't seek to extract advantage. He answered, "Thank you. I think I know how you felt at the time, standing by and watching a ship sink, unable to do anything to help."

The woman nodded, moved to the wheelhouse door then paused there a moment. He watched her and she knew

* *Thunder at Dawn*

34

it. She stared out at the cold sea, the weeping sky, and shivered. "Will the Navy catch that raider?"

"I hope so." But privately Smith doubted it. The German had played this game successfully before, the ocean was big and escorts stretched thin. Any ship sailing out of convoy, like the tramp the previous day, was easy game.

Elizabeth Ramsay left and Smith tried to put her out of his mind. He told Ross and McLeod to fetch the chart and led the way back to his cabin. The navigator spread the chart on the polished table and Smith dug his hands in his pockets, scowled down at it. He said, "Tonight's course."

Ross and McLeod stood by the table, eyes on the chart, and waited. There were three ways out of the Kattegat and into the Baltic. The first, the Great Belt, had been mined by the Danes, and besides, any passage of it took a ship past the doorstep of the German naval base at Kiel. The second, the Little Belt, was the route used by German U-boats and warships out of Kiel, partly mined and infested by destroyers. Any ship attempting to pass through the Little Belt would be boarded and searched.

Smith's finger went to the third option: the Sound, the stretch of water between Denmark and Sweden. He tapped the northern end of it. "There are no mines at this end and it's about ten miles from Kullen, on the Swedish side, to the Danish shore. *But* this is the main control point for German patrols, destroyers from Kiel that come out through the Little Belt. They stop and board every ship. From Kullen in the north to Skanor at the southern end of the Sound is about fifty miles as the crow flies but we're not aboard a crow, more of an ugly duckling."

Ross grinned and McLeod chuckled. Smith's finger traced down the Sound and paused: "There's a Danish minefield outside Copenhagen." He traced further south still: "Danish, German and Swedish mines close the southern exit between Skanor in Sweden and the Danish coast. There's a swept lane through the Swedish field, the Kogrund Passage, but ships only go through in daylight, escorted by the Swedes and, obviously, examined by them. So we can't use it." He tapped the chart again, south of the minefields that McLeod had earlier marked in pencil.

"More German patrols at the southern end of the Sound. They don't stop and search as a rule because they know any ship coming out of the Sound into the Baltic must be bound for a German or neutral port, while ships going in are either bound for ports in the Sound or they'll be checked at its far end."

McLeod asked, "So we don't need to worry about the southern end?"

"Yes, we do. Those destroyers patrolling south of the Sound know that ships only come out through the Kogrund Passage in daylight. We can't use the Passage, as I said, so we have to take advantage of our shallow draught and get round the minefields at night. And if those destroyers see a ship coming out of the Sound at night, or if the sun comes up and shows a ship steaming away that *must* have made the passage in the dark, then they'll smell a rat, chase and board her."

Suddenly their heads cocked, looking up at the deckhead, listening. There was the drone of an engine, heard faintly, like the buzzing of a fly, over the steady beat of *Audacity*'s engines. Smith went out through the wheelhouse to the bridge-wing and watched the seaplane fly overhead.

Ross spoke from the wheelhouse, "Danish markings, sir."

Smith nodded. The seaplane circled back, swooped low and he saw the heads of pilot and observer poked over the side of the biplane, peering down at the ship. He lifted a hand over his head. They waved in return and then the seaplane climbed and droned away on its patrol.

McLeod was looking over Ross's shoulder and said, "He was just having a looksee."

Smith said, "That's right. Clearly we passed muster."

It was comforting to know *Audacity*'s cover worked, but no amount of disguise would get her through the Sound. That was up to him. They returned to his cabin and he said, "So: we can't approach this northern end until after dark because if the patrols see us they'll stop us, and we have to be out of sight of the destroyers at the *southern* end by the time it gets light. We can't go in at the top one night, out at the bottom the next because we can't hang around in the Sound all through the day as we did in the Kattegat." For one thing, his orders – which Ross and McLeod hadn't seen – demanded haste. And for another: "We'd be in sight from either shore the whole time and there'll be Swedish patrols out of Hälsingborg or Malmö, Danish out of Copenhagen. If we steamed up and down they'd become suspicious. If we anchored they'd want to know why. Either way they might board us and blow the gaff. They don't have to tell the Germans about a British Q-ship in the Sound, but they don't have to keep quiet about it either. And we can't take that risk."

He stopped then, waited, and Ross said slowly, "So we have to make the entire passage in one night, starting from about ten miles out at sunset, to be ten miles clear of the other end by first light."

Smith nodded.

McLeod grumbled, not liking it. "That's cutting it fine, ower bluidy fine. It'll be a slow job working through the shoals at each end so we'll need to make a good ten or twelve knots for all of that middle passage, forty-odd miles of it. And all by night."

Smith asked, "What about the weather?"

Ross answered, "I think it's going to change."

McLeod nodded and added absently, eyes on the chart, "There might be some ice but it's unlikely. Nothing to worry us, anyway."

Smith asked, "Fog?"

The navigator shrugged broad shoulders. "There's always a good chance of it at this time of year. You could wait for weeks before being sure of a clear night."

But Smith couldn't. "All right." He talked them through his plan stage by stage and when that was done, asked, "Any questions so far?"

Ross rubbed at his long jaw worriedly, the stubble rasping. "It's going to be a close thing, even if everything goes right."

And if it didn't? If they ran aground, as one submarine did while attempting this passage back in 1914? If they strayed by a tiny error of navigation into a minefield? If they made not a single mistake yet ran into some mine that had broken loose and drifted? The risks were massive.

Smith gave orders for the gear to be made ready to haul *Audacity* off the ground by a kedge anchor if it became necessary, and a party detailed. He also ordered a damage-control party to be standing by to try to patch and shore up any hole made by a mine – though that was a forlorn hope; a mine would almost certainly sink her.

Finally he straightened from the table. He had tried to prepare for every eventuality he could foresee. Now he glanced at his watch and told Ross and McLeod, "I'm going to get some sleep. I suggest you follow my example when you're off-watch. It'll be a long, busy night."

McLeod picked up the chart and left with Ross. Both men were silent and thoughtful. Smith stretched out on his bunk. He was not tired but strung to a tight pitch. With his eyes closed the plans he'd made unreeled again and again as he sought to find fault with them. When he'd turned away from watching the seaplane he saw the girl walking the deck forward of the bridge, the hood of her cape pulled up against the rain. She looked up and their glances locked. Now her face and her eyes came between him and his plans, filling his mind . . .

The tapping at the door woke him and he lifted on one elbow, drowsily, to see McLeod's head poking around the door. The navigator said, "Sunset, sir."

"Coming." Smith rubbed at his eyes and sat up, swinging his boots to the deck.

McLeod had left the door ajar; his next words, to Ross, were low but audible: "Sleeping like a bairn, would you credit it? I couldn't get a wink."

And Ross's muttered answer, "Nor me."

Smith drew a wry satisfaction from that: they thought he was unworried. It was a good job they didn't know the truth. He splashed water on his face, picked up his overcoat and cap and went out to the bridge.

McLeod told him the rain had ceased an hour before. Now they steamed beneath a lowering sky. The sun set astern of them, a dull orange ball as if seen through smoked glass. The night would be overcast, dark, and that at least was to the good.

The sun was down and it was nearly full dark when they sighted the point of the Kullen promontory. They closed it, well to port of the central channel, *Audacity* steaming slowly, showing no light, and passed it breathtakingly close with a man in the bow again, casting the lead and calling the soundings. There was a Swedish lighthouse on a tower at the tip of the promontory but the lamp was not burning. Most of the navigation markers had been put out for the duration of the war. The tower was astern of them, off the port quarter when the lookout called from the starboard wing, "*Ship, sir! Starboard beam! I think she's a destroyer!*"

Smith used his glasses to pick out the furred silhouette in the darkness and Ross muttered at his shoulder, "Looks like a German destroyer to me." Smith grunted, watching the long, low vessel with her twin funnels trailing smoke and the hump of a gun forward. She was on an opposite course to *Audacity*. He thought the lookouts aboard the destroyer would not see his ship against the black loom of the land behind her and, steaming slowly like this, with no white water at bow and stern to give her away.

It was still a tense moment but the silhouette gradually lost shape as it receded, melted into the night and was gone.

Ross let out his breath in a sigh, then complained, "She was damn close in, well inside Swedish waters."

True, but so was *Audacity*.

And all the while the man at the lead had kept up his chanting and Smith listened, as he did now: "By the mark, two!"

Two fathoms: twelve feet of water and *Audacity* drew just five.

They saw no other patrol. Then McLeod reported quietly, "Viken on the port bow." The light at Viken had not been put out.

Smith ordered, "Starboard ten," to take *Audacity* out of the shallows and into the deeper water of the shipping lane. They had passed the patrols and were in the Sound. *Audacity* turned to port to follow the lane and Smith ordered revolutions for ten knots.

Ten minutes later Ross swore. Smith kept his face impassive but spoke on the voice-pipe to McLeod, now on the flying bridge above the wheelhouse: "Fog, Mr. McLeod."

"Aye, seen, sir." Then the pilot cursed in his turn.

Smith stepped out of the wheelhouse to stare at the grey mist that had already reduced visibility to a half-mile or less. McLeod came dropping down the ladder from the flying bridge and Ross stood at the door of the wheelhouse, both of them watching him.

He asked, "Local, d'you think? Reckon we might run out of it in a minute or two?"

McLeod shook his head. "It's possible, I suppose, but not likely. If you recall, sir, I said we could expect fog."

Smith nodded. The worst had happened. He had to be at Kirkko on the fifteenth. He had worried that fog might prevent him attempting the passage of the Sound and lose him a day or more in waiting for the weather to clear. But now he was into the Sound and he could not wait here. Should he try to return to the Kattegat? Getting this far had not been easy, but going back in fog would be worse. Then to lose a day and have it all to do again?

Time. Whether he went north or south he must be clear of the Sound *and* the patrols outside it by first light. Furthermore, if *Audacity* plodded on at a cautious snail's pace they would be safe from collision but still in the Sound when the sun rose. To be well clear by then they needed to make ten or twelve knots for most of the hours of darkness. Turning back offered no advantage; this fog might hold for days.

Smith made his decision. "Maintain revolutions for ten knots. Mr. Ross! Double the lookouts and clear lower deck."

"Aye, aye, sir!"

Standing outside the wheelhouse Smith watched the men come up on deck. Now, if *Audacity* were in collision with another vessel, the only men below would be those in the engine room. There was no shortage of lookouts and two were right forward in the eyes of the ship: whether they would see anything in time was another matter. The fog was patchy and one minute Smith could see for a mile ahead but the next, as the mist drifted, there was only an impenetrable grey wall beyond the fo'c'sle head.

McLeod bent over the chart table, head and shoulders pushed into the canopy rigged to prevent the light over the table showing outside. He emerged to say, "We should see Hälsingborg or Helsingør any minute now." The two towns stood on either side of the narrow passage. Helsingør, with Hamlet's castle, lay on the Danish side. Hälsingborg on the Swedish.

"Lights on the port bow, sir!" That came from a lookout.

Smith saw the spread glow as McLeod exclaimed, "Hälsingborg!" And then, prompting: "Change of course, sir?"

Smith ordered, "Starboard ten."

Audacity's bow swung and settled on a course to take her the length of the Sound, rushing on through the fog. Once he turned and saw Elizabeth Ramsay standing at the back of the bridge on the port side by the motor-boat. The order 'Clear lower deck' had meant everybody, even her. She wore her cape but the hood was thrown back, her hair blowing in the wind. Her face was only a pale oval in the darkness. He did not know how long she had been there, never knew how long she stayed. He turned to face forward.

McLeod muttered, "We won't see the Haken light."

The beacon on the island of Hven was not lit. But they soon saw Hven itself, and raced by it close enough to glimpse the loom of the plateau before it was lost once more in the mist. *Audacity* pounded on, making good her ten knots and more. That was only her clear weather cruising speed but the mist magnified the velocity until they seemed to be tearing along like a train. Smith mused ironically that even the fog had its compensations: at least no Swedish or Danish patrol vessel would be groping about on a night like this.

But suppose some nervous merchant skipper had anchored in the fairway? *Audacity* would be on her before the order to turn away could be given. At ten knots her bow would be stove in, and that would be the end of the mission. Before she sank he would have to try to get the gold off and dumped well clear of the ship where divers would not find it. He and his crew would be interned.

Was the fog thickening? Ross swore under his breath then said aloud, "Can't see a *bloody* thing!"

Then McLeod spoke, his voice coming muffled from inside the canopy: "I make it Copenhagen lies to starboard now, sir. Malmö on the port bow."

A capital city with all its lights lay only ten miles away but they saw only the grey banks rolling and streaming past *Audacity*'s side. Smith ducked quickly inside the canopy beside McLeod, peered at the chart and the navigator's calculations, then said quietly, "Yes, I see."

He backed out, straightened, then turned and leaned easily against the screen. That was a pose, for the benefit of the bridge-staff. In fact he was sweating. If their dead reckoning was correct he should order a change of course very soon or he would run her aground on the Swedish shore. But if he turned too soon – if their calculations were wrong – he would drive her on to the island of Saltholm or into the minefield off Copenhagen. McLeod was standing behind him now and knew the decision his captain was facing.

Smith took it, looked at his watch and said, "I think we should hold on for another minute."

"Sir." McLeod prayed to God that his captain was right.

The minute ran its course – and the portside lookout yelled, "Lights! Port bow!"

McLeod peered, then blew out his cheeks in relief and said, "Malmö, sir! No doubt of it!"

"Starboard ten!" Smith conned *Audacity* as she kept up that terrifying ten knots, past Limhamn where they saw lights gleaming, lights which were too close for comfort. They were on course for the Kogrund Passage, but that was mined and closed to them without a Swedish escort, so when the lookout picked up the glow of the light at Klagshamn Smith altered course to port and reduced *Audacity*'s speed to a crawl. Briefly they all breathed a little easier but they had only exchanged one terror for another. Smith was hoping to pick his way around the edge of the minefield through the shoals and shallows where no mines would be laid. *Audacity*, drawing only five feet, might do it.

That was the theory. The practice was like a blind man walking a tightrope. Smith ordered the motor-boat lowered and sent puttering ahead, taking the soundings and reporting them back to the ship in a muted hail. He had done this once before in the old cruiser *Thunder* but then there had been neither patrols nor mines. He strained his eyes against the fog as *Audacity* slipped slowly down the coast off Skanor with the shoals to port, sometimes barely a fathom under her, and the mines to starboard — somewhere.

Buckley, standing at the back of the wheelhouse, also remembered *Thunder*. He would never forget that night, leading the old cruiser down to the sea, nor the fight the next day. But he thought this night was a right bastard, too.

Smith stopped *Audacity* repeatedly when the hail from the motor-boat reported the bottom shoaling so even she could not pass, and took her out of it astern to seek another way through. He kept one eye on his watch because time was against them, ticking steadily while *Audacity* meandered slowly south. Her crew lined the rails, eyes narrowed to pierce the night and the fog as they searched for mines that might have broken loose and now be floating with the current. Nobody knew exactly how close the field itself was.

Until Ross said, "Lights, sir."

And McLeod sighed, "We're past Skanor. Thank God."

The minefield lay astern of them now and Smith ordered, "Starboard ten!" taking *Audacity* out of these shallows where she might run aground, to be held there until the dawn came and the patrols found her. The day would not be long in coming. The fog still wrapped them around, but he ordered, "Revolutions for ten knots."

"Ten knots, sir!"

Audacity was running again, bow shoving into the grey curtain that parted and streamed past the bridge like smoke, yet still rolled ahead of her. Smith speculated that if he

43

could be sure this fog would hold into the day he would reduce speed now to a more cautious, saner progress and creep away from the Sound under its cover. But would it? He dared not be seen anywhere near the Sound when dawn broke.

"Ship starboard bow!" . . . *"Ship!"* . . . *"Ship!"*

A score of voices yelled the warning and his shouted order came like an echo: *"Port twenty!"* He saw a ghost ship, dark grey in the lighter greyness, long and low, riding lights glowing. In the second's glimpse he had of her he saw that she was anchored and that she was a German destroyer. Then she was gone and only the fog remained.

He brought *Audacity* back on to her course. McLeod and Ross looked at him covertly, expectantly, but he did not order a reduction in speed. There was unlikely to be another destroyer on this Swedish side of the channel. There could be a merchantman anchored but that was a risk they had taken all through the Sound. Nothing had changed. The equation of time and distance was still the same: they must be out of sight of patrols when the day came.

It came with a steady shredding of the fog until all was gone except for a long bank of it falling astern. First there was twilight and then the first leaden light of day when they could see drawn faces and red eyes. And as the sun rose pale out of the east they peered astern and saw no ships, no land, only an empty sea. They had made the passage of the Sound.

Smith stooped over the chart with McLeod. "I want a course for Kirkko, Pilot. You know it?"

"Know *of* it, sir. We once called at Kotka, not far away on that coast." He glanced behind Smith's back at Ross, who raised his eyebrows and mouthed, 'Kirkko?'

Smith had caught that turn of McLeod's head and said drily, "It's in the Gulf of Finland, Mr. Ross. We have to meet someone there, but I'll tell you more about that later." Then he spoke to the navigator, "You've plotted the minefields ahead?"

McLeod stopped grinning at Ross. "Yes, sir."

The chart was spattered with his pencilled hatchings. They worked together to lay off a course through them

44

then Smith turned to Ross. "You have the watch?"

"Yes, sir." He had been on the bridge all that long night and it showed in his eyes and the lines of tiredness at their corners.

But so had Smith and McLeod, and it was worse for them. This was Smith's ship, his responsibility, while McLeod, as pilot, knew the risks they ran too well for his peace of mind. He looked an older man this morning and Smith ordered him to turn in.

McLeod did not argue, but produced his usual wide grin. "Aye, aye, sir."

Smith walked through the wheelhouse to his cabin, saw Buckley standing at its door and asked, "What are you waiting for?"

"'Case you wanted anything, sir."

"Are you on watch?"

"No, sir."

"Don't be a bloody fool, then. Turn in." He suspected that Buckley had waited there since dusk of the previous day, to try to save him if disaster struck. Buckley had waited like that before.

Smith lowered himself slowly to sprawl on his bunk. There was a hundred thousand pounds' worth of gold stacked under him. *Audacity* was alone in a German sea. He heard McLeod out on the bridge, taking his leave of Ross: "Well, maybe that's the worst over."

The worst? Smith thought it had been bad enough. But though they had broken through into the Baltic, they still had to get out again. After Kirkko he had to get them out.

This was only the beginning.

4

A German Sea

When they called Smith to the bridge he looked blearily at his watch and saw he had slept for a bare two hours. Ross apologised: "Sorry, sir, but I knew you'd want to see this." He pointed with one hand, with the other unslung the glasses from around his neck and passed them to Smith. He focused them, looking out on the bearing Ross indicated, searching . . . There. The Zeppelin was off the port bow, something like ten miles away and headed from north to south. The Swedish coast lay over the horizon to the north, so . . .

He said, "Flying patrol. She probably left Kiel, or somewhere on the German coast, at dawn. Flew north as far as Sweden and now she's on the return leg." The southern end of that leg might be Arkona. The neck of sea separating the German and Swedish coasts was only forty miles wide at that point.

Ross asked, "Could she be looking for us?"

Smith thought about it a moment, then: "We'll see." He handed the glasses back to Ross and leaned his arms on the screen. "Let's have some coffee up here."

A messenger went hurrying and Smith watched the Zeppelin, tiny with distance, seeming to hang almost motionless between sea and sky but in fact making fifty knots or more. Was it searching for *Audacity*? Had the anchored German destroyer seen them and sent a wireless signal to bring this Zeppelin out for the hunt? He did not believe it, remembering that mere second's glimpse he'd had of the destroyer. Any lookout aboard her would have had even less chance of seeing *Audacity*, a darkened ship.

The coffee came and he sipped at it while they ploughed

on, at twelve knots. There was no point in changing course, trying to run. The Zeppelin would have seen their smoke long before they saw it and could overhaul them at four or five times *Audacity*'s top speed of fifteen or sixteen knots. He watched it slide slowly across the bow then fly on towards the south. It did not turn aside for a closer look at the ship so it was not seeking her, just flying a routine patrol like a sentry patrolling his beat. Smith told Ross so, but stayed on the bridge.

In less than an hour they saw it return, coming up from the south and following the same line so that this time it passed astern of them. It still did not alter course to investigate one solitary tramp plugging on into the Baltic. It had no reason. Any ship here had to be neutral or German. But if a ship were headed outwards, for the Sound . . .? Smith shifted uneasily then glanced at Ross, saw his tiredness, and told him that he would stand the rest of the watch. Smith would not sleep now.

He paced the bridge on weary legs. Blackledge had not warned him of this Zeppelin. Did it patrol every day or was this an isolated flight? He worried at the problem until McLeod came to relieve him.

They sighted distant smoke several times that day but no ship showed above the horizon. Next morning they steamed through fog again that cleared in the forenoon. Smith was standing some watches so Ross and McLeod were not working watch and watch about, and he had the forenoon. He saw Elizabeth Ramsay come on deck to stand by the lee rail. She nodded when he put a hand to his cap in salute but then turned and walked away.

McLeod came to the bridge, worked on his chart for a few minutes then stretched his huge hands above his head, easing the muscles in his back. He glanced sideways at Smith and ventured, "This . . . reconnaissance, sir."

Smith smiled inwardly at the inflection on the word 'reconnaissance'. As he'd expected, McLeod was taking that story with a pinch of salt. "Yes?"

McLeod asked innocently, "D'you think it might be to see if we could get some ships into the Baltic?"

Smith let his grin show. "It could be, couldn't it?"

McLeod said, "Oh, aye." He gave that suggestion up, tried another tack: "What about after Kirkko, sir?"

Smith cocked an eye at him. "What about it?"

McLeod grinned openly, knowing that another captain might have snubbed him for his probing. "Sorry, sir. I'll mind my own business."

Smith understood his curiosity. Admittedly a Q-ship's job was a long way from routine patrolling, but this! He spoke easily, "One step at a time. Let's get our business done at Kirkko, first. I'll tell you one thing, though."

McLeod's head turned quickly and he snapped at the bait, "Yes, sir?"

"We could do with some coffee up here."

The lookouts reported smoke at intervals during that day, too, but it was late afternoon when McLeod called Smith to the bridge. "A ship, sir, and it looks like she'll pass us close."

She was off the starboard bow and some four miles distant, about the size of *Audacity* and looking flush-decked, like the German raider, though it was difficult to be sure, bows on as she was. Then as the two vessels steadily closed Smith saw she was not flush-decked, but only looked that way because there was a deck cargo of stacked timber filling the wells forward and aft of her bridge.

McLeod muttered, "Her colours are flying away from us so it's hard to tell – but they could be German: black, red, white . . ."

Smith used his glasses and read the name on her bow: *Anna Schmidt.* She was black and rust-streaked, deep-laden and low in the water. Now she was turning, marginally altering course towards *Audacity*. Her siren blared, two short blasts. A man stood outside her wheelhouse, waving his cap above his head and McLeod said, "Oh, hell! He wants to talk to us, sir."

The way came off the German ship, her screw was still and she was almost stopped now. Smith said, "All right." He was thinking of what he might learn from this meeting. "You say your German isn't much good but that doesn't matter. You're a Swede, remember." And: "Stop her."

The telegraphs rang and the pulse of *Audacity*'s engines ceased. She slowed and stopped almost abeam of the *Anna Schmidt* with less than fifty yards of sea between them. Her master was bawling through a tin megaphone now and McLeod stood out on the bridge with another. He lifted it as the bawling stopped and answered, "*Nein!*" Then he murmured an aside to Smith, lounging at the wheelhouse door: "He asked if I spoke German and I told him I didn't." But the skipper of the *Anna Schmidt* bellowed again and McLeod growled, "The bloody man speaks good Swedish! He's asking if we've come from the North Sea."

"Tell him."

Smith watched the *Anna Schmidt* as McLeod made his reply, not understanding a word but knowing it would be that the *Lulea* was out of Bergen and bound for Helsinki. The German master started again and McLeod translated: "He's warning us about the Russian minefields still in the Gulf of Finland, says some of them have been swept and we can get into Helsinki all right . . . He says they've been swept all along that coast but there are still big fields out in the middle of the Gulf between Finland and Riga."

Smith knew about them; McLeod had marked them on his chart. The pilot was going on: "He wants to know if we saw any U-boats in the North Sea and was there any British shipping?"

"Tell him we saw no U-boats but there were a few British ships waiting for a convoy from Bergen." That was nothing the U-boats did not know already, except that in fact there were more than a few British ships.

McLeod's tone dropped and became harder: "He says the U-boats have sunk many. His son is in a U-boat." There was the reason for the interest in the North Sea, that and a natural hunger for news. McLeod said, "He's out of Kotka" – Smith stirred; that was not far from Kirkko, McLeod had been there – "with timber for Kiel." The deck cargo of sawn lumber was self-evident, stacked so it showed two to three feet above the bulwarks of the *Anna Schmidt*. The German was laughing, a big laugh that came up from his belly, and McLeod explained: "His ship's due for an engine overhaul in the dockyard as soon as she's discharged her timber so he'll have nearly two weeks at home with his wife."

"Say you hope his son joins him."

McLeod looked oddly at Smith, but obeyed.

"Now tell him we saw a Zeppelin earlier on and we didn't know they flew this side of the Sound." Smith waited, wondering if the man's thoughts of his wife and Smith's good wishes concerning his son would soften the German skipper and remove his suspicions at such a question. Why should the master of a Swedish tramp be curious about a Zeppelin?

McLeod translated as the German boomed away cheerfully, unsuspectingly: "The Zeppelin just keeps watch. The ships that used to patrol these waters while Russia was in the war have gone to the North Sea. Most of the naval forces in the Baltic have now been concentrated at Danzig and Riga."

Blackledge had said that troops and ships were gathering there – for an attempt to grab the Russian Fleet? Was *Audacity* in a race, to help sink that Fleet before the enemy took it?

McLeod went on: "Now the Zeppelin only flies when the weather is good enough." That meant when it was fit to fly. "Almost every day now. There's only one destroyer at the Sound and you must have seen her. She did not stop you?"

He ceased his muttering interpretation and bellowed a negative.

They could see the German nodding: "Only the Swedes stop and board before leading the way through the minefield. The Zeppelin and the destroyer do nothing. They are a precaution, like a policeman, you understand?"

McLeod glanced at Smith, who said, "Wish him a safe voyage and wave goodbye." They had learned enough, more than Smith had hoped for, and further questioning might make the German skipper wonder at their curiosity.

The bellowed exchanges sounded across the sea for the last time. Churned foam showed at *Audacity*'s stern and then that of the *Anna Schmidt* as the screws of both ships turned and they got under way. The German master waved his cap and McLeod flapped a big hand. "Damned if I'm taking my hat off to him!"

Smith decided the Zeppelin made no difference to *Audacity* and her mission. On her way home she would pass through the Zeppelin's patrol area in the light of day and, inevitably, be seen. But she would be regarded as just one more merchantman approaching the Sound and, with a lot of luck, would evade the sole destroyer in the night by running in the shallows.

He went to his cabin, to read his orders again – *Audacity* would reach Kirkko the next day – and to sleep, because he would be on the bridge for most of the night as they passed the minefields at the mouth of the Gulf of Finland. He scanned the typed sheets again, arid sentences, flat statements: Germany held all the southern shore of the Baltic to and including Estonia; Russia, Denmark and Sweden were neutral, the last two as sympathetic to the German cause as to the British; Finland was neutral but a friend of Germany; the Bolshevik Russians were aiding and supplying the Red Guards trying to take over Finland while General Mannerheim and the White Finns fought them.

The agent at Kirkko, by name Robertson, would make himself known to Smith there, and would be informed by telegram to expect *Audacity*, as *Lulea*, on the fifteenth.

Smith did not need to read the orders, he knew them by heart now. He locked them away in his desk and sprawled on his bunk. In twenty-four hours he would be at Kirkko and in forty-eight hours his task might be completed. Though this would depend on the Russians, he was prepared to bet they would get their hands on the gold as soon as they could. And with it, Elizabeth Ramsay. He pushed her out of his mind and instead summoned up a picture of the chart, going over again the course he had plotted past the minefields. After a time he slept, but uneasily; his dreams full of Red Russians and White Russians, Red Guards and White Finns. Gold. And Elizabeth Ramsay.

They passed the minefields at the mouth of the Gulf in the night, running in the swept waters close to the Finnish coast, as the *Anna Schmidt* would have done. The morning was windless and they steamed through fog yet again. In the forenoon it thinned and visibility lifted to about two miles but the air still held a damp cold that chilled the men out on the open bridge. The lookouts stamped their feet and every now and again lowered their glasses to beat their gloved hands together. Smith strode steadily back and forth from one wing past the front of the wheelhouse to the other, twelve paces each way.

McLeod left his chart and came out of the wheelhouse to tell Smith, "We make the turn into the channel to Kirkko in two hours, sir."

Smith nodded. "Thank you." They were almost there and a day early. That extra day might be useful. The agent in Kirkko should know of *Audacity*'s coming but plans could always go wrong. They weren't home yet by a long –

"*Ship starboard beam two miles! A destroyer!*" That was a yell from the starboard lookout, grabbing his glasses and lifting them to his eyes.

Smith turned quickly, snapped, "Revolutions for eight knots!" Because this 'tramp' should only be making that speed, not the twelve knots at which she'd been cruising.

"Eight knots, sir!"

The other ship had appeared suddenly out of the mist on a course parallel to their own but now was leaning over under helm as she turned to close *Audacity*. McLeod said, "She's flying German colours."

Smith could see that for himself. He lowered his glasses and slipped quickly into the wheelhouse, the lookout's voice following him: "She's German, sir!"

Smith pressed the button under the screen that set alarm buzzers whirring throughout the ship. There came a trample of feet as the crew of the four-inch ran through the passages from their mess just forward of the funnel to the housing, just aft of it, where the gun was hidden. Ahead, and below him, the door of the fo'c'sle was hooked back and the crew of the twelve-pounder waited inside. He could see their faces, ready to pile out and up the ladder to the gun when it swung up out of its concealment below the deck of the fo'c'sle.

He stepped out of the wheelhouse on the port side where he would not be seen from the destroyer, looked aft and saw the door in the poop similarly open. Ross sauntered aft along the deck without apparent haste and passed in through the open door. His station in action was with the twelve-pounder on the poop.

Smith went back to the wheelhouse and the voice-pipes, heard and acknowledged the 'ready' reports as they came in but his head was turned to watch the destroyer closing them.

Two hours from Kirkko. They had passed the mines in the Kattegat, all the perils of the Sound and then the five hundred miles of the Baltic, only to run into this destroyer at the last. McLeod was out on the bridge-wing, ready to do his act as the Swedish master of *Lulea* but Smith could hear him swearing softly, savagely.

It was an old destroyer with a turtle-back fo'c'sle but she mounted as many guns as *Audacity* and had an extra ten knots of speed. *Audacity* was still some miles outside Finnish waters so there was no chance of claiming the haven of a neutral shore. Not that the Germans were likely to take much notice of the 'neutrality' of these waters; they were friends of the Finns and could expect their help. Five thousand young Finns, the *Jägers*, had been trained in Germany by the Kaiser's Army and were now back in Finland, serving under Mannerheim.

The destroyer was turning again now, and slowing to run abeam of *Audacity* and within hailing distance. Her guns were manned, the loading numbers standing by the open breeches, each cradling a shell ready to load when ordered. There was no doubt who would fire the first rounds if there was a fight. Either way, *Audacity* was unlikely to win. And there was the gold in Smith's cabin, Elizabeth Ramsay in hers.

There were two officers on the bridge of the German destroyer. No gold lace showed on the heavy coats they wore but their caps and their stances marked them. One of the Germans held a megaphone now and his voice came over to *Audacity*, hollow and harsh from the metal.

McLeod said, "He's asking where we're from, where

we're bound and what cargo. He can read our name; he's close enough to count the rivets!" He lifted his own trumpet and bawled his answer in Swedish, that *Lulea* was out of Bergen and bound for Kirkko with American canned goods.

The German reply cracked quick and brief: "*Kirkko?*"

McLeod repeated it: "*Ja! Kirkko.*"

The German lowered the megaphone and consulted with his fellow officer. Smith could see them studying *Audacity* as they talked. McLeod muttered, "I don't like this, sir. Seems as if something might be up. I hope to God he isn't going to try to board us." He and Smith could be killed in the next few minutes. One of those guns was trained on *Audacity*'s bridge.

The German lifted his megaphone again and McLeod translated: "How long are we staying at Kirkko?"

The plain truth might be the best policy – or some of the truth, for it was a cardinal rule never to let the enemy know more of your movements than you could help. Smith spoke for the first time: "Tell him, only long enough to discharge the consignment due there and to take instructions from our agent. We sail tonight for Helsinki."

McLeod did not know what the truth was, knew nothing of the agent Robertson or why they were in fact going to Kirkko. Possibly that gave his voice a ring of sincerity as he bawled across to the destroyer. Smith saw one of the officers nod and then the other was using the trumpet again. McLeod took a breath. "I think it's all right. He's warning us there's civil war in Finland, Mannerheim's fighting the damned Bolsheviks and there are Red Guards all along this coast. He says we're wise not to linger in Kirkko."

The German lowered the megaphone and lifted his free hand while McLeod waved in reply. The destroyer was cracking on speed, pulling ahead of *Audacity* and turning away. Her men were securing their guns fore and aft. McLeod stepped into the wheelhouse and let out a whistling sigh: "That was a bowel-opener."

Ross showed behind him. "I thought we were for it. I'm sweating."

Smith made no reply. He was cold.

The destroyer disappeared into the fog and *Audacity*'s gunners stood down in an atmosphere of relief and excited chatter. The tension had built in them as the destroyer ran close alongside, and for minutes they had been on edge, waiting for the order to load and fire. But now the ship settled back into her normal routine and Smith wondered at the Germans' reaction to the mention of Kirkko. They warned him not to delay there but he would have to, Red Guards or no, because he had come 'with all despatch' and arrived a day early. He would not have a rendezvous with the Russian officers before the following night. Kirkko could be a trap but he had no choice. He had to talk to Robertson.

5

The Russians

Audacity entered the Finnish port of Kirkko in the afternoon of the fourteenth of April. The fog and the damp, bitter cold of the morning had cleared and they closed the land in pale sunshine so they could see the densely wooded shore. Ice floated in patches that groaned and squeaked as they rubbed along the ship's hull. Smith and McLeod took *Audacity* in slowly, still disguised but with her crew closed up at action stations. They did not know what they would find in Kirkko, but hostile Red Guards who might try to board were a possibility. Smith was ready to fight his way out if need be, though that would mean the end of his mission.

All along that coast was a litter of offshore islands and shoals. The channel through them was buoyed, narrow, tortuous and it led to an opening between steep cliffs that hid the port. As they passed through the gap the channel curved sharply to the right and now they opened the anchorage with the little town a half-mile away at the head of it.

"Not much of an anchorage," muttered McLeod. "Room for two or three ships by the town but the sailing directions and the chart show shoals either side of the channel. There's enough water there for *us*, but –"

He did not need to finish: *Audacity* must not be seen to be of far shallower draught than any normal ship of her size. Smith, glasses to his eyes, gave his order. "We'll anchor here." He did not want to be close to the town. On the fo'c'sle the blacksmith knocked off the clip and the anchor roared out. *Audacity* lay close inside the entrance and to one side of the channel, leaving room for another ship to pass her if need be.

McLeod murmured, "There's the church, presumably the one they named the port after. That's what Kirkko means: church."

Smith saw it, set amid the straggle of houses that made up the town, hardly more than a village. There were a few solid-looking sheds and warehouses lining the quay and a sawmill with a jetty. The only other ship in the port lay alongside the jetty. She was loading sawn timber and flew the black, white and red ensign of the German merchant marine.

The guns' crews stood down from their action stations. Smith took Ross and McLeod into his cabin and told them, "I expect to be approached by a Mr. Robertson who is in business here as a shipping agent. You'll keep this under your hats."

Ross answered, "Aye, aye, sir."

McLeod asked, "Any idea when, sir?"

"No."

They left the cabin, silent but thinking.

Just ten minutes later a lookout reported a boat putting off from the shore and heading for *Audacity*. Smith told Ross, "Pass the word, we have visitors. The minimum of men on deck and make sure they all look the part and act deaf, dumb or stupid."

"Aye, aye, sir."

Audacity's deck stayed empty of men, save for a small party on the fo'c'sle and another on the poop, for appearances' sake because a totally deserted ship might excite suspicion. Neither party would be within talking distance of the boat when it came alongside. Smith took shelter in the wheelhouse with Ross while McLeod went down to the deck to meet the boat.

Ross muttered, "Suppose it's the P.M.O., sir?"

Smith had been told the agent here would prevent a visit from the Port Medical Officer. By what means? Bribery? And suppose Robertson had failed? Smith said, "McLeod will tell the doctor we've no illnesses on board and no one's going ashore."

Ross said doubtfully, "What if he insists on coming aboard to see for himself?"

The doctor would only have to talk to the crew for a few seconds to know they were not Scandinavian. Smith answered, "We can't weigh and run for it; that would look suspicious. So the doctor and his boatman will have an accident."

"Sir?" Ross shot him a startled glance, not liking what he heard.

Smith said drily, "Not murder, Mr. Ross. I'd keep them below and capsize their boat. There'd be enquiries but with any luck we'd have completed our business before they became pressing."

Ross probably wanted to ask what that business might be, but he held his tongue. And Smith was glad of that, listening for McLeod. He heard a voice, the words indistinguishable, garbled by distance, but then he recognised McLeod's bass rumble. Ross was chewing his lip anxiously, well aware of the danger. Smith stood with his hands in pockets, striving to appear unconcerned, but he let out a breath softly when McLeod's boots thumped on the ladder and the pilot said, "It's Mr. Robertson, sir, the ship's agent here."

Robertson followed him into the wheelhouse, a ruddy-faced man, stocky in a heavy fur coat, a homburg on his head. He looked from Smith to Ross in their shabby jackets without any badges of rank and asked, "Captain?"

Smith answered: "I command." He shook Robertson's hand then gestured to the others. "My officers." He gave no names.

Robertson shook their hands. "Guid to see you." The Scots accent was soft but clear.

Smith said, "We thought you might be the P.M.O. Can we expect a visit?"

"No." Robertson took off the homburg and ran fingers through short, grizzled hair. "There's only the one doctor here and he's away up country to see a case. When he comes back I'll tell him you're only here for instructions from me, that you've no disease aboard and you won't be coming ashore. He'll take my word for it. I've done business here as a shipping agent, and he's been the doctor in this town, these twenty years past."

Smith spoke to Ross. "Tell the steward we have a guest."
Then he ushered Robertson into his cabin and shut the
door, offered the single chair to the agent and sat down on
the couch.

Robertson said, "I didn't expect you so soon. Ye've
made a fast passage, Captain."

"Those were my orders."

Robertson chuckled. "Admiralty were pessimistic. The
coded telegram I got said *Lulea might* arrive tomorrow. It
also authorised me to raise cash locally, if you didn't get
here, and try to persuade the Russians to take coin and
paper for doing the job." He shook his head. "That's a
non-starter. There might be ways and means of getting the
money but my courier has talked to the Russians and he
said they made it plain they'll take only gold – *and* the lassie
has to go with it. He's arranged the transfer for tomorrow
night."

Smith asked, "Courier?"

"I have several; Russians and Finns, men who travel on
their own business and also make some enquiries, run some
errands on my behalf."

"Trustworthy, I assume."

"Absolutely." And Robertson pointed out drily, "My
life depends on it, and has done for some years now."

Smith took the point and nodded. There came a tap at
the door and he opened it, took the tray from Wilberforce
and closed it again. As he busied himself with the bottle and
glasses he realised that Admiralty had considered *Audacity*'s
mission unlikely to succeed, a desperate gamble they had
taken because they had to; the outcome of the war could
hang on it. He held out a glass and asked, "You know the
girl?"

Robertson took the glass and held it up, toasting. "Liz
Ramsay? Aye. I met her when she passed through Finland
on her way home. The railway from Russia runs just a few
miles inland. She's quite a girl. But I can't understand why
the Russkies insist she goes with the package, and I don't
like it."

Neither did Smith, but he asked, "The transfer? When
and where?"

Robertson savoured the whisky, then swallowed. "A drop of good stuff, Captain. Aye, well, our Russian friends sail from Petrograd in a fishing-boat, like a wee trawler, tonight. They'll be posing as fishermen and they'll follow the Russian coast as far as Kurgala Point, then cross the Gulf to Kirkko." The Gulf of Finland was only fifty miles wide between Kirkko and Kurgala. "They'll be here for the transfer tomorrow night then return the same way but not to Petrograd. That's too risky so they'll put into a quiet little port where they have friends, not far from Kurgala. It could be any one of a score and they haven't told me which. I don't blame them."

Smith frowned: "We make the transfer here? In the anchorage? In sight of the town and a German ship?"

Robertson lifted one finger of the hand holding the glass. "I can understand you not liking it, but wait a while. The Russkies don't fancy the idea of a rendezvous on the open sea. There's always the chance some other vessel might come along or that there might be bad weather which would make the transfer impossible."

Smith had a mental vision of two ships pitching and rolling while a fortune in gold swung precariously between them.

"Aye." Robertson went on: "And you'll know the situation in Finland. Mannerheim is leading the Finns, many of them German-trained, in a fight for independence from Russia, trying to throw out the Red Guards, Russian or Russian-supplied. There are Red Guards all along this coast. We might pick a quiet bay where there are none, or we might choose a wrong 'un and land up in trouble. But I *know* this town and harbour are free of them, there's not one within miles. And anyway, you're well away from the town. The German ship loading timber won't sail till the morning of the sixteenth, so she'll still be here tomorrow night, but you're a good half-mile away from her, too. You'll have no bother."

Smith still did not like the plan but this was the way the Russians wanted it. He could not contact them until they arrived the next night. Any attempt he made then to arrange a different rendezvous would mean delay and his

60

orders were to deliver his cargo with all despatch. "All right." He would not say 'very good', because it wasn't. "You spoke of the political situation here. What do you know of German naval strengths and movements, patrols and so forth?"

Robertson pursed his lips. "Very little. I only know what my couriers see, what I see myself, as we go about our business. There are destroyers and torpedo-boats, most of them ten or fifteen years old, a few a bit newer, but all dangerous to you. Some are based at Reval, others at Riga. There's a guard-boat that patrols outside of Reval, another in the Irbensky Strait – though I understand she lies more or less permanently at anchor at one side of the deepwater channel through the Strait."

Smith pictured the chart in his mind: the Irbensky Strait was the main entrance to the Gulf of Riga. The other –

Robertson went on, anticipating his thought: "The other way into the Gulf, through Moon Sound, is blocked by minefields. They were laid by the Russians last year when they were still at war and the Germans haven't bothered to sweep them yet."

Interesting, though not relevant to Smith. He waited and Robertson said, "As for patrols, there is the destroyer that comes out of Reval, sweeps all along this coast and goes back to her base. It may not be the same one all the time, but one of them shows up pretty frequently, every day or two."

Smith nodded. "We met her."

Robertson straightened in his chair. "Good Lord! When?"

"A couple of hours out. We told our tale, she looked us over and went away satisfied."

Robertson grimaced: "Nasty moment, eh?"

But Smith commented tersely, "Not nice." And prompted, "Any other patrols?"

"I understand there's an armed tug or a minesweeper that patrols out of Reval and along the Estonian and Russian coasts as far as Kurgala Point or thereabouts. Our Russian schemers know about both patrols. They'll stop a ship in case she might be carrying Russians or Russian supplies to the Red Guards – I told you the Germans were cultivating the Finns – but they don't bother fishermen." Robertson paused, watching Smith, then asked, "Anything else you need to know?"

Smith shook his head. "That'll do to be going on with."

Robertson stood up. "I'll tell them ashore that you're cleaning your fires tomorrow. That will explain your staying here."

"That's almost true, as it happens." *Audacity's* engineers did indeed want to let out the fires and clear them of clinker. But Smith would like them to do it now, so that it would be complete before nightfall and *Audacity* could raise steam then. He would not have his ship lying an immobile hulk all through tomorrow.

Robertson paused at the door. "This is a dangerous business you're on, Captain. If the Germans catch you, passing as neutrals in a disguised ship of war, I'm not sure how they'd regard you."

Smith was sure: as spies. He shrugged. He could do nothing about it, except: "We must try not to be caught."

"Mind you," said Robertson, moving out on to the bridge, "they're not averse to that kind of thing themselves. They've a raider out now. There was a report this morning, telegraphed from Norway, that she'd sunk a British steamer north of Bergen."

Smith told Robertson, "We know her." He did not explain but saw the agent to the side and his boat, then returned to his cabin and called for Ross and McLeod. "We lie here for the next twenty-four hours, but with steam just as soon as the chief has cleaned his fires. Tomorrow night we have a rendezvous here with a fishing-boat and we'll be transferring some cargo, three-quarters of a ton of it. It's in my cabin now. You'll need some strong hands to hump it down to the deck forrard of the bridge where the derrick can lower a line to it, and I want it done quietly and in record time. So make your preparations but no discussion with the men."

Ross asked, "Three-quarters of a ton, sir? In your cabin?"

Smith answered him poker-faced: "That's right. It's in

62

wooden boxes with rope handles and it takes up a space six feet by three by two."

He could see their minds working, saw McLeod's lips purse in a soundless whistle, and asked, "Understood, gentlemen?"

"Aye, aye, sir."

He went out through the wheelhouse, down the ladder to the empty wardroom below it and passed through to Elizabeth Ramsay's cabin. She answered his tap, opening her door wide, leaning on the frame. He said quietly, "Tomorrow night."

"I'm ready." One corner of her mouth twitched wryly. "You'll be glad to see the back of me."

"I don't think you should go, Mrs. Ramsay."

She shrugged. Then she lifted her left hand with the thick gold band on her finger. "I called myself Mrs. because it made matters easier in business than if I'd been a single girl. It's a kind of protective colouring." She looked him up and down in his crumpled blue cap and worn old overcoat. "But there's no Mr. Ramsay; there never was." She held his gaze a moment then shut the door in his face.

"Sir! Captain, sir!"

Smith woke at the call as the light glowed over his bunk. The time was shortly after midnight. He shoved up on one elbow and blinked at the man. "Yes? What is it?"

"Mr. Ross said to call you, sir. A boat just came in; about the size of a small drifter, she is, and making for the town." The officer of the watch had orders to call Smith at sight of any craft or of any unusual occurrence.

"I'll come." He swung his legs out of the bunk and hauled on his boots, buttoned his jacket and snatched his glasses, the old overcoat and plain blue cap from their hook on the door. He strode through the wheelhouse and out to the wing of the bridge. The night was moonless but with a bright dusting of stars.

Ross turned to meet him and said, "She came around the headland and was on top of us in seconds. She's closing the town now. I smelt fish as she passed us."

Smith nodded, used his glasses and saw the boat sliding

in to the quay, figures moving on her deck under a light. She had a single mast forward with the long boom stretching nearly to her stern where a man stood at the tiller. Her sail was lowered and he could hear the faint putter of her auxiliary engine. Doubtless fishing-boats used this port frequently and this could be one of them, but there was another possibility: a detachment of Bolshevik Red Guards using the boat to patrol. Ross had been right to call him but there was no need for action at the moment. There were sentries on *Audacity*'s fo'c'sle and poop, with rifles not obvious but ready to hand.

Buckley came on to the bridge and asked, "Fancy a drop of kye, sir?"

Smith grunted assent and lowered the glasses. But he still watched the boat as he shrugged into the overcoat, and wondered how Buckley knew he was on the bridge. He decided Buckley had probably arranged that he should get a shake whenever the captain was called.

He drank the cocoa when it came, absently at first because he was watching the fishing-boat and so burnt his tongue. After that he blew steam from it and looked over it at the boat with its solitary light, and waited.

A half-hour passed. The night was still, the riding lights of *Audacity* reflecting from water like a sheet of glass. Smith saw the lights of the German freighter where she lay upstream by the jetty of the sawmill. But he heard no sound from her.

Ross muttered, "She's started her engine again, sir."

He was talking of the fishing-boat. Smith nodded, watched it ease away from the quay and the bow swing until it pointed at *Audacity*, and steadied on that heading. He told Ross, "Call all hands. Action stations. But quietly." And to Buckley: "Get a Lewis up here." Buckley slid down the ladder from the bridge while Ross stepped into the wheelhouse, thumbed the button concealed under the screen and set muted buzzers whirring throughout the ship. Smith turned back to the fishing-boat and as he watched it closing *Audacity* he felt the ship coming alive beneath his feet. There was no pounding of racing feet nor bellowing of orders, but a quiet shifting, a murmur of voices from below the gratings on which he stood. That ceased as Ross bent over the voice-pipes and said, "Keep silence. Boat approaching, port beam."

McLeod stood beside Smith, fastening the toggles of a duffel coat, his plain blue cap jammed on hastily at a Beatty angle. Ross was at the wheelhouse door, looking out to the bridge, eyes watching the fishing-boat but head cocked towards Smith, waiting for orders.

Smith said, "It looks like the boat we're expecting but that's not due for another twenty-four hours. This might be any fishing-boat – or it might be Red Guards attempting to board the ship."

McLeod muttered, "Can't see many on her deck."

Ross answered, "There could be a hell of a lot below." He stood by the voice-pipes to the guns.

Smith said, "Tell the chief we may have to slip in a hurry and to stand by." He heard that order passed to the engine room.

The fishing-boat was closing, starting a long, curving turn to come alongside, the *chug chug* of her engine loud in the night, but slowing. There was a man forward on her deck, another aft, each holding a line. Two more stood in the waist and one of them raised a hand, waving.

Smith recognised the stocky figure, the homburg. "That's Robertson aboard her."

He heard a movement behind him, turned and found Buckley with a wide-barrelled Lewis machine-gun cradled in his arms. He faced outboard again as the fenders of the fishing-boat rubbed against *Audacity*'s side. The lines were tossed up from her and caught by the men on the deck abaft the bridge. Smith heard someone on the fishing-boat call out, the words incomprehensible. McLeod said, "Russian. Don't know what he said, though – *Jesus!*"

Men were pouring up through a hatch on to the deck of the fishing-boat below. Smith snapped, "Stand by with that Lewis!"

Then Robertson called up, "All right! They're ours!"

The men were not armed. They stood in a steadily growing crowd and, while Smith could not tell in the darkness whether their uniforms were khaki or navy blue, the style of their caps looked British. He told Robertson to come aboard.

He went down to the deck and met the Scot as he climbed the ladder, came over the side and panted, "Sorry, Captain! The first I knew about this was when that bloody Russian knocked on my door twenty minutes ago! This is your boat, come a day early to bring those men. They're Royal Navy."

"Navy!" Smith shot a glance at them. "Submariners?" Some of the crews of the boats scuttled when Russia surrendered and they were left without a base? Although he thought they'd been sent home through Murmansk.

"No." Robertson shook his head. "Royal Naval Air Service. Our embassy in Petrograd wanted them out of the Bolsheviks' way in a hurry so shoved them on this boat and sent her off. Their commanding officer will tell you the details but you'll have to give them passage. In Russia they could go to jail and if left here they'll be interned." Robertson took a breath and went on. "Now, the Ivans want to take the cargo. I told them they were promised payment on or after the night of the fifteenth/sixteenth, not *before*. But I said I'd leave the final decision to you."

Smith made it. His orders had said the fifteenth/sixteenth but they'd also said 'With all despatch'. And every hour *Audacity* lay here with the gold was another hour of risk. "How many of those Navy men?"

Robertson answered quickly, "Eighteen."

Smith shouted an order to McLeod: "Get 'em aboard and out of sight below as quick as you can." And to Ross: "Turn up the hands to transfer the cargo." He swung on Buckley: "My compliments to Mrs. Ramsay. Her friends are here and she'll be leaving within the hour."

He watched the R.N.A.S. men climb the side of *Audacity* then be hurriedly shoved below by McLeod and a petty officer, to be spread through the messes of the ship. Ross's voice, low and urgent, brought men running to the bridge. Smith showed them the hiding-place beneath his bunk and they shuffled in and out of his cabin, heaving the boxes, two men to each box. They used a block and tackle to lower them to the deck one by one. There they were

66

stacked on a wooden grating, secured in place by netting and hooked on to the dangling wire of the derrick. Smith had already warned Ross, "You'll need men on the derrick falls; we can't use the winch." They could not risk its clatter arousing curiosity on shore.

Ross had answered, "Told 'em off ready, sir."

Good mark to Ross. Smith did not need to guess what the men were making of his cargo. They had loaded ammunition often enough, and knew these boxes were far heavier. They would reach the obvious conclusion.

He leaned out from the wing of the bridge and made hand signals to the master of the Russian boat to work his craft along *Audacity*'s side until she was forward of the bridge. The Russian's orders to his men brought her there. His crew appeared uniformly bearded, huge and shapeless in oilskins, but he himself showed in the yellow gleam from the solitary lamp on the boat as clean-shaven. His eyes glittered wolfishly in the light.

McLeod came hurrying to the bridge and shouldered through the men labouring with the boxes. "The airmen are all stowed below, sir. The men in the bombers' messes forward, the two officers in one of those new cabins aft." Those messes for the crews of the bomb-throwers had been empty because the throwers had been taken out and their crews not shipped for this mission. McLeod went on: "Chap commanding them is a Flight Commander Gallagher. He insisted he had to see you but I told him he'd have to wait."

Smith nodded: "Very good."

Buckley appeared at the head of the ladder then turned to hand up Elizabeth Ramsay. She wore her cape and a triangle of silk covered her hair and framed her face. In the feeble glow that spilled out of the wheelhouse Smith saw her lips were parted, her eyes shining. That was how she had looked that first morning he saw her. He remembered her saying that she had no husband, that she was in business – but not what it was. He did not want her to go.

A dozen hands were manning the falls of the derrick, ready to heave the boxes up and over to the fishing-boat. The Russians were waiting expectantly, faces upturned. Smith pointed to their leader. "Can you trust him?" he asked the woman. The man had the eyes of a hungry animal.

Elizabeth Ramsay answered, "He'll keep his distance." She had taught him that at the point of a knife, for she had acquired some strange harsh ways in Russia – quickly and of necessity. But she would not try to explain to this silent, withdrawn young officer with the bleak gaze. Yet –

The net tightened around the boxes and they lifted slowly, checked, then the boom of the derrick swung and the boxes swayed out at the end of the wire to hang above the Russian boat.

Audacity's lookout called huskily, "*Ship bearing –*"

Smith spun on his heel and saw it, knife-edged bow pushing in past the headland. The gun on her fo'c'sle was manned and he thought he could make out figures on the bridge. As the searchlight mounted there sparked into life he grabbed the girl, dragged her into the wheelhouse and behind the open door, pressed her into the narrow space between door and chart table, protecting her instinctively with his body. The beam of the searchlight fell on the water of the channel beyond the fishing-boat, twitched on to it and Smith heard one of the Russians yell. The beam shifted again and now lit the dangling net with its three-quarter-ton burden, the bridge of *Audacity* and the men on it. From the wheelhouse Smith saw McLeod, with his hands lifted against the glare.

The girl whispered, her breath on his cheek, "What is it?"

"German destroyer."

He recognised her type, T class, two four-inch guns and three torpedo tubes. About ten years old. He remembered Robertson saying: ". . . a few a bit newer but all dangerous to you." The voice-pipes to the guns were only feet away from him. *Audacity* could fight if she had to, but not well, lying at anchor, stopped and tied up to the fishing-boat. She was expected to fight long enough to be rid of the gold but it could not be dumped here, in sight of the enemy and in barely four fathoms of water.

A voice hailed them in German. Smith could not make out the words but the tone held authority. He called, "What did he say?"

McLeod answered, "Wants to know what we're doing, sir."

"Tell him we're a neutral ship in a neutral port so what the hell has it to do with him!"

Smith saw the destroyer slide slowly into view from the wheelhouse, and stop right abeam as McLeod bawled his answer to the German challenge. Smith could see the other captain now, out on the wing of his bridge, hand lifting a megaphone.

The voice hammered back, guttural and angry. McLeod interpreted: "He says the Finns have asked the Germans to help and Von Goltz is landing at Hango with fifteen thousand men . . . He himself is escorting ships carrying a regiment, to land them here . . . and is an ally of the Finns so has the right to ask questions."

A regiment. One thousand, maybe two thousand men. Another ship was easing in cautiously around the headland. The gun on the destroyer's fo'c'sle, another aft, were both trained on the bridge of *Audacity*. A ransom in gold hung on the end of a wire rope, turning slowly.

Smith swallowed, then spoke: "Grovel a bit. Say we bought some fish from the boat. We're giving them canned goods in exchange and doing it now because the fishermen want to sail."

McLeod shouted the information, wheedled into it a tone of apology and respect. The megaphone lifted again and this time the rattle of German was less peremptory.

McLeod answered, then muttered, "The bastard said my German was bloody awful. And he asked about Red Guards here. I said there weren't any."

"Sehr Gut!" That echoed over the water as the destroyer edged forward slowly until she lay just ahead of *Audacity* and there came the rumble of her cable as her anchor plummeted down. The other ship came on, creeping, until she lay abeam of *Audacity* then she, too, anchored. There was a second troopship, just clear of the headland, but she followed suit and anchored there.

Smith rasped, "Tell Ross to carry on."

McLeod flicked a hand at Ross on the deck below. The laden net descended steadily and the wire went slack as the load disappeared inside the open hold of the boat. The searchlight's beam swung away from *Audacity* to sweep slowly around the harbour instead. On the bridge they were almost blind in that sudden darkening. Smith was still a moment, acutely conscious now of the girl's body under the pressure of his own, breast to breast, leg to leg.

He took a pace back and said, "There'll be a ladder over the side, just forward of the bridge. Ross will see you down. Tell the Russians to get out of here. Not in a mad scramble that might make the Germans suspicious, but with no delay, either." His voice sounded oddly formal, strange even to him.

He could hear the girl's quick breathing. She did not answer but in the door she looked back at him. Then she turned away to the ladder. But it was out in the open now. All the glances, the distant, awkward conversations, were done with. They knew too much about each other now. Like it or not.

Smith leaned over the rail of the bridge and told Ross stiffly, "See the lady safe aboard the Russian."

"Aye, aye, sir!" Ross answered from the deck below.

Smith watched him hold her arms as she swung over the rail and until she found her feet on the ladder; then she was climbing down. Buckley sent her big carpetbag down after her on the end of a line.

Movement caught at the corner of Smith's eye, a flash of silver in the black pit of the fishing-boat's hold. Peering, he made out men working down there and a shifting, silver flood. The Russians had stowed the gold at the bottom of the hold and now were covering it with fish – tons of it.

The boat's engine chugged, the lines securing her were cast off and she eased away. Smith caught a glimpse of the girl standing on the deck, her face turned up to him. Then the boat gathered way and Elizabeth Ramsay was lost, merged in the dark silhouette that held on steadily at the edge of the channel. The Russian obeyed Smith's instructions, went without unseemly haste but without delay, either. She passed the German steamer lying in the channel, rounded the headland and was gone.

The men disappeared from *Audacity*'s deck and Ross came up to the bridge. "That was a narrow squeak!"

"It's not over yet."

The German ships could not have come at a worse time. The Russians had escaped but *Audacity* could not. No freighter of her size and seeming tonnage could pass the German steamer anchored in the narrow channel. If Smith tried to slip out through the shoals on either side, taking advantage of *Audacity*'s shallow draught, it would raise suspicions. "We'll have to sit here and wait until the channel is clear, probably in the morning."

Robertson stood at the door of the wheelhouse, mopping his face with a handkerchief. "I'm breathing again, but only just. And to think it was me who actually told you this was the safest place for the transfer!"

Smith shrugged. "How were we to know this Von Goltz would choose tonight to invade, and land a part of his force here?" But now he understood the curiosity of the German patrol the previous day; they must have known of the projected landings here. "What about you? How are you going ashore?"

"Not tonight." Robertson was firm about that. "I don't want the Germans questioning a Scottish businessman found prowling about the harbour in the middle of the night. No. I left word with my housekeeper that I was coming out to you. If I'm not back by the morning she'll send my boatman to fetch me."

Smith pointed: "My cabin. Make yourself comfortable."

"Thank you, Captain. I'll not rest easy" – Robertson glanced towards the destroyer – "but I'll put my feet up for a while."

He retired to the cabin and Smith spoke to Ross and McLeod, "Stand down from action stations but crews sleep by the guns, the engine room staff stay on watch and keep steam up. I want an anchor watch on the fo'c'sle ready to slip if we have to run for it, but they keep under cover and everybody else stays below." Too many men on *Audacity*'s deck might again raise suspicions: she was supposed to be a merchantman with a crew of only twenty-odd, not the sixty she carried. He said, "Get some sleep yourselves. I'll call you quick enough if you're needed."

Ross hesitated, then suggested, "If Mrs. Ramsay isn't coming back to the ship, sir, then I could put those two Air Service officers in the cabin she was using."

Smith nodded. "Yes, but not now. They can manage for this night." He offered no explanation for the departure of the girl, nor for *Audacity*'s mysterious cargo. These were secrets Smith had to keep.

Ross and McLeod went away and Smith was left in the wheelhouse with Buckley and the two lookouts out on the wings of the bridge. Buckley leaned at the back of the wheelhouse and watched Smith standing silently at the front of it, arms crossed on the screen. Watching his captain Buckley felt relieved: That's all right, then. Nothing coming off at the moment. It's when the bugger prowls up and down like a caged lion then stops stock still that you've got to look out.

He had been with Smith for a year now and knew more about him than Smith suspected. Buckley was in a privileged position but wisely asked for no favours – that was just one of the things he knew about the captain. Buckley also knew about his women, again, more than Smith suspected. The leading hand could have got cheap kudos on the mess decks by telling a few tales but he never did so. It was none of their business. Smith wasn't a saint, Buckley knew that, but he was a bloody good man. The only one that would have got him here on this lot!

Flight Commander Malcolm Gallagher lay on the bunk in the new cabin once part of a bomb-thrower's mess. The mattress was hard and lumpy, the blankets seemed damp. Condensation dripped from the deckhead.

Still, it was not as bad as that billet he had shared with Johnny when they had first gone to France. The pair of them had slept in a corner of a barn, cold, draughty and with the rain coming in through the roof. That had been a good time, though. The Pups they were flying were new, and to them France was new and exciting. Johnny Vincent, always the joker when you were on the ground, had nevertheless been the wingman you could trust your life to when you flew.

Gallagher had boxed at light-heavyweight and very well; he bore no scars. He had come a long way since France: his black hair needed cutting now and dark eyes looked out sombrely from under thick brows. It was a hard face.

Sub-Lieutenant Edward Danby sat on the opposite bunk, fidgeting with his cap. Then he stood up to move nervously about the cabin. He was small and thin, pale and sandy-haired. Gallagher watched him with sour amusement that suddenly turned to irritation. "Can't you bloody well sit still?"

"Sorry!" Danby went quickly back to his bunk and perched on the edge of it. He looked towards Gallagher for approval, was instead confronted by his glare and dropped his eyes.

Gallagher wondered why the hell he'd been saddled with such a wet sub-lieutenant in His Majesty's Navy: Danby hardly knew one end of a ship from the other. Poking about now as if he'd never seen a mess deck before. Probably hadn't.

Gallagher knew ships. He was a regular officer and had been serving in a cruiser in 1914 when the flying bug bit him. He volunteered for the Royal Naval Air Service, went to Eastchurch for flying training then flew a succession of aircraft, leading up to Sopwith Triplanes and Pups before transferring to Camels. He had survived – successfully – and had the decorations to prove it.

Now his thoughts slipped back to his own last sea-time in the summer of 1917 before he had taken on this Russian job. He had been in a cruiser, flying Pups, with Johnny and a few more. Fred Rutland had been the first to fly off from a cruiser but others soon followed, Gallagher among them. Then came the Camels, Russia, and notching up more kills until on one mission he had flown into that wall of anti-aircraft fire. The Camel started falling apart around him but he got it back to that damn-awful field at Kunda Bay and landed it – just. They had carted him off to a Russian hospital – but only after telling him about Johnny Vincent. And Danby's part in the whole bloody mess . . .

73

He tore his mind away from that. Then he remembered the Camel, his Camel, where it was now. He swung his legs off the bunk, stood up and looked at his watch. "We've been down here an hour. I'm going up to talk to the skipper."

"Do you want me to come?" Danby asked.

"No, but you'd better. If you don't he might think I'm hiding you for some reason."

Smith leaned on the screen in the wheelhouse and stared out at the destroyer. Blackledge had said that the Germans were gathering ships and troops at Riga and Danzig: he thought it might mean an attempt to seize the Russian Fleet. Wrong guess; it was this force to invade Finland. So was the Russian Fleet still at risk? Smith heard the scuff of boots on the bridge gratings, turned, and saw two figures standing at the wheelhouse door.

The taller man asked, "Permission to join you, sir?" In the dim light of the wheelhouse his face was drawn and hollow-eyed, but still hard; this was a fighter and a winner. The shorter, younger man a pace or two behind looked tired and scared. They both stank of fish. Their uniforms were khaki service-dress but the tall one boasted the two rings of a naval lieutenant on his cuffs, and wings above them, the 'Bloody Duck', with a star that marked him as a flight commander. The younger had the single ring of a sub-lieutenant but no wings. He had obviously borrowed the jacket because it was too big for him and hung over his shoulders, almost hiding his hands.

Smith realised these would be the two officers who had come aboard earlier, brought by the Russians. They might well have had a hard time so, worried as he was, he said, "For a minute. You are?"

"Gallagher, flight commander. The sub here is Danby." That was said with a jerk of the head.

"Smith, commander, and commanding this ship." He held out his hand and they shook it in turn. Smith said, "You realise you're no longer R.N.A.S."

Gallagher sniffed. "So we heard. Since the first of this month we've been part of this new lot called the Royal Air

Force, us and the Flying Corps. Don't see that it's going to make any difference till we get home, though." He shrugged. "I see the *Anna*'s gone."

"*Anna?*"

"The Russian boat: that was her name. We were nearly two days in her hold." Gallagher grinned. "That's why we smell a bit."

Smith laughed. "We'll survive that! Sorry about your quarters. We'll try to improve them but we weren't expecting you. What are you doing here, anyway?"

Gallagher answered, "I brought a flight of six Camels out to Russia by way of Murmansk last September. It was supposed to be just a flag-showing exercise, Britain going to the aid of her gallant ally, but we did a bit more than that. We lost one officer early on and then there were others." Gallagher paused, remembering. Then: "We were flying from a field near Kunda Bay, that's in Estonia. I was shot down in November just a day or two before the Russians asked for an armistice, and wound up in hospital. There was only one real officer left with the Flight by then, Billy Williams, our armaments chap, and fortunately the first thing he did when he heard of the armistice was to send fifty-odd of the men back to Murmansk where they could get a ship home. That made sense because there wasn't a single serviceable aircraft, or a pilot, left. We'd lost some men invalided home with wounds." He paused. And there'd been the funerals, the thin note of the bugle, blown flat because of the bitter cold, the brittle crackle of volleys. "Billy kept a nucleus of sixteen: a few fitters and riggers, armourers, a couple of cooks. I was still in hospital. After the armistice everything in Russia went to hell. There was chaos. Billy and his men had no transport, got no supplies from the Russians. He did the best he could but Danby had only arrived as a replacement the week before I copped it so he wasn't any use."

Gallagher paused again, might have said more, but thought better of it. "In the end Billy set out for our embassy in Petrograd to see if they could organise transport. That was the last anyone saw or heard of him."

Gallagher took a breath: "Damn shame. Good man,

Billy. Anyway, the Russians were arguing the toss with the Germans about the peace terms but all the time Jerry kept on advancing. When they got close to Kunda Danby had sense enough to start bringing my chaps back on foot but then they were rounded up by some Russians and put under guard. The Russians were in uniform but whether they were Army or deserters, or just plain bandits is any-body's guess. They didn't speak English and none of my blokes spoke Russian. They had a rough time and after a few weeks they dug a hole in the back wall of the hut one dark night and slipped out. One of the fitters crowned a sentry with a chunk of wood and they headed for Petrograd again. They found me at the embassy – I'd arrived the day before after the hospital finally got me a lift in an ambu-lance. Even then I had to walk the last ten miles."

Smith said, "I understand the embassy got rid of you all in a hurry."

Gallagher nodded: "They said there was a possibility the Russians might bring some charges on account of the sentry being knocked out, so instead of trying to get us on a train to Murmansk they sent us over in the *Anna* to meet your ship."

Were they better off aboard *Audacity*? Smith wondered. Nobody knew what was happening, or going to happen, in Russia. But they had been on the bridge long enough. If the destroyer took to sweeping with her searchlight again and a sharp-eyed lookout spotted these two in uniform, the fat would be in the fire. The sooner they were safely below, the better. He said, "You're welcome aboard, but now –"

"There was something I wanted to ask you," Gallagher interrupted. "You'll remember I told you I was shot down. I got my Camel back but it was in a mess. We already had two busted machines on the ground so the fitters and riggers cannibalised them for parts to put mine together again but neither Billy nor Danby could fly it. Billy was armaments officer and Danby was – Administration. He took over that job from a chap who was killed. Danby had lost most of his kit when our field was bombed the night he arrived and that's why he's wearing the chap's jacket; it fits where

76

it touches. Anyway, they hid my Camel in the forest, stuck it up on blocks and wrapped it in a canvas hangar. Then Billy set off for Petrograd. A few days later Jerry overran the area and my Camel is presumably still sitting there at Kunda Bay. You see?"

"I do see. But what about it?"

"I want you to put me ashore so I can burn it." And Gallagher went on quickly, "On a show like this your orders are probably a bit elastic, with a lot left to your discretion. There's an old peasant, I suppose you could call him a farmer, lives nearby. We used to buy eggs and milk off him and he'll give me shelter if I need it, but this won't take long –"

Smith shook his head. "No."

"Listen, sir, please! From what the groundcrew say, with any luck it'll be in good condition *and* it won't have been found yet. And this is a first-line fighter, the best we've got. If Jerry does find it he'll learn from it and, damn it, he'll *use* it!"

Smith jammed his hands deeper in his pockets and hunched his shoulders. "No. If they don't learn from this one they would from another shot down in Flanders. And my orders are not elastic."

"But that Scottish bloke who came out with the Russians said they were twenty-four hours early so you have a day in hand. Surely you could –"

"Shut up, Mr. Gallagher!" And that stopped the pilot dead. Smith's patience had run out. His ship lay at anchor surrounded by the enemy and under their guns. So: "Get off my bridge and below or I'll have you put in the cells!"

For a second Gallagher did not believe him, took a breath to argue again but then read the promise in Smith's cold glare. He swung round, shoved past Danby and out of the wheelhouse. Danby waited until the rapid tramp of Gallagher's boots faded, then offered as part explanation, part apology, "It means a lot to him, sir, that Camel."

"I can understand that." *Audacity* and her crew meant a lot to Smith. He asked, "He's a man of some experience?"

Danby answered ruefully, "He was flying in action while I was still polishing an office stool with the seat of my trousers. He's an 'ace': twenty-three kills and he's flown all kinds. Triplanes in Flanders, Pups from ships. He was one of the first to do that."

"You've been under something of a strain yourself, Mr. Danby."

"It wasn't how I expected it to be, sir."

Smith grinned at him. "It never is! But it sounds to me as if you coped pretty well, notwithstanding. I suggest you get some sleep now. We're glad to have you aboard."

"Thank you, sir." Danby was smiling as he left the wheelhouse.

Smith leaned on the screen again and looked out at the ships and the low, lean shape of the destroyer seen beyond *Audacity*'s fo'c'sle head. How long before he would be able to sail her out of this trap? He was conscious of Buckley still standing at the back of the bridge, no doubt confident as always that the captain would get them all out of this. He wished he shared Buckley's confidence. He had sent his officers away to rest and given up his cabin to Robertson because he could not himself sleep this close to the enemy. He had to watch the destroyer. Although Gallagher and Danby were out of sight now the German captain might still become suspicious or simply curious. If he sent a boat to examine *Audacity* then Smith would have no alternative but to try to fight his way out to the sea. He swore under his breath. The night dragged on and he waited it out.

He was glad he was quit of Elizabeth Ramsay.

Wasn't he?

At dawn the first German troops were ferried ashore in boats. The destroyer's guns were manned and trained on the shore, ready to give covering fire if needed, but the soldiers formed up quietly into parties on the quay and marched off in various directions while the boats returned for more. There were spectators on the shore but no opposition.

Smith ate breakfast standing in the wheelhouse with McLeod for company while Robertson's boat came off for him and took him away. He told the navigator, "You did

78

well last night, talking to that German captain. We're lucky to have you aboard."

"Thank you, sir." McLeod pulled a face. "I don't want to do that too often, though. All the time I was talking I was looking down the barrel of that damned four-inch. Anyway, the best interpreter's left us."

"Interpreter? You mean Robertson? He's lived here for years."

"No, Mrs. Ramsay."

"What?" Smith had assumed that the woman spoke some Russian because she was the contact with the Russian officers, but he had not known . . .

"Oh, aye." McLeod grinned, remembering. "We talked a wee bit in the wardroom and she can speak every language around the Baltic like a native: German, Swedish, Russian –" He waved a big hand at the rest. "I learned by ear so I'm told I sound right, but I think in English then turn it into Swedish or whatever. She *thinks* in all these languages, I'd swear it. She must have been brought up in them. She'd have been the one to talk to that German skipper."

Smith knew that before the war it had not been uncommon for a merchant skipper to take his wife along. But now? He shook his head. "It would have looked odd, a woman doing the talking and being on the bridge at that time of night."

McLeod nodded agreement. "That's true. Good job you kept her out of sight." And then: "She's a real nice girl; Ross thought so, as well."

Smith had held her close. Now she was gone. He walked away, out to the bridge-wing.

Ross was on the deck below, supervising a few of the crew going about the normal work of a merchantman in port. One painted lethargically while others chipped at rust. The cook slopped out of the galley in pyjamas and plimsolls and dumped a bucket of rubbish over the side. Smith saw through glasses the same sort of domestic routine going on aboard the German timber ship lying by the sawmill. Her name, he saw, was *Königsberg*. She had not completed loading, confirming her master's intention of

79

not sailing until the next day. There was a small naval party from the destroyer stationed on the quay, acting as a signal link between their captain and the officer commanding the troops ashore. Their signal-lamp flickered rapidly at intervals to be answered by another from the destroyer. Her guns' crews had stood down and secured their pieces, so the shore must have been reported clear of any enemy.

At last the other ships weighed anchor and crept further into the harbour. The channel was clear and Smith took a breath, called Ross to the bridge and told him, "We'll get under way, but no fuss or rush."

"Aye, aye, sir." Ross took the point; they must not seem to be in a hurry to get away. The destroyer's captain would be watching them.

And when the anchor cable was 'up and down' a lookout reported Robertson's boat coming out from the quay. Calmly, 'no fuss or rush', they lowered the ladder again and he climbed aboard and up to the wheelhouse. "Good morning! You're off, I see. I don't blame you and won't delay your departure. Brought you this." He pulled off his gloves and took a folded sheet of paper from the inside pocket of his overcoat. "A coded telegram. It's for you. As soon as I decoded enough to know that, I left the rest for you to do and dashed out here to deliver it."

Smith quickly handed it to McLeod, whose duties included decoding, and he immediately went below to unlock his books and set to work.

Robertson, however, lingered. "The Hun is busy ashore and on his best behaviour, making much of being an ally of the White Finns. It's what I thought last night: they're here to sit across the railway line and stop any reinforcements that might be sent from Russia. The Finns talked to the Germans and I talked to the Finns, pointed out that I had a business interest and wanted to know how this convoy and maybe others would affect harbour and storage facilities here. They say the destroyer sails for Riga today to escort another convoy from there. The German commissariat are requisitioning stores and warehouses, some for immediate use but others to be available for the nineteenth, so that's when the next convoy is due to arrive here. I don't know whether any of that affects your movements but I thought I'd let you know."

"Well, at least that destroyer will be out of my way," Smith replied grimly, "I've seen enough of her."

Robertson held out his hand. "I'll be off. Good luck to you, Captain. By God! You're a cool one! When that destroyer turned up last night and you carried on with the transfer . . .!" He shook his head and climbed down to his boat.

Audacity got under way and crept around the headland until the other ships and the harbour were lost to sight. The open sea lay ahead and Smith stretched his arms, took a deep breath and grinned at Ross. "You can pipe: 'Up spirits!' The sun's over the yard-arm and I think I'll have a drink myself."

He had cause for celebration. In spite of German patrols, fog, minefields and the appalling bad luck of the previous night he had smuggled a fortune in gold into the Baltic and delivered it to the Russian plotters – under the very noses of the enemy. Now *Audacity* was on her way home and might well escape from the Baltic as safely as she had entered it.

Then he heard boots pounding the deck and turned to see McLeod running up the ladder to the bridge. He halted before Smith and said breathlessly, "The signal, sir!"

Smith took the telegram and read McLeod's transcription in pencilled capitals: NEGATIVE TRANSACTION. RE-TURN WITH CARGO. He stared at it, stiff-faced with shock for some seconds, and then he began to think again.

Blackledge had said the British government dared wait no longer for a positive guarantee from the Bolsheviks that they would not let Germany take the Russian Fleet. Now it seemed that guarantee had arrived in London and been accepted. So the operation was cancelled.

The Admiralty, knowing the transfer was scheduled, and *ordered* for this coming night of the fifteenth/sixteenth, believed that Smith still held the gold aboard *Audacity*.

He felt sick as the implications hit him: if the Russian plotters reneged, simply disappeared with the gold, he would be held responsible for its loss. Alternatively, if they carried out the plan and sank the ships, or tried and failed, he would be blamed for the consequences. And rightly so. His had been the decision to make the transfer a day early and his alone. Others might find excuses for him but he would seek none for himself. The guilt was his to bear.

6

Fight or Run?

"No sign of her yet, sir." McLeod's voice came down from the flying bridge to where Smith stood outside the wheelhouse door.

"Very good," he said, thinking that it was a bloody silly form of acknowledgment: the circumstances, in fact, could hardly be worse. Cape Kolganja lay off *Audacity*'s starboard beam and Koporja Bay opened ahead. Astern lay Kurgala Bay and across the ten miles of its mouth, low on the horizon and hazy with distance, was Kurgala Point. These were Russian waters and that was the coast of Russia. The sun was sinking and there was still no sign of *Anna*.

Smith saw Gallagher pacing the deck aft, scowling. He still smarted from having been ordered off the bridge. When questioned by Smith about the *Anna*'s crossing from Kurgala to Kirkko, he was polite and correct, but hostile. "She averaged about six or seven knots. They let me on deck after it was dark and I asked the chap at the tiller when we'd reach Kirkko and what speed we were making. He knew a little bit of English and told me six or seven knots."

"Thank you, Mr. Gallagher." And to hell with you and your injured dignity.

Danby was on deck but forward of the bridge. He seemed to be keeping out of Gallagher's way. He wore a greatcoat that fell to his ankles and made him look like a small boy dressed up in his father's clothes. But Smith remembered that he had led the surviving airmen out of a prison camp and back to Petrograd. So that when Gallagher gave him a hard time it was clearly not just a fighting-man patronising a chairborne warrior. There had to be some other reason.

"I think we should have seen her by now, sir." That was

Ross, cautiously voicing a conclusion his captain should have reached for himself – provided his captain was not a bloody fool, and had got his sums right. Was that what Ross thought, why he had spoken?

Smith just grunted in answer.

Audacity had worked up to fifteen knots after leaving Kirkko and held to it in spite of patchy, drifting fog; the seaward horizon was now blurred by mist, visibility three to four miles. So it was obvious to every man aboard that the captain considered it desperately important that the *Anna* should be caught. There had been just a chance that she would be. Robertson had said she would cross the Gulf of Finland from Kirkko to Kurgala Point and then head eastward along the coast to some little port where the Russians had friends. If she'd held to that course, and at the six or seven knots she'd made on the previous crossing, then *Audacity* would have come up with her before she raised Kurgala Point.

But they had not seen her. They had turned aside three times while crossing Kurgala Bay to look at fishing-boats but none was the *Anna*. She might have varied her course, but not by much because her destination had to be a harbour or inlet along this stretch of coast. Her speed was another matter. With a hundred thousand pounds in gold aboard her skipper would make the fastest passage he could; Smith was prepared to bet on it. By now the *Anna* was probably tucked away somewhere along this coast, along with a huddle of fishing-boats like herself, in any one of a score of little anchorages that were too shallow even for *Audacity* to enter.

Smith pondered the problem: should he send in the motor-boat to search every anchorage where masts showed above a breakwater? But any strange boat would be suspect, might get in but not out again. And if, by a miracle, the motor-boat found the *Anna* she would never get alongside her.

In a few hours it would be dark and the gold would go ashore – if it wasn't already there. If the Russians were among people they trusted they might well unload their cargo without waiting for night, and get it into hiding with minimum delay.

Smith stared out across the empty grey waste of Koporja Bay. He knew Ross was watching him, waiting. He could not wireless Admiralty because *Audacity* was far out of range of any British ship. Therefore he now had to go back to Robertson at Kirkko and ask him to send a coded telegram. *Audacity*'s return would look suspicious but Admiralty had to be informed that the plot was going ahead in contravention of their direct order.

Could Robertson's courier contact the Russian plotters and stop them? There might be a slender chance of saving that much from the wreck of the mission, though they would never get the gold back.

Smith made his decision. "Port ten."

"Port ten, sir."

"Mr. McLeod!" And as the navigator slid down the ladder from the flying bridge: "A course for Kirkko."

"Aye, aye, sir."

Smith knew that, even at fifteen knots, it would be dark long before *Audacity* entered Kirkko. Then he would have to find Robertson in the little town that swarmed with German troops.

Audacity was five miles north of Kurgala Point and running north-westward at her full speed. The mist had thickened and closed in again, visibility was barely a mile and sometimes much less, but Smith ordered no reduction in revolutions. He could not waste a minute in finding Robertson to pass the warning to Admiralty, and to send his courier to try to reach the Russians.

Nerves were strung tight by *Audacity*'s headlong rush. Smith stood immobile, silent, while McLeod shifted from one wing of the bridge to the other and Ross repeated, "Bloody fog! Can't see a damn thing!" Smith told himself that a collision was a million to one against. There would be few ships trading in the Baltic this early in the year and so soon after the ending of the war with Russia. They had not seen another ship since leaving Kirkko. Still, he had an extra lookout right forward in the bow because if they did come on a fishing-boat, that split second of advance warning might save running her down.

It was the man in the bow who yelled the report: "Ship on the starboard bow one mile!"

Smith's head snapped around and his hand grabbed for the glasses hanging against his chest. Even with their help the other vessel out there was insubstantial in the mist. It was hard to make out what she was, but certainly a ship and not a fishing-boat. She was a long, low shape – not a tramp like *Audacity* pretended to be – and Smith heard Ross curse softly as he reached the same conclusion. Moments later their fears were confirmed as the ship came out of the mist and her lines hardened, became clear.

Robertson had spoken of an old destroyer that patrolled out of Reval, along the Finnish coast then back across the Gulf. *Audacity* had met her not long before entering Kirkko. But this was a different destroyer. The Germans had probably added an extra vessel to their patrols because of their involvement in Finland. She would be on the lookout for ships from Russia and bound for Finland because, whether neutrals or no, they might carry contraband, supplies or reinforcements for the Red Guards fighting Von Goltz's troops. Smoke streamed from her two funnels and she was making around ten knots. She was older than the destroyer met off Kirkko, and weaker. Too old to serve with the Fleet, they had ripped the torpedo tubes out of her, and two of her three guns. Only one remained, right aft. As Smith studied her through his glasses he suspected that, while they had drawn most of her teeth, they had probably given her more bunkerage space for coal to extend her range for this task of patrolling. The aerials strung between her masts were connected to a superstructure abaft the bridge – that would be the wireless office: she was a pair of eyes – and a voice.

A light stabbed out from her bridge, stuttering a signal. McLeod said, "She's ordering us to stop, sir."

Smith judged she was less than a mile ahead off the starboard bow on a course almost parallel with *Audacity*'s but closing on her slowly. The gap between was narrowing fast, as *Audacity* overhauled her. The destroyer would probably have called on her to stop anyway, but the German captain would have added suspicions because

86

Audacity's speed was both out of character for the tramp she pretended to be, and out of reason in this mist.

There were men manning the German's gun now and others gathering around a boat. Her captain was not going to be content with howling questions across a neck of sea. When *Audacity* stopped, the boat would bring a boarding-party.

On the other hand, Smith could order an emergency turn to port and *Audacity* might escape in the mist. But the hunt would be up, and she might not get away.

He stepped into the wheelhouse, pushed the button below the screen and the buzzers sounded through the ship. He heard the trample of boots as the men ran to the guns, listened to the 'Ready' reports as they came in through the voice-pipes, watched the destroyer ahead. The lamp was flickering again from her open bridge, insistent. McLeod read it: "Stop or I fire."

The smoke from the destroyer's funnels was thickening. She was barely half a mile ahead, her skipper demanding more speed from his engine room so that this strange Swedish tramp would not get away.

Smith ordered, "Port ten," to bring *Audacity* around so the after twelve-pounder would bear as well as the other guns. He told McLeod, "Ensign." The navigator lifted a hand. Men crouching below the bulwarks let shutters drop down over the boards painted in the Swedish colours, covering them. Another on the poop snapped the Swedish flag from the jack and ran up the White Ensign. Smith rapped into the voice-pipe: "Ship starboard bow eight hundred! Midships and waterline! Fire!" Midships and waterline because he had to sink her. In exercises the guns had uncovered and got into action quick enough – but would they now?

Smoke jetted from the gun in the destroyer's stern. The flat thump of its report followed a second later and with it the shriek of the shell. It passed overhead, or more likely across the bow, where the forward twelve-pounder was swinging up on its revolving mounting from its conceal-ment under the deck of the fo'c'sle. Then the gun locked into place and the crew jumped in on it, training it round.

The breech was knocked open and the shell loaded. Smith heard behind him the clatter as the housing around the four-inch collapsed to the deck.

Audacity's head was turning. "Meet her . . . steady!" She was broadside to the destroyer, and fore and aft the twelve-pounders fired almost as one; *crack! – crack!* Then a second later the four-inch banged. Flame bit on the destroyer as the rounds struck, smoke drifted to match the wisping mist, and a hole showed in one of her funnels, another in the superstructure. The gun on the destroyer spurted smoke once more but Smith never heard the shell nor saw where it went. Heavier smoke drifted along the old destroyer's length as she was hit again and again. She pushed out of it and now her gun was cocked at the sky and no men stood near it. *Audacity*'s guns were firing faster and more accurately than ever they had done in practice.

McLeod bawled exultantly, "I haven't seen one round go over yet!"

The German had been pounded from stem to stern and every time she came out of the smoke she showed more wreckage. Both masts were cut and collapsed, the foremast a jumble of steel crushing the superstructure abaft the bridge – that took yet another hit as Smith watched. The bridge itself was empty, mangled. But she had not stopped, and if anything was cutting faster through the flat sea, so that while *Audacity* had worked up abeam, she was not headreaching on her, no longer had the edge in speed.

The destroyer turned away. Smith had been half-expecting it: "Hard astarboard!" he shouted, to bring *Audacity* around after her. Was the destroyer out of control? Not yet. She turned more quickly, more tightly than *Audacity* could manage with her bigger turning circle, then steadied to run back along her own wake. *Audacity* was still under helm so the range was opening. Her guns weren't firing so rapidly nor hitting so regularly. The heel of the ship in the turn, and the changing relative positions of guns and target, accounted for that. There were splashes of near misses astern of and alongside the destroyer.

"Meet her . . . steady!" *Audacity* straightened out, racing after the destroyer. It was a stern chase now. The four-inch and the after twelve-pounder had ceased firing, no longer able to bear. Was the range still opening? Smith was not sure, but *Audacity* had lost ground in that turn and the destroyer was now a mile ahead. Smith used his glasses, and saw that everything along her deck – masts, super-structure, bridge – was smashed flat.

McLeod shouted, "She's on fire, sir!"

She was. Smoke streamed from her that was not from her funnels, and Smith glimpsed a yellow glow under it. But she was not slowing. Then her smoke and the mist veiled everything and she was as insubstantial as when they first sighted her, smoke and mist drawing a gauzy curtain.

The twelve-pounder in the bow ceased firing, the layer no longer able to see the target. Now there was only the mist, banks of it lying a mile away or in places less than half that distance. The guns waited, breeches open but empty, the ammunition numbers breathing hard as they stood by, cradling the shells snatched from the magazine hoists. The tang of cordite still hung about the ship.

The men on the twelve-pounder were grinning. A burst of laughter came from the crew of the four-inch, only ten yards from where Smith stood outside the wheelhouse. They had fought and punished the enemy, seen him run, were still in the grip of that excitement, a mixture of fear, tension and exhilaration. They had not thought the situation through yet, but they would. They weren't stupid.

Ross had. And McLeod. No grins or laughter there. *Audacity*'s chief protection had not been her guns or her disguises but the fact that the enemy did not know, had no reason even to suspect, that she was in the Baltic. And now that protection was gone.

Smith said, "A course for Reval, Pilot." Because that was where the destroyer would be headed. *Audacity* hunted along that course, in the hope that the destroyer might have broken down, or at least been forced to slow by the hammering she had received.

McLeod reported: "Sparks doesn't think she sent a wire-less signal." The wireless operator was keeping his listening watch. "The only traffic he heard was weak and distant."

Smith nodded. "Thank you." If the destroyer's wireless had been wrecked before she could send out a warning then *Audacity* had a few hours' grace, at least. But if the destroyer reached Reval she'd raise the alarm soon enough.

At one point they thought they heard distant gunfire, but no one could be sure of its bearing. It lasted only a second. They searched until the mist became dusk and did not find her.

Smith spoke to Ross: "Pass the word to the men that it was good shooting, better than ever they did in exercise." That was true and the praise well-deserved but even so the shooting had not been quite good enough. The destroyer had got away.

There was something else these men deserved. Soon they would realise they were under imminent sentence of death – or a prison camp if they were very lucky. His mind went back to before he had set out on this cruise, the determination formed then: "And you can tell them I am now taking this ship and her crew back to Rosyth."

"Aye, aye, sir." Ross looked startled, relieved – then unconvinced.

Smith could understand that. The intention was one thing, the achievement another. One decision at least had been taken, that getting a message directly to Robertson was out of the question. But the length of the Baltic still lay between *Audacity* and the Sound, six hundred miles of sea that the enemy controlled, and once the damaged destroyer reached port they would be hunted throughout that length. Then there was the passage of the Sound – and before they ever reached it there would be the patrolling Zeppelin . . .

McLeod was waiting, expecting to be asked for a new course. What should it be? *Audacity* was dawdling along at eight knots while Smith made up his mind. He paced the bridge rapidly, his thoughts churning. The length of the Baltic . . . run for it, fast and straight? Or hug the northern, neutral shores . . .? Change the identity of the ship with a fresh disguise? But then there was still the Sound. He had to pass through it in the night but to have time for the passage he must make his approach before then, in the light of day. And now the Zeppelin would suspect every merchantman, neutral or no, reporting to the destroyer which would intercept, board and search. The Zeppelin was the key to the door –

He halted suddenly as the pieces clicked into place, turned and stared at McLeod. "Let's look at the chart, Pilot."

Buckley, at the back of the bridge, thought, Here we go!

Then Smith turned to him and spoke abruptly: "Ask Mr. Gallagher to come up, please."

7

"Sink her!"

The night was still and a low covering of cloud hid all but an occasional star. Smith stood on the flying bridge above the wheelhouse with McLeod and Gallagher. The navigator crouched knees-bent by the compass, taking bearings. Gallagher waited silently. He had known about the mysterious boxes transferred to the *Anna* at Kirkko and had been privy to the guesses of the rest of *Audacity*'s crew as to their contents. That was inevitable in a ship with the gossip circulating. Now he had been told the part he must play in their escape. Smith, glasses to his eyes and looking out over the port side, knew that Gallagher would have plenty to think about; he could be landing on the enemy coast very soon. The shore was a low, ragged black line set in silhouette against the night sky, and, less than a mile distant, a tall rectangular tower stood up from that line.

Audacity crept through these shallow inshore waters with a man at the lead. Smith passed the glasses to Gallagher, who trained them on the land. McLeod straightened and said, "It looks right from the chart, sir."

Smith nodded. "Yes, it does." And it *had* to be right. They must not put Gallagher ashore miles from his destination, lost at the outset.

McLeod went on, certain now: "That's Kunda Bay opening ahead of us." Beyond the tower landmark the shore fell away, a receding blackness.

Gallagher returned the glasses to Smith and said positively, "That's the tower. And that's the bay; God knows, I've flown over it and walked along it often enough."

Smith slipped the strap of the glasses back over his head and let them hang on his chest. "That's a fine piece of work, Pilot. A good landfall." And it was, considering

McLeod's last sighting had been off Kurgala and they had then fought the destroyer and searched for her, fruitlessly.

McLeod answered honestly, "Bit of luck, sir." Some parts of his calculations had been by guesswork, guided by instinct.

Smith went down to the wheelhouse with Gallagher and stood by Ross as *Audacity* edged cautiously into the bay. The man at the lead softly called the depth under her. "By the mark, four! . . . By the mark . . ." The guns were hidden but their crews stood ready to bring them into action. Outside the wheelhouse were three of Gallagher's groundcrew: a petty officer, a fitter and a rigger. Each carried a haversack holding the minimum of the tools of his trade. And like Gallagher, each man had food for a day and a water-bottle, a pistol belted around his waist, and a rolled blanket slung over one shoulder and fastened at the belt. The pulling boat on the starboard side was swung out, hung in its davits ready to be lowered and a party stood by at the falls. The motor-boat would have done the job faster, but the noise of its engine would have alerted any enemy on the shore.

Smith stared out over the bow at the low, black outline of the shore, underlined by a thread of silver where the sea gently washed the beach. There was no ice here, nor fog, but the night was dark enough for the job. No light showed on *Audacity* bar the glow from the compass. The man at the lead read its markers by the touch of his fingers.

The lookout in the starboard wing of the bridge called, "Light! Starboard bow!"

Smith saw it, then it was gone. Broad on the bow. A mile away? More? On the shore? He was outside the wheelhouse now, using his glasses, ordering, "Stop her."

The lookout said, "Hard to tell against the land – but it looks like a ship o' some sort. Think I can see a funnel. And maybe a mast."

Smith thought so, too. There was a low, lumpy outline, but that *might* be a funnel. And a mast. For a moment he wondered if this was the destroyer they had sought. Then he discarded that idea. She would have been showing more light, would have been a hive of activity as her captain tried to repair some of his damage and looked to his dead and wounded. So – a fisherman, perhaps? But whatever it was . . .

He turned to Gallagher. "Go now." He'd intended to creep in nearer the shore, but: "I don't think that ship's seen us, or will see us, but we won't risk going further in. Make a wide circle round her. We'll take you off tomorrow night."

Gallagher nodded; they had been through his plans and Smith's orders to him. "If you don't come, I use my initiative." He paused, then added sardonically, "Bloody long walk home, though."

Smith had said, hours ago, stooped over the chart, "I'll let you go after your Camel, on certain conditions." And Gallagher had seized on the offer, not even asking what the conditions were, accepting them with a shrug when Smith told him.

The boat was lowered. Then its crew, with Gallagher and his men, climbed down to it and it pulled away. Buckley was at the tiller because he had landed on an enemy coast – and more than once before . . .

Smith saw young Danby on *Audacity*'s deck forward of the bridge, watching the boat disappear into the night. Should he invite that lonely young man on to the bridge? It was surprising that Danby had turned out to see Gallagher go – the older man's treatment of him verged on contempt. Or was it hatred?

Smith checked the thought, wondering if he was exaggerating what could be no more than two officers of differing personalities getting on each other's nerves. That was common enough. But he had problems of his own and he did not want company, so he left Danby where he was.

He paced the starboard wing as he waited. Gallagher should be all right. He had been confident this coast would be thinly held by the Germans – with probably not one posted for miles – and Smith had agreed. Now he went over in his mind the plans he had made so rapidly, examining, seeking to improve them, looking for faults. All the time he listened to the cast of the lead, a monotonously repeated,

"By the mark, three!" *Audacity* lay like a log on the water; McLeod, up on the flying bridge checking his bearings to marks on the shore, confirmed that by not reporting any change, any drift. There was virtually neither current nor tide here.

The ship was still but not completely silent. Men talked in whispers, shifted position and stretched as they waited by the guns. The lookouts ceaselessly searched back and forth through their arcs from bow to stern. The ship across the bay, whatever it was, showed one more brief gleam of light then became dark again – as if a man had opened a door or a scuttle to look out at the night, then closed it. Danby wandered the deck between bridge and fo'c'sle.

Smith had wanted to send him after the Camel because it would be no use saving it if Gallagher was killed in the process. But the pilot would have none of that: "It's my Camel. I'll trust nobody else with it, especially –" He broke off there, then challenged Smith: "If it was your ship, would you send anyone else?"

So Gallagher had gone.

"Boat's coming back, sir." That came from Ross.

Smith halted and watched the swift rhythm of the oars as they swept the boat towards *Audacity*, could imagine Buckley's hoarse growl, "*Put your backs into it!*"

The boat was hooked on, hoisted inboard and Buckley reported to Smith. "Went sweet as you like, sir. Gave that craft a wide berth – 'cept it looks like it could be two of 'em when you're a bit closer, though we didn't get *that* close, one tied alongside the other. We never saw a soul on the shore. Mr. Gallagher and his lads nipped up the beach and in among the trees at the back of it. I saw that much and all was quiet so we come away."

"Very good." Smith hoped it was, that he had not sent the four men to their deaths. One more calculated risk. He thrust that thought from his mind. "Mr. Ross!"

"Sir?"

"I want a man who's handy with a needle."

"A needle, sir?" Ross shifted his mind to this new tack. "Well, Fenwick is a dab hand, does a bit of tailoring."

Smith had been calling rapid orders into the wheelhouse

but now turned back to Ross: "Get him up here. I want him to make a couple of ensigns for me."

Audacity's engines thumped slowly as she turned and slipped out of the bay as quietly as she had come.

"Morning, sir. Gettin' light." Wilberforce, the little steward, stood by Smith's bunk, a steaming mug held in one skinny hand. Smith took it and sipped at the coffee while Wilberforce rattled on: "Mr. Ross said I was to tell you we're on station an' cruising west-nor'-west at eight knots."

Smith nodded. So they were now patrolling off the mouth of the deepwater channel leading out from Kirkko, where he had handed the gold and Elizabeth Ramsay to the Russians. *Audacity* had made the passage through the night from Kunda at a leisurely ten knots. Back to Kirkko after all, but no chance of contacting Robertson, or through him the Admiralty. He scowled at the irony. But the gold was gone – and probably his career with it – and that was that.

Wilberforce breathed at a mark on the table and used his cuff to polish it clean. "Pity we didn't come up with them Russians, sir. I'd ha' liked to see that Mrs. Ramsay again. Very nice to me, she was, always a word and a smile –"

"Get out!" Smith shoved the half-empty mug at him.

Wilberforce took it and went, muttering under his breath, "Not like some foul-tempered bastard I know!"

Smith had turned in all standing. Now he had only to pull on his boots and the old overcoat. He picked up his cap, went out to the wheelhouse and grunted, "Good morning!" at Ross.

"Good morning, sir. Nothing seen of *Königsberg*."

"Early yet." Smith went out to the starboard wing. The sun had not risen but it reddened the eastern horizon. He thought that was appropriate because over that horizon lay Bolshevik Russia. The sea was the colour of pewter, and cold, though there was no ice this far out. The land and Kirkko were hidden behind the rim of the sea to the north. Fog wisped in patches and Smith's breath steamed on the air.

He should not have snapped at Wilberforce as he had, but he'd been caught off-guard. That was a sign of the pressure on him and his need to hide it. How deeply was Elizabeth Ramsay involved in the anti-German plot? Why had the Russians insisted she went along with the gold? Would they secretly betray the Allied cause? Would *she?* He remembered the contact between his body and hers. Would he ever see her again?

"Excuse me, sir."

He turned and saw the seaman Fenwick, tall, thin as a whippet, but now as bulky as the rest of them in layers of clothing. He carried two rolled bundles under one arm. "Got them ensigns you wanted, sir."

"Let's have a look at 'em."

Fenwick put one bundle down on the gratings, shook out the other. It was the black, white and red-banded flag of the German merchant marine. Smith saw Ross watching from the wheelhouse and nodded, "Good." Fenwick rolled it and spread the other: a blue St. Andrew's cross on white. Smith nodded again, "That's a good job. Mr. Ross said you were a dab hand; he wasn't exaggerating. Thank you."

He took the rolled ensigns from Fenwick and passed them to Ross. "Keep them handy."

Would there be a use for them? If the German freighter *Königsberg* and her load of timber did not come, there would not. His plans would have gone awry. He had promised every man aboard that he would take them out of the Baltic. It had been a bold statement, one he might live to regret – die regretting it. He did not let his fears show in his face but said casually, "Tell Wilberforce I'm ready for my breakfast."

Smith ate slowly, forcing himself to swallow every mouthful, then climbed the ladder to the flying bridge. No one was up there now. He paced rapidly forward and aft, eight strides each way. *Audacity* was steaming on the westward leg of her patrol. Now and again as he turned he swept the northern horizon with his glasses. That horizon was murky and close, the visibility limited by low cloud, mist and drizzling rain.

Robertson had said *Königsberg*'s master intended to sail

this morning. In other words he would finish loading late yesterday and wait until this morning to make his passage of that winding channel out of Kirkko in the light of day. That made sense. Smith had told Ross: "Early yet." It was not early now. If *Königsberg* had sailed on time they must sight her soon. He halted and used the glasses but saw only leaden sky and that sea of pewter ending in a grey line of rain and cloud.

He turned away. He had gambled that the destroyer, battered and on fire as she was, would not make good twenty knots, that once her captain thought he had shaken off pursuit he would reduce to half that speed or less, to fight the fire and see to his wounded and dead, the damage to his ship. So he would not reach Reval to raise the alarm until this morning, so that by the time the signals warning of a raider, *Audacity*, had gone out, *Königsberg* would have sailed. She had no wireless, her masts had carried no aerials, Smith remembered that. But if her sailing was delayed for some reason? What if the warning signals had reached her?

He had thought there was a good chance that his gamble might succeed. All his plans for escape from the Baltic were based on that. First of all, he needed *Königsberg* and her cargo – for a disguise. Most Q-ships could change their appearance. They usually operated by trudging back and forth, alone, inviting attack along a shipping lane where U-boats were known to be active. But a U-boat commander was not a fool. If he saw a ship running eastward one day and recognised the same ship steaming westward the next, then he would smell a rat. So *Audacity* already had a dummy deckhouse that could be erected forward or aft, bands of various designs and colours that could be bolted to her funnel, different names painted on boards to bolt to her bow and stern, strips of black-painted canvas that, stretched along between fo'c'sle and superstructure, superstructure and poop, gave her the appearance from a distance of being a flush-decked ship instead of a three-island tramp. She also carried a carpenter, Bennett, mainly for the purpose of knocking up fresh disguises to order. But now Smith wanted a particular new identity for *Aud-*

acity, for a special reason, though that would depend on Gallagher's report. If the airman lived . . .

"Ship! Starboard beam!"

Only seconds ago the horizon had been empty. Smith set the glasses to his eyes. *Königsberg?* Or had he calculated wrongly; was the hunt already up and this a destroyer seeking his ship? She was hull-up but blurred in the murk out there. Gradually easing out of it now, Smith could see the outline of her taking shape. He ordered, "Starboard ten!" and dropped down the ladder to the bridge below.

Ross stood at the wheelhouse door. "Looks like her, sir."

"Yes. Got those ensigns?" Ross snatched them from a locker in the wheelhouse and Smith slapped the top one of the two. "That one and ours. Put the other away." He looked at the ship's head, *Audacity* still turning to starboard. "Meet her . . . steady . . . steer that." She straightened on a course to intercept the other ship, now on the starboard bow. *Königsberg*'s black, rust-speckled hull was low in the water, deep-laden with timber. She also carried it as deck cargo, the sawn lengths stacked in the wells between fo'c'sle and superstructure, superstructure and poop, higher than the heads of the men he saw moving on her deck. "Pass the word for the carpenter." And to Ross: "Close up the four-inch but keep it under cover until I give the word."

"Aye, aye, sir." Ross's eyes gleamed and his teeth showed in a shark's grin. "We're going to sink her, sir?"

"Eventually. First I want you to get a boarding-party together. McLeod will lead when it boards but you will later take command of the prize, so bear that in mind when you pick your men."

That shook Ross: "*Prize*, sir?"

Smith read the first lieutenant's mind and grinned. "All right! I'm not asking you to sail her back to Rosyth."

"Thank you, sir." Pretended relief; possibly not all pretence?

"You'll want engine-room staff so take the second engineer and tell him to pick some off-watch stokers. You can have ten men for the boarding-party but most of them will be working for Bennett." The carpenter was now climbing the ladder to the bridge. Smith rapidly gave Ross the rest of his orders then turned to Bennett. The old jacket buttoned over his blue jersey was strained tight as he caught his breath from the hurried climb. He kept his cap on though in front of his captain and did not salute; someone aboard *Königsberg* might be watching and Bennett was supposed to be a merchant seaman. Before the war, he had been. Before that he had served twelve years in the Navy.

"Sir?"

Smith's gaze was trained over Bennett's shoulder and fixed on *Königsberg*, now broad on the starboard bow, and closing every second. Smith's eyes shifted fractionally to focus on Bennett. "Take a good look at that ship." And as the carpenter half-turned: "I want this ship to look like her, with her deck cargo. I'm going to put you aboard her. I'll tell you now what I want done and you'll work out how much timber you'll need. Be sure you've got enough, allow a safe margin, but that's all. There'll be some seamen aboard but you can take the rest of those airmen as well." They could earn their keep. "Find out which of them knows a hammer from a saw."

Bennett got out a dog-eared notebook and the stub of a flat, carpenter's pencil. He scribbled quickly as Smith spoke his orders then tucked the pencil behind his ear and hurried away. After the man had gone Smith took off his cap and ran fingers through the fair hair that the cap had pressed flat. He had not taken his eyes from *Königsberg* for a second but he had heard the crew of the four-inch running to the gun, the report to Ross that it was closed-up. *Audacity* was still on a course to intercept the timber ship. Smith jammed the cap back on his head. "Port ten." Then as *Audacity*'s bow swung, "Ease to five . . . meet her . . . steer that."

Now the two ships ran level, barely a hundred yards between them and *Audacity* was still edging in on *Königsberg*, if slowly. The few hands working on *Königsberg*'s deck drifted to the port rail to stare across at *Audacity*. A stumpy figure in a short, black overcoat and peaked cap emerged from *Königsberg*'s wheelhouse and waved at the Swedish ship he might be remembering from Kirkko. Smith trained his glasses and saw a man of maybe sixty, round-faced and scowling. He would be wondering why this stupid Swede had come so close.

Close enough. Smith lowered the glasses and his eyes swept in one swift glance from McLeod and the boarding-party, kneeling hidden behind the starboard bulwark forward of the bridge, to Ross in the wheelhouse, the signaller and the bosun's mate with the two ensigns bent on and ready to hoist. Then from the innocent-seeming housing that concealed the four-inch gun to Bennett and the group of airmen lying on the deck below the bulwark aft of the bridge – finally down at the machine-gunner squatting on the gratings near his feet, the Lewis gun in his hands.

Smith ordered, "Hoist the ensigns! Lay the four-inch on her!" And leaning over the rail to call down to McLeod on the deck below, "Say your piece!" McLeod stood up by the bulwark, but the boarding-party, armed with rifles, still lay in its cover.

The roof and the sides of the four-inch housing fell away and the long barrel of the gun swung to point at the bridge of *Königsberg*. The White Ensign broke out, and another with a blue St. Andrew's cross on a white background – the ensign of the Imperial Russian Navy.

McLeod was bellowing through a megaphone, ordering *Königsberg* to stop or be fired on. Smith watched the round scowling face through his glasses and saw it lengthen as the jaw dropped. For a second the German master gaped into the muzzle of the four-inch, then he turned, to shout his orders. Smith let the glasses hang. Would the old man try to turn away and run for it, even with the gun trained on him at point-blank range? Or would he turn towards *Audacity* and try to ram? Either way, Smith would order the four-inch to fire. A murderous decision, but one he would have to take for the sake of his men.

He let out his breath in a whistling sigh. *Königsberg* was slowing, her single screw stopped and the way coming off her. *Audacity* slowed, too, at Smith's order, edged in closer, and rubbed gently against *Königsberg* as both ships lay still, fenders between their steel sides. Lines flew across and were caught and made fast by the German seamen, bewildered by this sudden attack and under the threat of the

Lewis machine-gun now mounted on the wing of *Audacity*'s bridge.

The boarding-party, McLeod at their head, swarmed across and Smith ordered him to tell the German master, only feet away now, to lower his boats. He dropped down the ladders to the deck forward of the bridge as McLeod bawled a translation. The grating now lashed between the two ships tilted gently as they rose and fell on the sea. Smith crossed it quickly, light-footed.

The rest of the German crew were assembling on deck, routed out by the boarding-party: seamen from the fo'c'sle, stokers and the engineer from the engine room. McLeod already had some of them working at lowering the ship's boats on the starboard side. They stared at Smith as he climbed to the bridge with McLeod hurrying behind. The master waited sullenly, flanked by his two mates, men as old as himself, their status as officers marked by weather-worn, peaked blue caps set square on their heads. All three glowered at Smith in his old overcoat, and at McLeod, who had shed his duffel for the sake of speed and wore one old jersey pulled over another. McLeod launched into carefully rehearsed German. Smith hardly understood a word but he had told McLeod what to say anyway: that Smith had been captain of a British submarine but now commanded this Russian ship out of Petrograd. There was an angry outburst from the German master and McLeod reported, "He says we're breaking the rules by not being in uniform and we'll be shot as spies. He says our stay in Kirkko, under the Swedish flag, was spying too. And Russia is supposed to be neutral."

Smith pointed to the Imperial Russian ensign flapping over *Audacity*. "Tell him the Red Russians made peace but the White Russians did not. Tell him his Navy has got to catch us before they can shoot us – and laugh as you say it. Then tell him the four-inch is only one of our guns. We met one of his destroyers yesterday and she was glad to run for her life. But we mean him no harm and as seamen feel sympathy for him. Then get down to the rest of it."

Smith smiled pleasantly at the master and his mates. McLeod went on with his speech, his laugh coming on cue, and the Germans exchanged uncertain glances. Smith leaned against the rail, smiling easily, seemingly without a care in the world. Now McLeod would be asking if the *Königsberg* was bound for Helsinki. Wasn't there a lot of German shipping plying into and out of those waters – and in the Gulf of Bothnia further west?

All the while Smith was aware of the boats on *Königsberg*'s starboard side being lowered, her crew going down into them with pathetic little bundles of hastily snatched belongings. Smith hardened his heart; this and worse had been done to British seamen by U-boats – and by the raider they had seen off Norway. The airmen had come aboard and were trooping along behind Bennett as he bustled around inspecting the timber stacked on *Königsberg*'s deck.

The conversation on the bridge flagged, then ceased, the master and his mates standing scowling and silent. Smith said cheerfully, "All right, they've guessed what we're trying to worm out of them. What results?"

McLeod grinned at Smith, trying to indicate satisfaction, the Germans watching him. "They began by saying there was some German traffic with Helsinki and now there might be more with Von Goltz's troops landing nearby. Then they started nudging each other and shut up."

Smith nodded; he'd seen the Germans' flicker of wary interest as Helsinki was mentioned. "Tell the captain we're casting off now and once we're clear he'll be able to lower the boats on the port side and get away. I regret it, but I'm sending his ship to Russia under a prize crew. Fortune of war. He has my best wishes."

That did not mollify the German skipper. He growled something clearly offensive and McLeod stiffened. "You bastard –"

Smith stopped him. "I can guess what he called me and in his position I might have done the same. Come on."

He touched his cap in salute, went back to *Audacity* with McLeod and climbed to the bridge. Ross crossed over to take command of *Königsberg*, with the course McLeod had given him on a piece of paper tucked into his pocket. The captured ship was cast off and now the boats on her port side could be lowered. The remainder of her crew and her officers climbed down to them. They pulled clear of the ships and then rested on their oars, watching intently. Smith bellowed across to Ross on *Königsberg*'s bridge, "Get under way!"

"Aye, aye, sir!" Ross worked the handle of the engine-room telegraph himself and Smith heard its jangling. *Audacity*'s second engineer and a party of stokers were below in *Königsberg*. Her screw turned and she moved ahead, then began a slow turn to starboard.

Smith ordered, "Half ahead!" *Audacity* trembled again to the beat of her engines. He watched from the starboard wing of the bridge as she headed westward, on a course that would take her to the waters off Helsinki. *Königsberg* was steaming away in the opposite direction, eastward towards Russia.

The German boats were under way again, creeping across the surface of the sea like beetles as the oars swung, pulling back towards the Finnish coast. It was out of sight beyond the mist-shrouded horizon but they should make a landfall before the night. And tomorrow their story would be told: that the disguised raider had struck again; that she was a White Russian out of Petrograd but com-manded by an English naval officer and was last seen bound for Helsinki and the Gulf of Bothnia.

Smith held to that course until not only *Audacity* but her smoke would be out of sight of the men in the boats. Then he turned her in a wide circle to port and headed eastward again. In the late afternoon they sighted a long smudge on the horizon ahead that was the island of Gogland, midway between Finland and Estonia. Off its southern tip they found *Königsberg* but with most of her deck cargo of timber gone, jettisoned in passage. The two ships came together again and rubbed side by side, stopped out of sight of land.

Bennett and the airmen aboard *Königsberg* had not been idle while she had made her passage and then waited at the rendezvous for *Audacity*. They had started knocking together timber frames, four sets of each, and each set comprised four sides and the top of a box. So when the first set was swung aboard *Audacity* by the derrick and erected forward of the mast over Number One hold, the hollow box so formed was a replica of the deck cargo as carried by *Königsberg*. A neat piece of work.

As the day wore into evening the mist rolled in over the sea again. There was a lot of work still to be done, sunset little more than an hour away and no question of using lights. Smith lifted the megaphone to call over to the carpenter: "Leave the airmen to finish the frames! You come back aboard and deal with Number Two hold!" That was between the foremast and the bridge. "Mr. McLeod will detail a party to give you a hand!"

Bennett waved acknowledgment and returned to *Audacity* with his bag of tools. Despite the damp cold his face was red and sweating and he carried his jacket over his arm. He bawled at the men McLeod had assembled for him, "C'mon you lot!" Together they dropped the hatch covers of Number Two hold, down into its cavernous depths. It was empty, the bomb-throwers taken out before *Audacity* sailed from Rosyth. With timber swung over by the derrick from *Königsberg* Bennett and his gang erected a new deck inside the hold and lower than the deck outside. When a box was set up over the hold and the new deck there was headroom inside it of ten feet. The box stretched almost the width of the ship, some twenty-eight feet, leaving a gangway three to four feet wide on the deck at either side. It was twenty-five feet long.

Bennett picked up his tools and hurried aft with his mates. The derrick there was swinging frames across from *Königsberg* and he set about erecting two more boxes over the holds abaft the superstructure. These, like that on Number One hold, were a comparatively simple job; no new inner deck was called for.

These were hours of fast and furious work for every man except the lookouts and guns' crews who remained at their posts. *Audacity*, stopped and lashed to *Königsberg*, had to be ready to fight at a moment's notice. The mist kept visibility down to two miles or less – a blessed cloak for this transformation – but it also meant that if an enemy chanced on them it would be at short range and without warning.

McLeod approached Smith on the bridge. "The painters

have finished, sir." There was now a broad, red band around *Audacity*'s funnel, the boards with the name *Lulea* had gone and others were bolted on which read: *Anna Schmidt*. These were the colours and the name of the German timber ship they had met when first entering the Baltic, on her way to Kiel and, according to her captain, a spell in the dockyard.

The sun was down when Bennett came wearily to report to Smith: "All done, sir. Not exactly what you might call a cabinet maker's job but they're all good an' solid an' I reckon they look right."

"So do I. Well done. *Mr. Ross!*" That last he bellowed.

"Sir?" Ross answered from *Königsberg*'s deck.

"I'm sending two of those scuttling charges over." Smith's voice was harsh: "Sink her!"

"Aye, aye, sir!"

Now the prize crew returned to *Audacity*, one of them carrying a sack stuffed with papers from the captured ship. Ross was last of all and as he reached *Audacity*'s deck the lashings were cast off and her engines started, the screws turned and she began to ease away. Ross came to the bridge, breathless and filthy. "All aboard, sir. I set the scuttling charges myself. Hatches are off so a lot of the timber below deck should float out of her as she settles. She'll take a while to do that, but she'll go down."

Then they heard the charges explode, the thump of one followed seconds later by the other. Smith nodded. With the hatches battened down, the timber in *Königsberg*'s holds might have given her just enough buoyancy to keep her upperworks above the water. But not now. "Very good, Mr. Ross."

Night shrouded them. *Königsberg* was going to her grave, already perceptibly settling lower in the dark sea as *Audacity*, now *Anna Schmidt* with her four rectangular boxes of timber 'deck cargo', headed south again.

Smith wondered if Gallagher would be waiting for them. Or was he a prisoner now – or dead?

8

Kunda Bay

It was the same low, ragged shoreline, just a blurred, black silhouette in the night. But the darkened vessel, or vessels, that had lain in Kunda Bay twenty-four hours before had gone. The shore seemed quiet and the pulling boat had been sent away with Buckley at the tiller. *Audacity* lay still and silent.

Smith stood outside the wheelhouse, his eyes and his mind on the shore – most of the time. In the waiting silence his thoughts slipped back increasingly to Elizabeth Ramsay. He wondered how she would fare in Russia. Was there a lover waiting for her? The leader of the Russian plotters, perhaps? He told himself he was finished with the woman but her image kept coming back nevertheless.

"Light, sir! On the shore. Gone now but it could ha' been a signal from a torch." The voice of the port side lookout came low.

Smith too had seen the winking light. He grunted acknowledgment. Was that Gallagher? He should have been all right, had said he had a friend ashore if needed: "He's a peasant or farmer. Lord knows how old he is but we used to call him Crusoe because he has a beard down to his chest and a fur hat like a chimney-pot. He used to sell us eggs and milk. We got on all right in Indian language, signs and a few words. He doesn't like the Germans."

Smith shifted restlessly. The Germans would be hunting *Audacity* by now, maybe along this very coast. He stood still, head cocked, listening, and heard the faint splash of oars. Ross, beside him on the bridge spoke quietly. "That sounds like them coming back." Smith nodded. Had they found Gallagher and his men? And the Camel? The boat took shape out of the night and curved in towards *Audacity*'s side. He saw there were more men in her now but could not make out anyone in particular until Gallagher appeared at the head of the ladder and swung his legs over the bulwark to stand on *Audacity*'s deck.

He came quickly to the bridge. In the faint light in the wheelhouse Smith saw him scowling and asked, "No good?"

"No bloody good at all, sir. You want to get out of here. Fast."

So that was that. Smith spoke to Ross, "Turn her." It seemed the bad luck still dogged them. Or had he hoped for too much, that the Camel would be intact and they could bring it off? Now he would have to recast his plans without it. If he could.

The boat was hoisted and swung inboard. *Audacity*'s screws turned, bringing her around. Gallagher took the mug of coffee Wilberforce brought him, sucked at it and shuddered. "I needed that. Hell's teeth! What a country!" Then he noticed Danby standing at the back of the wheelhouse and glared at him. "What about seeing to my men?"

Danby moved towards the ladder but Smith held up a restraining hand. "No need. I've given orders and they'll be looked after. Now tell me what you found."

Ross was conning *Audacity* out of the bay, creeping. The call of the man at the lead came up to him: "By the mark, four!"

Gallagher gulped coffee and rubbed his mouth with the back of his hand. He glanced down at the boxes of timber 'deck cargo' and said, "You've certainly changed the look of her. Well, when Buckley put us ashore last night we doubled across the beach and into the trees . . ."

He'd taken the lead, the other three airmen following in a single file, working around the edge of the wood. The night was dark and under the trees it was as black as pitch. Gallagher had been told by Danby that the Camel lay in a clearing close to the field, two hundred and five paces along from the corner of the wood. Now Gallagher counted each stride, eyes trying to pierce the darkness ahead but able to see to his right the open field from which they had flown the Camels. They had lived in huts across there in the far corner. He had shared one of them with Johnny Vincent.

One hundred and eighty-one, two, three . . . mush of wet leaves underfoot so his boots hardly made a sound and he couldn't hear the men behind him – eighty-eight, nine, ninety, ninety-one –

Christ!

He had frozen in his tracks, breath held. There was a muffled thudding ahead of him and now he could detect a flicker of movement on the other side of this tree. Ten yards away? No more. One man, stamping his feet to keep warm: *thud-thud-thud.* That's all that had saved him from walking into the bastard. Was that the shape of a helmet? *That* was the barrel of a slung rifle. One man. Just one sentry but there'd be others about, maybe a platoon or a company, bedded down somewhere.

Gallagher had eased back cautiously, eyes never leaving the man, one hand on his pistol, the other gesturing: *back! back!* He retired about twenty yards before halting and collecting the others under the trees, whispering the news of the sentry. "I'm going to look around, see if I can find the Camel. You wait here. Keep still and quiet and under cover."

He had worked deeper into the wood and edging to his right, making a circle to pass behind the sentry and well clear of him. He thought it was probable that the man was standing in the clearing where the fitters and riggers had stowed the Camel, a score or so yards inside the wood. Afterwards they had used uprooted bushes to close the entrance. That should have worked, provided nobody had actually poked into the wood, but it looked as if . . .

He had smelt the tobacco-smoke as he saw the light, a pin-point of brightness between the trees. He moved slowly towards it, planting each foot slowly, carefully, pistol in hand but not cocked. He halted because now he could see two more men – and the Camel. It was just a lumpy, irregular shape in the night, still apparently wrapped in the canvas hangar as it had been hidden, the wings removed and stacked alongside.

The two men were crouched in the corner formed by

the fuselage and undercarriage, where the light would not be seen from the outskirts of the wood. It might have been a proper lantern but Gallagher guessed it was more likely to be a candle under a tin with a hole cut in the side. It shed a circle of light the size of a plate, just enough for the men to see the cards they held. The pipe in one man's mouth glowed red as he drew on it. Gallagher could not see their rifles but they would be there. He was certain of it.

He had turned and carefully retraced his steps, found his men and whispered, "They've set a guard on the Camel. Three men at least." He hesitated. They could probably overpower the guards, but the rest of the platoon would come looking for them. Then there would be more troops about when Smith returned the next night and little chance, if any, of escaping from the beach. But if he waited until tomorrow night, then with Smith's help a surprise attack could rout the guards, even a platoon of them, and whisk the Camel away aboard *Audacity* as Smith had planned.

He had said, "We'll go up to the house and see if we can talk to Crusoe." They nodded; all knew the old man and the house.

They made another circle, wider and deeper into the wood to pass well behind the Camel, and came to the edge of the trees close by the house. It squatted long and low, smoke trickling from its chimney. One window was lit and that was the kitchen. Gallagher approached softly, peered in, froze. A German non-com sat at the table, a book propped open in front of him, chin on his hand, spectacles on the end of his nose.

Still, Gallagher thought, at least the Germans were clearly rear-echelon troops, all over-age or under-fit. A surprise attack tomorrow would see them away.

He and his men had then retired deeper into the wood and spent the rest of an uncomfortable night huddled in their blankets. In the morning Gallagher watched as German troops paraded outside the house; twenty-four men with a couple of non-coms and a *Leutnant*. There was one horse, for the *Leutnant*, and one mule. It packed the wireless; Gallagher had seen plenty of them. They marched down towards the Camel and Gallagher waited until they were out of sight then moved to the edge of the wood, waited again.

He had seen Crusoe earlier but then the soldiers were present. Now the old man was somewhere around the back of the house. The old woman was in the kitchen but Gallagher had never had any dealings with her. He knew there were sons but they had been conscripted into the Army and their father hadn't heard of or from them for a long time. Gallagher suspected they had deserted. He waited patiently for Crusoe.

When the old man finally trudged around the corner of the house the woman had gone from the kitchen. Gallagher whistled softly and Crusoe's head turned. He was too old for life to surprise him any more. Calmly he crossed to the trees at Gallagher's beckoning. He wore a thick felt coat that came to his knees and a high fur cap that covered his ears. His brown face showed yellow teeth and a wide grin.

Gallagher said cheerfully, "Hullo, old cock." He shook Crusoe's hand then pointed after the departed soldiers and grimaced. Crusoe spat. They talked in the shelter of the trees; with hardly a dozen words in common they communicated in signs. It was a slow business, with Gallagher always on the watch for one or more of the soldiers returning. He learned that they had come along the coast only the previous day and found the Camel. Or perhaps Crusoe had led them to it; he looked uneasy at that point in the exchange. Gallagher thought it possible that Crusoe had concluded the British had gone and weren't coming back. So he'd decided to make a few bob while he could; Gallagher could understand that. Anyway, the troops had found the Camel and that night a tug had turned up – Crusoe indicated one boat pulling another.

Gallagher worked that out; the *Leutnant* had sent a signal to his H.Q. They had told the Navy, who had in turn sent a signal to the tug. It had been her light he had glimpsed from *Audacity* before he was put ashore. He came to another conclusion: that the tug was there to take away the Camel. When? And where to?

He embarked again on his laborious questioning. Crusoe did not know when the Camel was going; he shrugged at that. But when Gallagher pointed west, he nodded, conveying that the Germans had told him the Camel was bound for Riga. At least, Gallagher thought that was the destination: he wasn't sure about the old man's pronunciation. He hesitated before pulling out his map because he thought the old man might not be able to read, doubted if he had ever seen a map. But Crusoe's stubby, black-nailed finger jabbed confidently at the distinctive bowl of the Gulf of Riga. Gallagher wondered where he had learned about maps. During military service? Had he been to sea? God only knew.

Riga. It sounded reasonable because the Germans had an Air Force base there. He dug into his pocket for the tin of tobacco he had brought for the purpose and gave it to Crusoe. They shook hands again and the old man patted the pilot's shoulder. Gallagher lifted a hand in salute and farewell, retired into the trees and sought his men.

He led them through the woods then watched the German soldiers manhandle the Camel to the shore where Crusoe had said the tug was waiting. Crawling close to the edge of the trees, he settled down in what comfort he could to watch them embark the Camel. The water was shallow and he was impressed with the soldiers' ingenuity. He was still there when, the Camel long gone, night fell, and he saw *Audacity*'s boat, and flashed his torch.

Now Gallagher drained the mug and banged it on the shelf under the screen. "They sailed around noon. We had to lie on our bellies under bushes on bloody freezing ground and watch them take my Camel. The soldiers marched off straight after."

"By the mark, five!" That was the call of the man heaving the lead. *Audacity* was emerging from the bay into deeper water. Soon she would be able to crack on speed.

Smith's mind was busy making calculations. The Irbensky Strait, the entrance to the Gulf of Riga, lay roughly two hundred-odd miles west of *Audacity*. The tug had sailed thirteen or fourteen hours ago and she would be making around eight knots. If Audacity steamed at fifteen . . .

Gallagher said, "Another thing –"

But McLeod broke in, "Wouldn't it have been easier to send a pilot up from Riga? They could have flown him up as a passenger in a two-seater and he could have taken the Camel back."

Gallagher glowered at the interruption, and answered, witheringly, "Not bloody likely. For one thing, the wings have to be put back on it – and any pilot would want such a machine overhauled before he took it into the air. And that would be a job for the workshops at Riga. Another reason is that Jerry may also have heard that the Camel's not the easiest aircraft to fly. Anyway, he'd prefer to try it out close to home, friends – and an ambulance, just in case it produced some unpleasant tricks."

Ross nodded. "I've heard rumours that Camels are killers."

Gallagher snapped irritably, "Balls! You have to fly them all the time, that's all. Far more pilots are killed by incompetence and funk than by Camels."

Danby stood back in the shadows. Even so Smith saw a flicker of emotion pass across his face. Anger? But it was gone too soon for Smith to be certain.

He moved towards the chart table. "You said there was another thing?"

"That's right." Gallagher's teeth showed in a grin. "I'd reckoned the tug would draw eight to ten feet and couldn't get close to the shore, so I thought they'd have to dismantle the Camel and ferry it out a piece at a time. But it turned out they didn't have to. There was a fishing-boat with the tug, they beached the boat stern to, ran some planks from her stern to the beach and shoved the Camel aboard. The tug took her in tow."

Smith stood suddenly very still by the chart table. "A fishing-boat."

Gallagher nodded. "I see you're with me, Captain. Those boats may all look the same but there's no two of them *exactly* alike. There was a rope lashing like a Turk's head on her tiller, some new timber showing where they'd patched her side – I spent a day and a night in her on the way to Kirkko and I'd know the bastard anywhere. It was that Russian fishing-boat, the *Anna*."

9

Riga

"Boat!"

"Hard astarboard!" Smith saw the ship's lifeboat as the lookout's mouth opened to bellow the sighting. It lay right ahead and close under the bow, *Audacity* charging down on it at fifteen knots, a low smear of black with a flecking of white where the sea broke against it.

In seconds it would disappear under the bow but *Audacity* was answering to the helm, the stem swinging aside. "Meet her!" The engines had slowed, he could feel that through his boots, hear the slower thumping. "Steady! Steer that!" He had been just in time to save the boat; a second later and *Audacity* would have run it down. Did it matter? He snapped at the port side lookout, "Anybody aboard?"

The boat was sliding past close alongside, bouncing on *Audacity*'s bow-wave. Smith hardly needed the lookout's answer, was sure he saw —

"There's men aboard her, sir! Maybe half a dozen!"

"Stop her!" The tremor of the gratings under his boots was stilled. *Audacity* was bound for the Gulf of Riga as fast as she could because he thought that she might, just, come up with the tug towing the *Anna* — and the gold — before they entered the Gulf. He did not want to stop but there were men down there on the cold, black sea. "Slow astern." He moved out of the wheelhouse on to the port wing to see better, followed the line of the lookout's pointing finger, and nodded as he picked out the craft rocking astern, rolling in *Audacity*'s wake.

Ross and McLeod arrived on the bridge together, coats flapping as they dragged them on. Smith had conned the ship since leaving Kunda Bay an hour before and sent his officers below to sleep, but the stopping of the engines was as good as any alarm. He told them, "There's a boat astern of us. I'll take her alongside, port side to. Get a net over, Mr. Ross, and some good men on it. Make sure they're on lines."

"Aye, aye, sir." Ross dropped down the ladder. Smith watched the boat but spoke to McLeod. "There are some men aboard her. None of them has moved but rouse out the S.B.A. all the same." *Audacity* carried no doctor, only a Sick Berth Attendant, a trained medical orderly, a man who could lance a boil, dress a wound – or try to revive a man in the extremities of exposure.

Smith stopped *Audacity* so she drifted down to nudge against the boat just forward of the bridge. The men were already clinging to the nets there, the safety lines holding them but hanging slack to let them move on the net or enter the boat. Two of them dropped down. Smith watched from the wing and saw them picking their way about the boat. He could see now that there were six men in her. His own seamen were reporting now and Ross, at the side above them, passed it on to Smith. "Five of them frozen stiff, sir; stone dead. One still alive – just. Out cold but still breathing."

"Fetch them aboard." He saw Pearson, the S.B.A., down there with Ross, two of the hands with him, their arms filled with blankets. McLeod had returned to the bridge and Smith told him, "Pass the word for Fenwick." There was work for his sailmaker's needle; he would need canvas and Smith would have to stop *Audacity* again at first light to bury the dead. But now – the last corpse was swinging up at the end of a line and the empty boat was drifting away. He must wind *Audacity* up to fifteen knots again. They did not have a minute to spare and they had to steer clear of Reval because Robertson had said that a guard-boat, probably an old destroyer, patrolled outside the port.

At first light they were off Reval but well out to sea. Ross had the watch but Smith turned out of his bunk, dressed in uniform for the first time in weeks and took his prayer book and Bible from the drawer of his desk. Outside in the wheelhouse Ross said, "They were German Navy men, sir. McLeod's looked at all of them and he's got their effects and notes of identities. The one we brought aboard alive is still hanging on but Pearson says it's touch and go. McLeod is sleeping by him in a chair in case the chap wakes."

"Thank you." Smith wondered – German Navy men? He went steadily down the ladders to the deck aft of the bridge, in no hurry for this. Fenwick's handiwork was there, five neatly stitched canvas bundles, weighted with fire-bars and resting on hatch covers. McLeod had examined all of them, men dead of exposure, and now if he was sleeping his dreams would not be pleasant. A petty officer and two seamen stood by, bare-headed, waiting to launch the bodies. Smith glanced up at Ross, who was waiting on the bridge for that sign, and the engines stopped. The less time they spent stopped, the better, but you could not simply dump men over the side like sacks. So he tucked his cap under his arm and opened the prayer book at the marker . . .

While still off Reval they saw distant smoke inshore, but no ship. Then in the late afternoon a seaplane flew low overhead. Gallagher, in the wheelhouse, squinted up at it and said, "A Brandenburg. Slow as hell. Used for reconnaissance." It circled once and then swept in low enough to see the colours of *Anna Schmidt*'s Line painted on the funnel, and her name on the stern. The four big boxes of simulated deck cargo must have looked real enough. The pilot and his observer flapped gloved hands in answer to the waving of the few men on deck, all of them in rough working clothes. The Brandenburg banked away, showing the underside of its big boxy floats, and headed eastward until it was only a speck in the sky astern and then was lost. No destroyer came bustling to investigate.

McLeod came to the bridge. The burly navigator looked pale and drawn. "That chap's awake, sir, the one we took out of the boat. He rambled a bit and I couldn't make any sense out of a lot of it. *But*" – he paused to take a breath – "him and the others came off that destroyer we fought.

He shakes all the time he talks about it, goes on and on about the shelling and the fire. I gather he was in some sort of damage-control party trying to put it out, but then it blew up." He glanced at Smith. "You remember we thought we heard gunfire? That could have been her exploding. He's not very clear about what happened after that. He just remembers being in the boat with the others. He doesn't know yet that they're dead."

Smith asked, "Were there any other boats?"

McLeod shook his head. "I asked him. He didn't seem to know but he did say she went down very quickly."

With the belly blasted out of her, she would, and Smith doubted that there were any other boats. "How is he?"

McLeod pulled a face. "Not good. Shock. Some burns. Nearly frozen." He glanced aft and spotted the steward, Wilberforce. "I didn't feel like any breakfast. Wonder if I can get a bacon sandwich?"

Examining frozen corpses was not good for the appetite but that was past now. Smith told him, "Try your hand."

"Thank you, sir." McLeod went hungrily away.

As far as the *Anna* was concerned, Smith could make a fair guess now at the succession of events. The tug was the one mentioned by Robertson, the one that carried out the inshore patrol of the Estonian and Russian coasts. She must have stopped the *Anna* and taken her prisoner not long before *Audacity* appeared in those waters, searching for her. Not long before, but long enough to have received the signal ordering her to Kunda Bay to pick up the Camel, and to be on her way there and out of sight when *Audacity* arrived. Smith paced across the bridge and turned abruptly: he'd missed the *Anna* by mere hours, possibly minutes.

They'd run into the destroyer, and wrongly believed she'd got away and would give the alarm. Clearly *Audacity*'s identity had still been a secret – if the destroyer *had* sent a signal and alerted the enemy to her presence then the tug would not have sailed from Kunda unescorted. If Smith had known all this then once he'd abandoned all thoughts of recovering the gold he need not have captured the *Königsberg* or sent Gallagher seeking the Camel. He could have taken *Audacity* quietly home as she had come, a 'neutral'.

But it was a waste of time to speculate on what might have been. The plot to sink the Russian Fleet was dead, he had needlessly taken *Königsberg*, and now *Audacity* would be hunted. But at least the 'cargo' was still hidden aboard the *Anna*. Of that he was certain. If the crew of the German tug had found that pile of gold they would not have dawdled at Kunda nor made the long voyage to Riga. They'd have taken it straight to Reval.

McLeod, sandwich in hand, clattered down the ladder from the flying bridge and entered the wheelhouse. "Odensholm bears 190 degrees and we'll be opening Moon Sound in a minute, sir."

Smith nodded. What of Elizabeth Ramsay? Was she aboard the tug? And – he suddenly remembered guiltily – what of the Russians? Then he was honest with himself: he didn't give a damn about them, bearded strangers seen vaguely in the night. He cared about Elizabeth Ramsay. He guessed that she and the others would indeed be prisoners aboard the tug because it would be easier for their German captors to keep an eye on them there and feed them. If they were locked below deck in the *Anna* there was always a chance they might break out and cut the tow.

If, of course, there *were* any prisoners. Gallagher had seen none. They might all be dead.

"Smoke bearing red seven-oh!"

McLeod came quickly out of the wheelhouse, followed Smith to the port wing and they stared out through glasses. That was all it was, smoke, the sign of some ship hidden below the horizon. It could be the tug. It could be anything.

McLeod said, "That's Moon Sound, sir."

Smith turned and went back to the wheelhouse. He studied the chart. The port of Riga lay at the bottom, on the southern end of the Gulf of Riga. *Audacity* was on course for the Irbensky Strait, the main entrance to the Gulf and still some hundred-odd miles south. Moon Sound was another way in for vessels of shallow draught; ordinarily a tug would make the passage easily. But Robertson had said that Moon Sound was blocked by Russian mines which the Germans had not swept.

Had they swept it now?

If so, then the smoke could be from the tug heading into the Gulf by way of Moon Sound. That would be easy to find out, simply by altering course to close the smoke so the ship, now hull-down beyond the horizon, would be in sight within the half-hour.

But if it was *not* the tug then another thirty minutes would have been lost before *Audacity* was back on course, and the tug ahead of them would have increased its lead by eight miles or more.

If it *was* ahead of them? If it *was* bound for Riga? Smith was taking the word of an ill-educated local peasant as reported by Gallagher. But Gallagher had been sure, and it did make sense for the Camel to be taken to the German Air Force workshops at Riga.

Smith was painfully aware that he had transferred the gold too soon, missed catching the *Anna*, taken the *Königsberg* when he need not, and missed the tug and the gold when they lay under his hand in Kunda Bay the night he put Gallagher ashore. A succession of disastrous errors.

If he did not change course and that *was* the tug steaming into Moon Sound then he would lose her, the gold, the Camel, Elizabeth Ramsay. And perhaps *Audacity*, too?

Behind him Ross leaned in the doorway, silently rubbing at his long jaw. He and McLeod both watched Smith. This was not their decision to make, but it could still kill them.

Robertson had been right about the destroyer patrols and the tug so it was odds-on that he was right about the mines laid in Moon Sound. After all, the Germans were fighting a war on the Western Front and in the North Sea, and were now involved in Finland. Why should they use precious ships and men, needed elsewhere, to sweep a passage through Moon Sound; a passage they did not want? They had good reason to leave well alone. As it was, they only had to guard one door to the Gulf of Riga: the Irbensky Strait.

Smith made his decision: "Keep her as she is." Then he went to his cabin and threw over his shoulder, "Call me when the watch changes." He shut the door between him and the rest of them.

And told himself that was another mistake. He needed to be out in the air and on the move but instead he was cooped up in this cabin like a cell. Because he wanted to appear calm, unworried, confident. Why bother? They all knew he desperately wanted the tug, the fishing-boat, the Camel – and the 'cargo'. Just as they knew what that 'cargo' was. He was a posturing fool and was now paying the penalty.

Smith lay on his bunk and, when they called him at the end of the watch, pretended he had been asleep. He passed a few restless minutes in the wheelhouse but there was nothing in sight but the long finger of Cape Ristna to port. That ran out from Dago Island, one of the two big islands closing the northern end of the Gulf of Riga.

He returned to his cabin, sat at the table and tried unsuccessfully to read. Worry and ill-temper mounted inside him, his mind chewing at all the possibilities, trying to plan a course of action for each of them but knowing there was the unforeseen always waiting. The crew of the four-inch, in their mess right abaft and below his cabin, were singing. It got on his nerves. He only had to speak a word to McLeod outside to stop it. He was the captain and could do what he liked, couldn't he? No, he couldn't. The song finished in a burst of laughter: it was a good sign that they were cheerful. Now came a touch of sentiment: "There's a long, long trail a-winding . . ."

There was; they were on it and not knowing where it would end.

He thought, David Cochrane Smith, part-time philosopher. That was when he laughed at himself and he was grinning as McLeod rapped at the door and put his head around it. "Smoke ahead, sir. Port lookout just spotted it."

The lookout had bellowed the information from the wing of the bridge but Smith had not heard him through the singing and his preoccupation. "I'll come."

McLeod looked mystified by his captain's good humour as Smith followed him out through the wheelhouse on to the bridge. An overcast day but no fog. He used his glasses, picked up the smoke and saw the black speck under it. Impossible yet to make out what ship it was, but soon . . .

McLeod said, "We're overhauling her fast."

They were. Smith knew that if it *was* the tug, with the *Anna* in tow, then *Audacity* would be making almost twice her speed. Ross was on the bridge now, Gallagher right forward in the eyes of the ship, Danby below on the deck.

Ross said, "That must be her, sir. Two vessels in close line ahead. One of 'em *must* be in tow. They've altered course to port now and you can see 'em."

Smith saw two specks, one astern of the other. Presumably their course alteration was to enter the Irbensky Strait, the entrance to the Gulf of Riga.

And Robertson had said there was a guard-boat, a destroyer, anchored in the Irbensky Strait.

The wind froze Gallagher's face as the ship punched into it at fifteen knots. Could this be spring? He remembered Paris in the spring, when the Fokkers were annihilating the squadrons and he and Johnny Vincent were the only survivors of theirs at the end of one bad, black week. They'd been sent on four days' leave to Paris, got drunk on the train, and had stayed drunk or at least half-drunk, anaesthetised, until they went back to the squadron, one now full of the fresh, new faces of the replacements. Gallagher thought of those four days now, the brandy Johnny'd put away. The brandy they'd both put away. He hunched down into his jacket.

Was that his Camel ahead? It was freezing cold up here at the sharp end. Johnny Vincent. His eyes watered so he turned his face from the wind and saw the small figure standing on the deck below the bridge. Bloody Danby.

Audacity turned to enter the buoyed channel that wound between the shallows on either side of the Irbensky Strait and Smith called his officers to him. "Robertson told me there was a guard-boat in the Strait and I expect he was right. After *Königsberg* being taken, only twenty-four hours ago and less than three hundred miles away, that guard-boat will probably stop us. We have to assume she will. She may accept us as the *Anna Schmidt* carrying timber, but if she does then that identity will be linked to any action we take in the Gulf and that disguise will be useless to us afterwards." He paused, then finished: "Unless we deal with the guard-boat."

McLeod chewed his lip, thinking about that 'deal with'. Ross asked, "Suppose we knocked down the boxes and went in as another ship? Say the *Friedrich Wilhelm*?"

Smith shook his head. "They'll know by now that *Königsberg* was captured by a three-island tramp so they'll not let one near them, hang what name on it you like. A timber ship is something else. I think as the *Anna Schmidt* we can get a lot closer to the guard-boat before they start shooting."

Closer. Shooting. Ross and McLeod stood silent, imaginations at work. Smith went on, "Mr. Ross, you'll want a boarding-party and you'll lead it yourself. I suggest a dozen men, active and quick. I want two good men with Lewis guns in the bow of this ship. Now . . ."

As they listened to him the sun was slipping down towards the western skyline and the coast that lay some eight miles distant. To port but out of sight beyond the horizon lay the long point stretching out from the island of Saaremaa. *Audacity* crept in through the Irbensky Strait, ahead of her the bottle-neck between the shoals, a mile-wide channel – and the guard-boat that held it. Beyond lay the Gulf of Riga.

The guard-boat lay at anchor on the eastern side of the marked channel, the buoys in a widespread line running away into the Gulf. She was a twenty-year-old torpedo-boat, like a small destroyer, half the length of *Audacity*, low and narrow, her deck barely six feet above the water-line. Her two funnels showed only threads of smoke from banked fires; she would be keeping a sufficient head of steam to be able to get under way and manoeuvre if she had to. But she probably swung to her anchor there for weeks on end.

Smith thought that, because of her immobility, it was

likely she would be carrying less than her sea-going complement of twenty-four or -five men. She mounted a single
four-pounder gun forward of the small, open bridge.

Audacity plugged towards her slowly, reduced to seven
knots and slowing still. The tug and her tow, steaming on
about five miles ahead now, were just visible through
glasses. Smith stood in the wheelhouse with McLeod and
edged his glasses down until the guard-boat leapt into
focus. She lay a scant half-mile over the bow and a light
now blinked from her bridge. He could see the two men
there clearly, the officer and his signalman working the
lamp, their heads and shoulders showing above the canvas
dodger around the bridge. As Smith watched, three men
gathered around the gun forward of the bridge and its
barrel swung until it pointed at him.

McLeod was at the wheelhouse door, lifting the signal-
lamp in readiness for his reply to the guard-boat's bridge:
"Usual challenge, asking who we are, telling us to stop."
Blasé-sounding, but he wiped his sweating hands one by
one on the front of his jacket. He could understand German
if it wasn't too quick or complicated and could get ready
the sort of signals he'd likely have to send. But if the
guard-boat sprang something on him that he couldn't get
the hang of, then they'd be in real trouble.

Smith kept the glasses at his eyes. "Answer." He heard
the clacking of the lamp, already knew the message he'd
told McLeod to send, limpingly, as a merchantman would:
"*Anna Schmidt* out of Kotka with timber for Riga, ordered
to load cargo and join convoy for Hango."

He hoped it sounded plausible. The main body of Von
Goltz's troops had landed at Hango, eighty miles west of
Helsinki. The captain of the guard-boat would know that
– but a German merchantman would not, would just be
following orders.

The shutter of the lamp was silent a moment as McLeod
paused in sending, letting the captain of the guard-boat
think about this evidence that the *Anna Schmidt* was genu-
ine. Then he went on: "Have German and Swedish newspapers. Will pass to you on line. News from the Western
Front is good." For the Germans, maybe it was; probably

by this time the divisions transferred from the Russian Front were having their effect.

There was a man at *Audacity*'s side bent over a convincing-looking bundle of papers, knotting a line around them. Another just aft of the bridge was hanging out clothes to dry. Wilberforce emerged from the wardroom, a merchantman's saloon, and shook imaginary crumbs from a table-cloth. A cook came out of the galley and threw a bucketful of slops over the side then stood leaning on the rail, pipe in mouth, watching the guard-boat. The German captain had glasses at his eyes, would see all these signs of normality and the ensign of the German mercantile marine flapping from the jackstaff on *Audacity*'s poop; she was less than a quarter-mile from him now.

The lamp winked from the destroyer's bridge in reply and McLeod read with relief: "Keep clear of my paint." He laughed. "I know that one; seen it before!"

It seemed the *Anna Schmidt* had been accepted. The guard-boat's captain could not see the man lying on the deck by the staff, clutching the other ensigns ready to hoist, nor the two machine-gunners kneeling in the bow with the Lewis guns in their hands. The bulwark hid Ross with his boarding-party crouching forward of the bridge and the other men on the port side with fenders. The motor-boat – Smith could hear the putter of its engine – had been lowered and kept pace off *Audacity*'s starboard quarter, out of sight of the guard-boat, a petty officer and a dozen men aboard.

Danby and a furious Gallagher were below, ordered there by Smith, because there was no task here that he would entrust to the untried Danby, and Gallagher would be too important when – or if – the Camel was recovered.

The guard-boat lay off the port bow and less than a cable's length away. "Port ten!" *Audacity*'s bow edged around and Smith called softly, "Steady . . . steer that." Her stem pointed at the guard-boat. "Stop engines." The telegraph rang down to the engine room, the slow thumping of the engines ceased, and *Audacity* slid on with the way on her.

The man forward of the bridge stood upright, the bundle

of newspapers in his hand, poised as if ready to throw. The officer over on the guard-boat's bridge would be watching that bundle. Smith was prepared to bet that other ships had come alongside the guard-boat before now to pass over papers to men hungry for news from home. But when that German skipper saw how close *Audacity* was steering –

Smith saw the man's mouth open to yell, his arm outflung as he pointed at *Audacity*.

Now!

Smith stepped out of the wheelhouse and lifted the megaphone to bawl at the machine-gunners: "*Fire!*" He saw flame at the muzzle of the guard-boat's gun, staggered as something smashed howling through the wheelhouse, saw the jagged hole punched in the screen where he had stood. The Lewis guns hammered, sweeping the guard-boat's deck, and the men on it scrambled for cover. The heads disappeared from the bridge, and the gun stood abandoned on its mounting.

Audacity loomed over the old destroyer, so that the machine-gunners had to depress the guns nearly vertical to hit her. Smith bawled, "Slow astern!" Then to the gunners in the bow, "Cease fire!" And: "Get those fenders over!"

The fenders, huge mattresses of rope, were swung over the bulwark to thump against *Audacity*'s port side and hang there from the lines. The Lewis guns were silent though still trained on the guard-boat. *Audacity* slipped through the last few yards of sea that separated them, her screws turning again but now in reverse, slowing her. "Stop her!" She slammed against the guard-boat, the shock cushioned by the fenders dangling between, but heeling her over as Ross and his men got to their feet. The tall figure of the first lieutenant led the way, jumping down the six feet or so to the guard-boat's iron deck, sprawling on hands and knees then getting up and running aft, pistol in hand. The others followed, all but two who hesitated as *Audacity* swung away again and a gap appeared between the two ships. One of them jumped but fell short into that widening strip of churned foam. "Get a line to that man!" Smith shouted.

The motor-boat swept around *Audacity*'s stern, bumping

in her wake, and curved in to slide alongside the guard-boat, her men swarming aboard. Men of the first boarding-party were already on her bridge but there was no sign of Ross. The gap between the two ships continued to widen. From the corner of his eye Smith glimpsed a figure diving from the deck aft of *Audacity*'s bridge, saw him hit the water: it was Gallagher.

"Sir!" That was Ross, standing in the guard-boat's bridge, bawling through a funnel of his hands. "Found their Sparks lying in the wireless office. Out cold. I think he must have been knocked flat when we bumped her and got laid out! Couldn't have sent a signal!"

Smith waved acknowledgment and took a breath. So that was all right. But – he leaned over the rail beside McLeod and saw that the navigator had organised a party to rescue the man in the sea. They had lines over the side and now Gallagher grabbed the bowline on one of them, worked it over the arms of the spluttering man he was holding up.

Smith straightened. *Audacity* had drifted astern and there was a gap of twenty yards or so between her and the guard-boat. Men crowded the German's waist now, prisoners under guard.

Smith shouted through the megaphone: "Mr. Ross! How long?"

Ross sounded cheerful: "Soon as you like, sir. We've got all her crew: one officer, one chief P.O. – sixteen all told."

As Smith had guessed, not a full sea-going crew. "Casualties?"

"None, sir. Only their Sparks and he's awake now and nursing a sore head."

Smith gave thanks for that, recalling the Lewis guns sweeping the iron deck; some men had been very lucky.

The party at the side hauled the man in, spewing sea-water, and Gallagher was clambering up at the end of a line. Smith called across to Ross, "I'm coming alongside. Stand by to transfer those prisoners. I'll send over two of those scuttling charges. Use them."

"Aye, aye, sir!"

So *Audacity*'s bow was laid alongside that of the guard-boat and lines passed to secure her there while the prisoners clambered aboard, preceded by some of Ross's boarding-party and followed by the others. They stood under the muzzles of rifles in a tight-packed crowd below the fo'c'sle. Buckley passed the scuttling charges over to Ross in a canvas sack and the first lieutenant disappeared through a hatch abaft the guard-boat's bridge. Smith had laid the two ships bow alongside bow so that *Audacity*'s midships would not be covered and the motor-boat was able to come alongside, be hooked on and hauled up to the davits, then swung inboard.

Ross appeared on the guard-boat's deck, empty-handed, cast off the lines and climbed aboard *Audacity*.

"Charges set, sir."

"Very good. Lock those prisoners away under guard." Smith entered the wheelhouse, stepping around Wilber-force who was busily sweeping up splinters of wood from the hole the shell had smashed through the screen and muttering resentfully under his breath. Smith ignored him and ordered, "Slow ahead." By a miracle the glass in the windows of the wheelhouse had not been broken. He chided himself for not seeing that the windows were lowered before the action, then snapped, "Didn't anyone have the sense to make those windows safe?"

No one answered but there were withdrawn expressions on the faces of McLeod and the bridge-staff. Smith could guess why: it had been a quickly prepared but neatly planned operation in which – save for that one man falling over the side – everything had gone like clockwork. Yet now Smith was carping over one very minor detail. In fact, he was impatient to be away. They had lost enough time. There was a little over an hour before sunset and the tug was now only a streak of smoke on the horizon.

The guard-boat lay astern now as *Audacity* swung away. "Full ahead." And to McLeod: "All officers on the bridge in fifteen minutes, please, and get Bennett up here." There was work for the carpenter: the shell had come in through the bridge screen and smashed its way out through the deckhead. The damage must be made good.

The two explosions were muffled and a minute apart.

Smith went out to the wing when he heard the first, was watching the guard-boat when the second came. He thought he saw the old destroyer shudder though that might have been a trick of the light. But when Ross came to the bridge ten minutes later he reported with satisfaction, "She's over on her beam ends and going down."

They had forced the gate and *Audacity* was loose in the Gulf of Riga.

10

Night Action

Smith gave his orders to his officers. They sat about his cabin while he leaned against the desk. Ross had come straight from putting the prisoners under guard, still dirty from worming about in the belly of the guard-boat, planting the scuttling charges. Gallagher was towelling his hair but wore dry clothes borrowed from McLeod. The navigator sat by the door, one ear cocked for any call from the wheelhouse. Danby, typically, had tucked himself unobtrusively into a corner.

Smith said, "We'll be up with the tug inside the hour. I intend to call on her to stop then go alongside and Mr. McLeod will lead the boarding-party this time because there may be need of his German. I want to know if the tug carries the crew of the *Anna* – and if not, what happened to them. Whether she sent a warning signal before we took her. And I believe the cargo is still aboard the *Anna*, in her hold, and I want that confirmed. Understood?"

"Aye, aye, sir."

Gallagher asked, "What about the Camel, sir?" Naturally he was eager, wanting his precious plane. Both were precious in Smith's eyes and he had blasted the flight commander for risking his life diving over the side to save the seaman – if they ever got the Camel it would still be useless without its pilot. "I'd foreseen such a possibility," Smith had told him angrily, "and posted lifesavers at the side for exactly that purpose!"

Gallagher had answered simply, "I didn't think of that at the time, sir. I just saw the man in the sea and went in after him." There was no doubt he was brave.

Now Smith said, "As soon as McLeod has secured the tug I will put you aboard to inspect the Camel, and, if it seems sound, see to its transfer. Take any of your own men you'll have use for. Are any of them seamen?" Because transferring the Camel would be a task for men used to working afloat.

Gallagher combed his thick, still damp hair with his fingers. "A few regular Navy, the P.O. for one, but the rest" – he shrugged – "a trip in a pleasure-boat off Southend is about all they've seen. Some never went to sea till they were drafted across the Channel to France." They were 'hostiles', signed on in the Royal Naval Air Service for 'the duration of hostilities', as mechanics, riggers or armourers. Gallagher said, "But I can find what I want among 'em."

Smith nodded, pushed up from the desk, and smiled around at them. "I think there's time for a meal for all hands, Mr. Ross. See to it."

He wondered if there were prisoners aboard the tug. He would know by nightfall. And then? He wanted the gold and they all wanted the Camel for the desperate gamble that might get them out of this trap that was the Baltic.

Ross came out of the wheelhouse to stand at Smith's shoulder. "She's less than a mile ahead now, sir."

Smith nodded. *Audacity* had worked up to fifteen knots, hammering after the tug at twice her speed. Beyond the tug, a low, black line on the horizon marked a headland. Once around it the course for the port of Riga was south-east, a turn to starboard of nearly ninety degrees. The tug held a course close inshore, her master probably knowing these waters well and heading to cut the corner by passing close off the headland. The sun was down and the sky to starboard lit red by the afterglow of its setting. There lay the shore, a muffled dark edging above the pale line where the sea washed it in foam.

"Smoke – red two-oh!"

Smith swung to focus on this new factor, the dark smear off the port bow that marked a ship, probably coming up from Riga, but still hull-down, ten miles or more to the south. He acknowledged the report: "Seen."

Audacity closed rapidly on the tug and would soon be abeam of her. The Russian fishing-boat nodded rhythmically at the end of the curved line of the tow. The fuselage of the Camel was lashed squatting on the deck, its detached wings standing beside and propped between wooden supports. There was no one to be seen aboard the *Anna* and Smith thought that the prisoners – if there *were* prisoners – must be aboard the tug. He had expected that but he swore softly under his breath because it could make his task more difficult. There was a man standing aft in the tug, peering back at *Audacity*, and another leaned out of her wheelhouse. Her master perhaps, his curiosity aroused by this ship overhauling him? But clearly only his curiosity, not his suspicion, because no one had been sent forward to man the six-pounder in the bow.

The crew of the twelve-pounder on *Audacity*'s fo'c'sle lay on the deck there, hidden from the sight of anyone aboard the tug. They were ready to man the gun but had orders not to load: it was a bluff. McLeod crouched on the deck forward of the bridge with his dozen or so men armed with rifles, his face turned up to Smith.

The lookout reported again: "That smoke off the port bow, sir. It looks to be more than one ship, maybe two or three or more."

Smith swung to the smoke again, saw the spread of it now but only grunted agreement and returned to the tug, almost abeam and a cable's length away. One thing at a time. "Starboard ten!"

"Starboard ten, sir . . . ten of starboard wheel on."

Audacity's bow turned on to a course that would take her across the bow of the tug and Smith ordered quietly, "Ease to five . . . steady . . . steer that. Eight knots."

There was a sudden commotion aboard the tug. Men appeared on her deck, her master ducked inside the wheelhouse then emerged again with a megaphone and his voice boomed brassily, angrily across the narrowing gap between the two ships. McLeod called, "He's asking if we're drunk or mad, sir! Says we have to haul clear!"

Smith ordered, "Port twenty!" And *Audacity* swung back so she ran close alongside the tug. "Tell him to stop or we'll sink him." He lifted a hand in signal. As McLeod rose to his feet and bellowed back at the tug the forward twelve-pounder swung up from its hiding-place in *Audacity*'s bow and its crew trained it around to lay it on the tug – which began to turn away.

"Starboard ten!" Then Smith snapped at the two men with the Lewis guns on the bridge-wing: "Mount 'em!"

They swung the guns up on to the rail, cocked them. The tug had steadied on a course headed for the shore, her deck was deserted and her master gone to cover inside the wheelhouse, although he must know that would give him no protection against the shells of the twelve-pounder; he had stared into its muzzle. Smith accepted that he was dealing with a brave man. He could not order the twelve-pounder to fire because of the prisoners who might be aboard the tug. Even though her master did not know that, the bluff had failed.

He ordered, "Sweep her deck from stem to stern."

The Lewis guns hammered in irregular short bursts, their muzzle-flames red in the dusk. Smith could see them hitting, splinters flying all along the tug's deck and glass bursting from the windows of the wheelhouse, but the tug held to her course. He told the Lewis gunners, "Keep it up. Point of aim her wheelhouse, and low. Whoever's steering her is lying on the deck." Or the wheel was lashed and men lay dead around it.

Ross glanced at the shore coming closer with every second, then worriedly to Smith who kept his face impassive. Should he drop back then turn to run across the tug's stern, cut the tow and so capture the fishing-boat, the Camel and the gold? But *Audacity* might ride over the tow without cutting it. Then it would slide along her bottom, foul her screws and she would be left a motionless hulk. Besides, if Elizabeth Ramsay were aboard the tug . . .

If . . .?

He must not run *Audacity* aground. He ordered speed reduced to five knots and saw relief in Ross's face, warned the Lewis gunners: "The range will be opening."

Audacity fell astern of the tug then astern of the fishing-boat, while the gunners fired bursts, reset the range, fired, reset. Sometimes they were missing now.

133

Ross muttered, "If he doesn't stop or turn soon – Christ! He's struck bottom!"

The tug faltered, ground on, then was checked completely.

Smith snapped, "Stop both! Slow astern both!"

Audacity slowed, then briefly stopped as the screws went astern. "Stop both!" The engines were still and *Audacity* lay only yards off the tug's port quarter. Another second's turning of her screws and her bow gently nudged the tug.

McLeod and his party were now gathered in the bow and he went down on the end of a line to stand in the stern of the tug. He was followed by others, and *Audacity* was secured to the tug, bow to stern. Germans showed on her deck, seen only as darker shadows in the gloom but their hands were held high: the crew of the tug.

Smith chafed with impatience. What was McLeod doing? He should have reported by now.

He turned to peer out over the port beam to where the distant smoke had been sighted but he could see nothing in the dusk. Those ships would be only six miles or so away now. He knew what they were. Several ships sailing in company, headed out of Riga for the Irbensky Strait: they would be the convoy Robertson had told him about. This was around the time they would be sailing if they were to arrive at Kirkko on the nineteenth. He should have remembered that convoy. There would be at least one destroyer as escort – the destroyer had sailed from Kirkko for that purpose. So – had the tug sent off a signal? *Audacity*'s wireless operator had not reported one but that didn't mean a signal had not been sent; he may have been combing the wrong frequencies. If a signal *had* been sent and received that destroyer could be here in half an hour or less, even though she had to work up from the convoy's speed of eight or nine knots. Where the *hell* was –

"Captain, sir!" McLeod stood in the stern of the tug.

Smith lifted the megaphone. "Report, Mr. McLeod!"

"Four prisoners, sir. Found 'em below. The lady's one of them." Smith thought, Thank God for that. But McLeod was going on: "One man dead in the wheelhouse, but we found her master in there as well and he's not hurt.

Twelve of a crew, alive that is, but none of them are saying a word except the master. He knows some English, a bit more than he lets on, I think." That was a warning to Smith to guard his words. "I asked if he'd sent off a wireless signal and he told me to go to hell."

The master could be bluffing. He had been in the wheel-house and probably didn't know whether a signal had been sent or not.

"The lady says the fishing-boat's all right, sir. I've talked to her privately. She says the tug put a couple of shells into the *Anna* when she captured her, killed three men and wrecked the engine, but otherwise – *everything is all right*."

That last was said with emphasis. Clearly the gold was still hidden aboard the fishing-boat, under a ton of fish and under the Camel. It would take a lot longer than the thirty minutes at most that they had to get it out of there. No question either of the boat getting under way, without an engine, and not even any way of setting her sails with the Camel on her deck.

"Sir?" Gallagher was becoming impatient now.

"Wait!" Smith barked it, angry from frustration. There lay the gold, the Camel and the girl, all in his grasp. Tow the fishing-boat? But if *Audacity* had to run for her life or fight for it then a boat in tow could mean capture or death.

Either that escort destroyer was working up to full speed and would be on them in less than thirty minutes, or she had not heard any wireless signal, did not know of *Audacity*'s presence here, and was dawdling along at the speed of the convoy.

He dared not assume the latter. If he did and he was wrong then *Audacity* would be caught, stopped and help-less, a sitting target for the destroyer's guns.

He could take Elizabeth Ramsay and the Russians aboard then run for it, but he needed the Camel – and the gold. Still, the destroyer had its burden too: the convoy. And Smith's orders, if *Audacity*'s disguise were stripped away, as it had been, were to do what damage he could so as to draw at least some extra German ships out of the North Sea and into the Baltic. Besides . . .

135

Smith put himself in the enemy's place, men who did not know that *Audacity* had entered the Baltic through the Sound but *did* know there were White Russians who wanted to continue the war against Germany. *Königsberg*, furthermore, had been captured by a raider claiming to be White Russian and whose captain said *Königsberg* would be taken to Russia. Now the obvious course for a lone British raider without a base and seeking to escape from the Baltic would be to avoid naval forces, try to remain unobtrusive. But a ship that sought action, risking damage – he swallowed at that – argued a ship with a base not too far away. In Russia. A Russian ship, therefore. What else?

Audacity could run, twisting and hiding, leaving behind the gold and the Camel, trying to evade the pack in howling pursuit. Or she could . . .?

Audacity. God alone knew why Admiralty had chosen that name for her but Smith knew that now she must act the part.

"Mr. McLeod!"

"Sir?"

"I'm sending Mr. Gallagher and his men over to relieve you."

"Aye, aye, sir."

Smith leaned over the rail to address Gallagher on the deck below, his plan forming as he spoke: "Put the prisoners below under a guard. He's to shoot to kill if they try to give any trouble." It would do no harm for the German master to hear that. "The Russians and the lady stay with you." He had strained his eyes but still had not seen her, hidden by the dark and the crowding figures aboard the tug. She would probably be safer there. "Get all the *cargo* out from under the plane and on to the tug. See if you can raise steam on her and haul her off that bank. Use a kedge if you have to. One man to ready that gun for action in case you need it; you're not far from the shore." The firing might have been seen on land and there might, though it was unlikely, be German troops nearby. "Don't use a light, but one hour from now show a green one. We should be back for you about then. If we don't come back sink all the cargo in deep water and then it's up to you." That was an unpleasant prospect for Gallagher. Smith asked, "Understood?"

"Aye, aye, sir."

Smith was risking Gallagher now, but McLeod was needed aboard and Gallagher and the Camel were a team. Together, but only together, they might save *Audacity* before this voyage was ended. He had no other choice.

The transfer of men was carried out and as McLeod panted up to the bridge Smith ordered, "Cast off forrard. Slow astern both."

In the bow they hauled in the lines and *Audacity* backed away from the tug, turned at Smith's orders and headed out to sea. "Mr. Ross."

"Sir?"

"Tell Bennett I want that timber disguise flattened and lashed down. There's a convoy out there and we'll be in action shortly."

"The *convoy*, sir?" Ross asked disbelievingly, eyes turning back to the tug now only a blur in the night. Then as he caught Smith's cold glance, "Aye, aye, sir."

Smith was prey to doubts and fears now but nevertheless he was determined to hold to his decision. *Audacity* had been steaming for ten minutes and had almost worked up to her full speed of sixteen knots. Bennett and a gang of men, sweating and swearing, had knocked the four timber 'boxes' apart, so that the four sides of each lay flat under its top. They were lashed down and would not show above *Audacity*'s bulwarks. Buckley stood at the back of the bridge. He was the reserve quartermaster, there to take the wheel if anything happened to the coxswain. Ross was aft, to direct the fire of the twelve-pounder on the poop and to lead a damage-control party if need be. Danby was with him. If the bridge was hit and Smith killed then Ross would take command. Smith thought what a mess Ross would inherit. He reflected that Danby could learn from Ross this night. Or he, too, could be killed. But there were all kinds of fearful possibilities because Smith had been forced to choose a desperate course of action. But they were as ready as they could be.

When McLeod turned from the chart where he had been bringing his plot up to date, Smith stepped quickly out of the wheelhouse on to the bridge. Not to take the air; at nearly sixteen knots a freezing gale whipped into the wheelhouse because this time the windows had been lowered to save them from the blast when the guns opened fire. But Smith did not want to talk to McLeod or to anyone. He stood with the lookout, a seaman who would not speak until addressed, except to report. He had promised to take these men home: but now he could be the death of all of them.

The convoy was close and off the starboard bow. The night was dark under a cloud-scattered sky but he could see the green and red navigation lights of the ships. The convoy showed lights because there were no British submarines now in the Baltic. A raider, a small armed tramp, had been reported but she had last been seen off the coast of Finland and then apparently had headed for the Gulf of Bothnia. Besides, the convoy was still inside the Gulf of Riga, a German lake, and the captain of a small armed tramp would be a suicidal lunatic to attack a convoy escorted by at least one destroyer.

The destroyer's captain, seeing *Audacity*'s lights, would still be curious – but no more than that because this strange ship must certainly have passed the scrutiny of the guard-boat in the Irbensky Strait. Smith could make out the ships as well as their lights now; four merchantmen steaming two by two, and the lower, slim shape in the lead. She would be the destroyer, presumably the one seen at Kirkko, better armed than *Audacity* and ten knots faster. If the tug had sent off a warning signal then the destroyer had not received it, or she would not have been steaming placidly at the head of the convoy at this moment.

So could *Audacity* steal quietly away into the night and return to claim the Camel and the gold? No. Because the destroyer would pass within a mile or two of the beached tug. It was hidden in darkness but there might be a curious patrol on the shore to burn a flare and so bring down the destroyer. Or if the convoy steamed on then they would find no guard-boat in the Irbensky Strait and raise the alarm. It would be better if the destroyer's captain were presented with other problems to absorb his attention.

And Smith had made up his mind.

McLeod came out of the wheelhouse to stand at his side and Smith glanced at him, bulky in duffel coat, cradling the signal-lamp in his gloved hands. "Know what you have to send?"

McLeod nodded. "Yes, sir."

"Remember to keep it slow." McLeod was acting the part of a merchantman's mate. The rapid Morse that was his pride would be out of character.

"Aye, aye, sir."

Smith had composed the signal and McLeod translated it into German: *ANNA SCHMIDT* FROM DANZIG BOUND FOR RIGA. The destroyer would challenge soon. *Audacity* carried a green navigation light on the starboard wing of the bridge by the lookout, a red to port. The destroyer must be able to see them . . .

And there came the challenge, a brief, rapid flicker of Morse. Smith cautioned, "Wait." It would not do to respond too quickly because that also would be out of character. The mate of a tramp would have to find his lamp, arrange the reply in his head . . . "Now!" He turned to call, "Starboard ten! Steer seven-oh!"

"Starboard ten, sir, steer seven-oh!"

The aim was to bring *Audacity* a little closer to the convoy as she passed. Smith turned back as McLeod worked the key of the lamp, slowly, hesitantly. It was not only play-acting but also gave Smith time while *Audacity* and the ships off the starboard bow closed the gap between them at their combined speeds of about twenty-three knots, *Audacity*'s fifteen and the convoy's eight. The destroyer at the head was only pottering along at convoy speed. She was coal-burning and would take time to work up to even fifteen knots. And by the time she did it should all be over. McLeod lowered his lamp when *Audacity* was almost abeam of the destroyer. While the signal was limping out Smith had heard and acknowledged the coxwain's report: "Course seven-oh, sir!" *Audacity* was now heading to pass the convoy with less than half a mile between them.

"That escort looks like the boat we saw at Kirkko, sir," McLeod said.

Smith nodded. "Man the voice-pipe to the guns." McLeod went into the wheelhouse. Smith thought that the destroyer's captain must be suspicious now, must see that this strange ship heading to pass close by his convoy was steaming at far more than the eight to ten knots he would expect of a merchantman.

Light sparked again in rapid Morse from her bridge. That would be an order for *Audacity* to stop and be investigated. The destroyer was turning, but the leading ship in the column nearer *Audacity*, three or four hundred yards astern of the destroyer and broad on *Audacity*'s bow, would be abeam of her in half a minute. "Hoist the ensigns! Douse the lights!" Smith shouted. He saw the lookout reach for the green light and switch it off; the red glow to port blinked out. At foremast and main the blue and white colours of the Imperial Russian Navy, and the White Ensign, broke out at the yards and streamed on the wind. And while all this went on he shouted again, "All guns commence! Ship starboard beam!"

That was the only order needed. The twelve-pounders forward and aft swung up to stand on fo'c'sle and poop, their crews leaping in on them to train them around. The screens around the four-inch abaft the wheelhouse crashed down and the slender barrels of the three guns swung almost as one, seeking, then settling. The breech blocks clashed shut behind the rounds thrust in by the loaders. There was a breath-held second as each layer brought his sights on – then all guns fired.

The leading cargo ship was almost abeam, bulking out of the night, and Smith saw the shells burst low on the waterline, two under the lift of the superstructure, one just forward of it. He swung away, looking for the destroyer and saw her off the starboard quarter, more than half a mile astern and dropping back still in the turn. He jerked his head around to stare forward, saw that on this course *Audacity* would pass even closer to the next ship in the column than she was to this one . . .

The twelve-pounders fired again, the *thump* of the four-inch coming a split second after. Three hits again, and this time all under the superstructure. The engine and boiler room lay there. Some of those shells would be exploding among the coal in her bunkers but others would find their way into the heart of the ship. She was falling astern as *Audacity* pounded past her. The four-inch and the twelve-pounder aft would still bear but the gun on the fo'c'sle would get off only one more shot at her, so: "'A' gun shift target! Ship starboard bow!"

He heard that passed by McLeod through the voice-pipe: the forward twelve-pounder fired with the others and then its barrel swung to point at the next ship in the column. Smith peered astern through his glasses, seeking the destroyer, but his night vision had been destroyed by the flashes of the guns. Then he found her, saw her lights, green and red, and made out the narrow bow-on shape of her. So she was after them and trying frantically to work up steam. Light blazed into his eyes and he winced them shut against it, lowered the glasses then looked again. The destroyer was using a searchlight. Its beam lit *Audacity* so that he could see her two ensigns laid out flat on the wind. The crew of the destroyer would see them, too. There were the men working the four-inch, and the twelve-pounder right aft on the poop, Ross's tall figure standing straight behind the gun as if in the drill-shed, Danby a pace or two away. The gun swung around to point over the stern, fired down the beam of the searchlight – and it snapped out. Smith did not see the shell strike but it must have passed close to the light. There was no answering gun from the destroyer. Her captain might well hesitate to open fire on *Audacity* because a small error in training his gun could hurl a shell past her and into the merchantman ahead. Smith swung to look for that ship, for a moment could not see her in the sudden darkness after the searchlight's glare. Then she took form, huge and close, turning away as the forward twelve-pounder hit her low and amidships. She was trying, hopelessly, to run away from the guns –

No, more than that. She was also turning to steer clear of the ship ahead of her, that *Audacity* had just left astern, that was blowing off steam in a whistling roar. *Audacity*'s shells had told and her head was falling away and she was slowing. There would be a scene from hell down in her boiler room. He remembered there were men in those ships and swallowed.

Audacity was now abeam of the second ship and all guns were firing into her. The regular salvos had become ragged as the action went on, each gun firing individually just as fast as it could be loaded and laid, an irregular but rapid hammering. The shooting was good, had been very good throughout. Smith nodded with cold professional approbation. It was not easy to hit a particular section of a ship when it was roaring past you at twenty-odd knots.

"Starboard twenty!"

"Starboard twenty! . . . Twenty of starboard on, sir!"

To swing *Audacity* around the tail of this little convoy, cutting across the wake of the ship they were pounding. She towered close, barely a cable's length away, and sliding past so now some of the shells were hitting her aft, so close there was only a heart-beat between the flame of discharge and the orange burst of the shell. *Audacity* was heeling in the turn, running past the high poop, and there was a gun up there, men working at it, trying to bring it into action. He saw them thrown from their feet as a shell burst under them in the stern.

"Meet her! . . . Steady! . . . Steer that!" He bawled it through the din and heard the order acknowledged. *Audacity* straightened out of the turn to run across behind the convoy.

"Ship – port bow – two – cables!"

The high and piercing shriek from the port side lookout jerked Smith around. A ship, not a merchantman? She was bearing down on *Audacity*, narrow and low, looking to be another destroyer, but old like the guard-boat at the mouth of the Gulf. He shouted, "'B' and 'Y' engage to port!" He heard the order repeated by McLeod, saw the four-inch and the after twelve-pounder start to swing. Flame licked out of the night from the second destroyer, from the little four-pounder she carried forward of her bridge, and again she was so close that the *crash* of the hit came immediately after the flash. The shell exploded somewhere on *Audacity*'s superstructure. Smith saw the orange burst light up the port wing of the bridge in a blink of flame that was instantly gone, and felt the jar of it through the deck.

The old destroyer was coming on, would pass astern of *Audacity*. She fired again and Smith heard the howl of the shell hurtling past the bridge. The after twelve-pounder flamed, the four-inch slammed and the *crack* of the forward twelve-pounder came like an echo as it engaged a fresh target, the rear ship in the port column of the convoy.

"Starboard twenty!"

The coxswain did not hear him but McLeod did, repeated the order into his ear and the helm went over. McLeod yelled, "Twenty of starboard on, sir!"

Smith was turning to run up the other side of the convoy and the old destroyer was passing astern now, *Audacity*'s after twelve-pounder swinging to follow her but silent, unable to depress far enough to hit her. The four-inch was silent too, for that same reason and because if it fired it would hit the mast or blow off the heads of the twelve-pounder's crew. But the destroyer was turning away, *her* gun wasn't firing either and there was the glow of a fire aboard her.

"Ease to ten! . . . Midships! . . . Steady!"

Again McLeod passed on Smith's orders. He realised there were other fires; one aboard the first ship they had engaged, a pulsing glare amidships; another on the second that had steamed past the first now lying still, and that was a bigger blaze just aft of the superstructure. He could not see the destroyer that had led the convoy and thought she must be beyond those blazing ships by now, would be hastening around after him.

Audacity was hauling up on the rear ship in this port column, passing close again but more slowly, at only the six or seven knots' difference in their speeds. So now all guns, trained to starboard, were pumping shells into the merchantman. She was already turning away so most of the hits were amidships or aft. She too carried a gun on her poop that fired now, but the shell must have passed high overhead because Smith did not even hear it. She was slowly falling astern and ahead was the leading ship of the port column, but she had already turned away, was half a mile distant and opening the range. She was still a good target. At Smith's order the guns shifted their aim to her as *Audacity* held on the course that would take her back to the mouth of the Gulf. Smith watched the orange winking as the shells burst. There was a red glow covering the whole of the convoy now, lighting them so that Smith could see the two ships running away, the one that was stopped and burning, and the fourth that still had way on her, although most of the red light was cast by her fire.

Suddenly the fire became a soaring pillar of light that hurt the eyes. Smith's cap was snatched from his head and he was hurled back by the blast to slam against the side of the wheelhouse. Then the thunderclap of the explosion reached him, numbed him. For seconds he was blinded. Then, as his sight returned, he saw the black humps that were ships under a sky that was still tinged red by fire, but the main source of that furnace glow had gone.

His ears rang. The lookout, thrown sprawling by the blast, climbed to his feet. McLeod came to the wheelhouse door and mouthed at Smith who could not hear him but saw McLeod's lips forming those words that were in his own mind: "Ammunition! She's blown up!" *Audacity's* guns were not firing. Doubtless the layers could not yet focus on their target. Smith pushed past McLeod into the wheelhouse, stooped over the voice-pipe to the guns and ordered, "Check! Check! Check!" He heard his own words, though distantly, and the acknowledgment from each gun, the reports that no gun was loaded. "Port ten! Steer two-two-oh!" That was a course that would take *Audacity* away from the shipping lane and heading in towards the coast.

He went out to the starboard wing again and used his glasses to search the sea astern. There was the red wash under the clouds. He counted the scattered ships slowly as he found each one, steadily sweeping an arc. He was sure but he asked, "How many do you see?"

The lookout answered, "I make it five, sir."

Smith heard that more clearly, his hearing returning as

the ringing subsided. He lowered his glasses. "Yes." The two escorts and the three surviving merchantmen, though one or more might not survive for long. One was certainly stopped and on fire. The captain of the destroyer would yearn to hunt for the stranger come out of the night to tear his convoy apart, but she had gone into the darkness and with only the other old destroyer to help him, and she damaged, it would be like hunting a black cat in a very big, very dark room. And at the same time the ships of his convoy were in desperate straits and needing his aid. Suppose another sank with loss of life while he was off on a wild-goose chase, when he might at least have saved her crew?

Smith was prepared to bet that the German captain would stay with his charges. Just the same, he ordered or reminded both the lookouts to keep a sharp watch for any pursuit.

Audacity showed no light now, was silent but for an occasional quiet voice, the steady beat of her engines as she ran along off the coast at eight knots, and the banging of hammers as Bennett, the carpenter, and his mates re-assembled the sides of the 'box' forward of the bridge. The red glow still lit the sky astern. When the guns ceased firing there had been a release of tension, loud laughter, shouted talk because ears rang and some men were excited, others relieved. Smith had cut it short: "I want silence, Mr. Ross! We're not out of the wood yet!"

He stood outside the wheelhouse, hands jammed in pockets. He did not think they would shake but still did not want to risk it so kept them hidden. "How long since we left the tug?"

McLeod answered, "The hour's nearly up, sir. She should be ahead of us now."

Smith nodded. Gallagher was somewhere in the darkness ahead. He should show a green light – if he was still able to, if a party from the shore had not surprised him before he could bring the gun into action, overrun the tug and killed him and his men.

Were there guns sited on the coast here? It was unlikely,

and Smith wondered if he should take *Audacity* close in-shore to creep through the shallows searching –

"Green light, port bow, sir!" The lookout bawled his report as McLeod's mouth opened, as Smith himself saw the pin-prick green glow.

"Port ten!" *Audacity* came around so she headed for the light. "Slow ahead." She closed the tug and Smith stopped her only yards away. He saw a cable running out from the tug's stern to disappear in the sea and that would lead to the anchor Gallagher had used as a kedge. Had he got her off the bank and afloat?

Smith called, "Mr. Gallagher?"

"Sir!" He stood in the stern of the tug. His voice came up to Smith: "We're very glad to see you! And surprised, to tell the truth! That was quite a fireworks display!"

Smith was in no mood for chatter. "I trust you didn't spend your time watching it!"

Gallagher answered, "No, sir! We used the tug's derrick to get . . . everything out of the boat. The cargo is forrard by the wheelhouse, on gratings and netted, ready to load. We raised steam on her, used the kedge and she's afloat – just. I can feel her bumping still as the current takes her. I didn't haul her off altogether because she's holed forrard where she went on the putty. There's two feet or more of water in her now and it'll be up to the stokehold fires before long; the pumps can't hold it."

"Any sign of activity ashore?"

"Not a cheep."

"We're coming alongside. Stand by to load the Camel."

Ross was on the deck forward of the bridge, his party gathered behind him, a man at the winch. As *Audacity* nuzzled alongside the fishing-boat the winch hammered and the wire from the derrick wriggled down to be hooked on to wire strops looped around the Camel, while the men with it cast off the lashings. Gallagher lifted a hand, signalling, and the Camel swung up, then inboard, to be guided down to rest on the staging the carpenter had erected in the hold just forward of *Audacity*'s bridge. The undercarriage and the rear half of the fuselage were below the level of the deck, the cockpit and the engine above it.

Thus only six feet of its nine feet of height stood above the deck but even these were still below the top of the 'box'. The wings followed, to be slotted into the wooden supports Bennett had prepared on Gallagher's instructions, inside the 'box'. They rested on their leading edges, well padded with canvas.

Minutes later the gold was also aboard and being packed away, with sweating and swearing at the weight of it, back under Smith's bunk. *Audacity* went astern. Gallagher jettisoned the anchor and its cable, eased the tug clear of the bank, then turned her and followed *Audacity* out to deeper water. There he stopped her and left her sinking, the engine-room plates already awash.

Audacity took the fishing-boat in tow while Gallagher came aboard with his men, the German prisoners, the three Russians – and Elizabeth Ramsay. Smith glimpsed only fleetingly her slim figure among the bulky men. Then McLeod, speaking of the ship far astern that had burned since *Audacity*'s attack, said, "She's gone!" The red glow on the horizon had suddenly ebbed and was snuffed out. The sea had claimed her. Two merchantmen sunk out of the four.

Smith ordered, "Mr. McLeod! Half ahead. I want a man at the lead and a course as near as we dare to this southern shore. Mr. Gallagher! Dismiss your men below and take Mrs. Ramsay and the Russians to the wardroom. See to their comfort. And, Mr. Gallagher!"

"Sir?"

"Have a drink on my bill. You've all earned it."

"Aye, aye, sir. Thank you."

"Mr. Ross! Lock those prisoners away under guard below. The master on his own."

"Aye, aye, sir!"

A problem for Ross, but that was what first lieutenants were for. Smith had his own problems. He believed the destroyer would stay shepherding the remnants of the convoy, but he could not be certain. She might be hunting him, or her captain might have taken her at full speed to the Irbensky Strait, to close the door in the hope that his attacker was still in the Gulf of Riga. Smith did not want to run into him there without the advantage of surprise. *Audacity* would come off worst in that kind of action. So he conned his ship through the shallows off the southern shore, one ear cocked for the low call of the man at the lead, the other for McLeod's murmured promptings: "The chart shows a bank running out about here, sir, and the soundings confirm it. We'll need to ease a point or two to starboard."

So they felt their way cautiously out of the Gulf and through the narrow neck of the Strait, with no light showing and the guns manned. The guard-boat was of course gone, scuttled, and they saw no destroyer. When they were out in the deeper water of the Baltic again, Smith told McLeod, "A course to take us northabout around Gotland, Pilot. We'll make for the Swedish coast." Not heading directly for the Sound because they could expect to meet enemy patrols on that course. This northabout way, he hoped, would steer them clear of patrols for a time, and once off the Swedish coast they could take shelter in those neutral waters – if they had to.

Then he sent for Elizabeth Ramsay and the three Russians. When they crowded into his tiny cabin the latter looked exactly what they purported to be: bearded fishermen in heavy coats and sea-boots. They stood in an awkward row in front of the leather couch near the door. Elizabeth Ramsay had dark circles around her eyes but her face was scrubbed and, despite the lines of strain and weariness, she looked younger. This was a tired girl, not the hard, painted woman with the bold eyes.

Smith said, "I'm glad to see you, Mrs. Ramsay. Please be seated." She sank into the single chair and smoothed out her dress. He gestured the Russians down on to the couch, and turned back to the girl. "I gather you had a rough passage. Will you tell me about it?"

She shrugged. "I heard McLeod tell you most of it. The tug intercepted us off Kurgala and called on us to stop. The Germans had never stopped fishing-boats before. Maybe they thought we'd been running supplies to the Red Guards in Finland. We made a run for it, of course, but she fired her gun and killed two, one of them our captain, and wounded another. He died soon afterwards." Her hands twitched in her lap and she laced her fingers firmly together. "They took us aboard the tug and questioned us. The Russians claimed they were fishermen and I said I was the wife of one of those killed. The captain of the tug only had a few words of Russian and I didn't let on I knew German. He wasn't satisfied, told his crew we were up to something and he was taking us back to be interrogated by an interpreter. Then a man came along with a piece of paper, a wireless message. The captain was surprised. He said they were orders to go to some place and load an aeroplane. They locked us up; I was on my own in a little cabin. I had plenty of time to think. I knew once they got the fishing-boat into port and unloaded it they would find the gold. And then –" She broke off there.

Smith thought: then the interrogation, the story told by each checked against the others and its discrepancies challenged over and over until someone virtually talking in his sleep let slip the truth.

The girl looked up at Smith with a half-smile. "I was going to try to escape but I couldn't see how. I'm very grateful to you. We all are." She pointed to the Russians, spoke to them and they answered with smiles, nodding their heads. "They know how close they were to being shot as spies – if not by the Germans, then by the Bolsheviks, because the Germans would have handed them over."

And with them the details of the plot to sink the Russian Fleet. Smith nodded. Now for it. "I want you to tell them the plot is finished. I had orders from the Admiralty to cancel it and return with the gold."

For a moment she stared, disbelieving, then: "You mean you're giving up, you're not going to try again?"

Smith explained patiently: "My new orders came just after you left Kirkko. I was trying to find you when the tug captured you. Those orders are clear: I take the gold back and the plot is finished. Please tell them that, Mrs. Ramsay."

She pushed at her hair with one hand, dazed, but complied, speaking slowly, heavily. When she had done the Russians muttered among themselves. It was difficult to tell whether they were cast down or relieved. Smith could understand that, after their experience of the last few days, and now that their leader was dead the risks must have loomed larger than the rewards. Or was their reaction just Russian stoicism?

He said, "If they stay aboard this ship they will land up in England – if they're not killed, or captured again. On the other hand, they can take their boat and go home. She's been damaged but she's seaworthy and I'll give them the tools and timber to make the damage good. They can sail her." He had got Gallagher's word for that. "They stand a good chance of getting there."

Again the girl passed on his words. And again the Russians muttered among themselves, then came to a nodding agreement.

Elizabeth Ramsay translated wearily, "They'll take the boat. They have families in Russia, and what money they have is there." Then, with bitterness, "They say they would be beggars in England. I can understand that."

Smith heaved an inward sigh of relief: three fewer bodies to squeeze into his ship. "It will be in their own interest to keep silent about the plot. I want their word that they will say nothing about this ship; they don't even know it exists. In return I will keep silent about their part."

They agreed. He thought they would probably keep their word: they had nothing to gain by breaking it. *Audacity* stopped, the *Anna* was hauled in and the Russians went down into her with the tools and timber, water and supplies. The boat had a compass and McLeod gave them a course. Smith, through Elizabeth Ramsay, had hammered into them that they should use the fishing tackle they had aboard. "If they're stopped, there's no need for them to try to run again. There's nothing aboard now to incriminate them. They're just fishermen – a long way from home, admittedly, but they can cook up a story for that."

They had shaken hands before they went down into the boat. Elizabeth Ramsay stood a yard away now. He watched the *Anna* fall astern as *Audacity*'s screws turned, saw them start to hoist the sail. Then they were lost in the night.

He turned and came face to face with the girl, thought he saw tears on her cheeks. She said huskily, "Damn you to hell, Smith! You and the bloody Admiralty! Damn you all to hell!" Then she walked away quickly, her head down.

Smith went to his cabin, sank down into the chair at the little knee-hole desk behind the door and stared at his hands spread flat on the top of the desk, at the grime on them and the broken nails, watched the fingers tremble. He tried to stop that shaking but he knew he would not. It always came after an action, the visible manifestation of the shuddering inside him now that the danger was past.

It was over – for now; they were clean away. They lived on a knife-edge of risk, might run into a powerful enemy at any moment but for now that was only an outside possibility and there were long odds against it. But tomorrow . . .

Ross and McLeod had clearly thought the attack on the convoy suicidally dangerous but they had underestimated the twin advantages of surprise and the confusion of a night action. Smith had cold-bloodedly assessed that an attack was possible, at small risk and at disproportionately great gain.

There would not be another convoy with just a pair of escorts, let alone unescorted, after tonight. Smith suspected that the damage wreaked by *Audacity* would have left the Germans, fighting in darkness and dazzled by muzzle-flashes, with an exaggerated estimate of their enemy's firepower. He could imagine the German naval reaction: this must not happen again. So that meant more convoy escorts and fewer ships free to engage in the hunt for *Audacity*. And he had drawn attention forcefully to this area, had again laid the false trail that this ship was a White Russian raider with a safe base not far away. That should seem logical to German eyes since it would be unthinkable that a solitary British ship could somehow enter the Baltic without detection and then commit the lunacy of attacking German naval forces on their doorstep. So the risks taken were not only acceptable, but justifiable.

He was thinking ahead now, staring not at his hands, but unseeingly at the grey-painted, sweating steel side of his cabin, unaware that his fingers had ceased trembling and lay still.

Tomorrow?

He pushed up from the desk and began pacing his cabin, the eight or nine feet from the door to the rear and back again, brushing between the round table and the leather couch.

Mcleod had the watch and was on the bridge. Elizabeth Ramsay was in her cabin, the door firmly shut behind her. But below, in the wardroom, they heard Smith's pacing, faintly. Gallagher, Danby and Ross sat at the table, washed now and free of the smoke-grime and sweat-streaks of action. Wilberforce, the steward, had produced sandwiches and whisky. Gallagher's gaze lifted up to the deckhead and the sound of that pacing. He raised his glass and said, "You're a mad, hard-nosed bastard. But here's to you."

Ross echoed deeply, "Aye!"

Up on the bridge Wilberforce entered the wheelhouse bearing a tray and spoke to McLeod, "Brought you some sandwiches and a little something, sir. And for the captain."

Buckley, his back against Smith's door, said, "Leave his."

Wilberforce objected. "He'll be expectin' something and I'll be in the rattle if I don't –"

"He won't be and you won't be," Buckley told him flatly and not moving from the door, "but you will if you barge in there now. Leave it, I'll take it in later."

Wilberforce gave him the tray and went off, muttering, "Bloody officers!"

Buckley thought, "I'll give the captain ten minutes to work the worst of the mood off him. Then he can swear at me as much as he likes. He's done enough."

The pacing went on.

11

The Trap

In the last of the night they encountered fog again, but Smith did not order a reduction in speed and *Audacity* tore through the grey veils at a pounding fifteen knots. Only on changing course to round the north-west tip of Gotland did he slow the ship to an easier ten. *Audacity* was safely across the shipping lane that ran east to west the length of the Baltic and now headed for the neutral coast of Sweden, on her way, ultimately, to the Sound. And he had always to keep in mind the consumption of coal. *Audacity* started this voyage with enough for ten days' steaming but that was at an economical speed of eight or ten knots. At fifteen she ate coal and he would get none in the Baltic.

That morning off Gotland he stopped *Audacity* and they buried the dead seaman off the tug and the man taken from the lifeboat the previous day. He had died in the night of shock, exposure and pneumonia. Smith had the two German officers brought up for the ceremony, the *oberleutnant* of the guard-boat and the tug's master. It was bitterly cold as *Audacity* rolled slowly in the dank mist that glistened on the canvas shrouds wrapped tight by Fenwick's neat-stitched twine. Afterwards the sun sucked up the mist and it was a fine day.

He paced the flying bridge in the late forenoon, eight strides forward, eight strides aft. He was alone but for the two lookouts, one on either wing of the bridge. They kept out of his way but eyed him covertly now and again as he strode restlessly, scowling. He glanced at them, gauging their mood. He always tried to gauge the mood of every man aboard as he saw them going about their duties and today was satisfied that his crew was cheerful. This was a sparkling, bright morning: they had smashed a German convoy, and then got away without a scratch. Well, not entirely: there were the usual bruises and scrapes inevitable when hands and arms and shoulders work with the hard, moving steel of a gun.

Audacity herself had been equally lucky. The single shell that hit her had missed the wireless room with Sparks at his post inside and burst in the empty mess of the four-inch gun's crew. Bennett fixed a patch on the hole and now a man was daubing on paint. Every time Smith turned at the port side he saw him, brush in hand. He sang softly and out of tune but in time to the wheezing of Wilberforce's concertina that the steward was playing in his pantry.

Ross and McLeod were happier men, relieved that last night's wild escapade had not ended in disaster, and that *Audacity* was now on a course that might take them to safety. Some of Ross's charges, the prisoners, were on deck now in the well between superstructure and poop: the *oberleutnant* and crew of the guard-boat. The master and the crew of the tug had been up for exercise earlier. While their officer tramped the deck to starboard the guard-boat's crew strolled or lounged along the port side. They already appeared reconciled to being prisoners of war; an armed sentry watched them from the poop. The *oberleutnant* was a man in middle-age, obviously long since passed over for promotion and Smith's capture of his ship had ended his career. His crew had simply changed from one form of captivity, weeks spent swinging around their anchor, to another.

The prisoners were still an infernal nuisance, however, and Smith wished there was some way he could be rid of them. But if he put them ashore in a neutral country to be interned they would tell their tale to a German consul and they knew about *Audacity*'s disguise – the four boxes of timber 'deck cargo' now erected again by Bennett – and the Camel.

He glanced forward and saw the carpenter and his mates now at work in the opened box below the fo'c'sle, measuring, sawing, hammering. Bennett knew what he had to do; Gallagher had sketched a plan for him, of a platform sixty feet long, and there was plenty of timber for the job.

Gallagher was also forward of the bridge. The lid of the 'box' that held the Camel was also slid back so the fitters and riggers could get in and work on the aircraft. Gallagher was with them. He had told Smith happily: "Her tyres were soft but they just needed pumping up and we've done that. Jerry had packed up all the spares and stores he found with her, and the petrol; there's all we'll need. We're stripping and overhauling the engine but we know already there's not a damn thing wrong with it. The wings were stowed on their leading-edges all the time so *they're* all right. There are holes all over the fuselage, one or two broken spars and snapped wires, but nothing we can't repair as good as new."

Danby was not with Gallagher. Of course. That was still the only jarring note. The armourers had the Camel's twin Vickers machine-guns out on the deck, stripped down for cleaning and overhaul. A half-hour ago Gallagher had fired practice bursts at a barrel towed astern. Now Danby stood by the men, hands in the pockets of his oversize jacket, smiling. He got on all right with them, anyway. He might not be a pilot, let alone an ace, but he had got them safely to Petrograd.

Even Elizabeth Ramsay was quiet. Wilberforce, the steward, had earlier brought up a chair for her and set it on the deck in the lee of the forward 'box'. She sat there in the sun, sheltered from the wind and with a blanket wrapped around her, reading a book, presumably from the dog-eared collection in the wardroom. Smith occasionally saw her turn a page but he never saw her look up at him, though she did and more than once.

He thought that there was only one discontented man aboard, himself, and that because of the girl's reaction. Why had she been so bitter on learning she was not to risk her life in Russia? Relief would have been a normal reaction, possibly tinged with the disappointment of anticlimax, but not that emotional outburst wrung from her: "*Damn you all to hell!*"

He tried to put the girl from his mind, continued pacing. He should count his blessings: *Audacity* had not been captured nor sunk and he had not lost a man. So far as the enemy knew, after capturing *Königsberg*, *Audacity* had headed for the waters off Helsinki. She was not seen there but nor was she sighted anywhere else so they might reasonably conclude she found no pickings off Helsinki but evaded capture, then crossed to attack in the Gulf of Riga, and would now be running for her Russian base. So the search would be concentrated eastward but there would still be patrols at this western end of the Baltic.

Gallagher, standing with one of the fitters on a makeshift staging by the Camel's engine, could see over the side of the 'box' to the girl sitting only a few yards away. He watched as she rose and walked aft towards the bridge, thought she was well worth looking at.

She reminded him of the girl in London. Well, there were really two girls, one dark, one fair. They rented a flat and Johnny Vincent and he had shared it with them during the week before they sailed for Murmansk with the Flight. They had a fine time. Lying in late in the morning, having a few drinks before lunch – and a few after. Playing billiards, golf; talking, arguing, laughing. A show every evening, and the girls . . . Johnny said he wanted to ask the fair one to marry him but Gallagher laughed him out of it: "Get married? When we're going to Russia? Come off it, Johnny!"

He shifted on the staging and saw Danby with the armourers, smiling. What did he have to grin about? What was the little bastard thinking?

Danby was happy for a little while. The armourers were joking as they worked on the guns and he was one of them. They'd gone through some hard and dangerous times on their way out of Russia and there was mutual respect. On their part not the hero-worship they had for Gallagher, but respect nevertheless. He could do their job as well as they. He sniffed at the faint aroma of gun oil and the penetrating reek of the dope the riggers were painting on the repairs made to the fuselage. When the dope dried it would tighten the fabric, but now it only made the stuff hang damply loose over the ribs like an old man's skin.

This was the life he wanted. It was a far cry from the

dusty office in Eastcheap and he could smile at that now. Junior clerk, the junior clerk of a dozen. The senior clerk was old Jameson, sixty-five and looking more like ninety-five after a half-century in that cramped, dark, little hole. That had been Danby's destiny, to fill old Jameson's chair after a lifetime of working for the firm. A family firm in which the family took the top jobs, while the Danbys waited for the Jamesons to die.

The war had been his chance to break out. He'd volunteered as soon as he was old enough, though well aware that three of the clerks older than himself had regretted their eagerness and been buried in Flanders. That was a risk he was ready to accept in order to get away, to become *somebody*; an officer in the Royal Naval Air Service.

He looked up and met Gallagher's bitter stare, knelt quickly and said to one of the armourers, "Here, let me give a hand with that." He kept the smile fixed in place.

He had thought he'd escaped from the office, that instead he would serve in a profession even after the war, live with a little dignity and a deal of pride. But Gallagher had destroyed that hope. With Gallagher's report on his record there would be no question of him staying in the R.N.A.S., or the R.A.F. as it was now. And there was nothing he could – or, rather, would – do about it.

Smith's thoughts were interrupted: "Begging your pardon, sir." A man stood at the head of the ladder.

Smith halted. Why couldn't they leave him in peace? He rasped, "Yes?"

"The lady would like a word with you, sir. Mr. Ross told her you were busy and not to be disturbed, but . . ." His voice trailed away before Smith's glare.

But Elizabeth Ramsay was a law unto herself. Should he send her away, to rub in that he was captain of this ship and she only a passenger? But was she not more than that? Last night she had cursed him – out of disappointment and anger? She had blamed him once before, equally unfairly. So . . . "Ask her to come up." Was it possible that she wanted to apologise? Or rather, not wanted, but thought that she should?

He met her at the head of the ladder, handed her up to the flying bridge and said, "We can talk here. It's private."

She looked forward, then aft, the length of the ship. "Is it? Everyone can see us."

Exactly. For safety's sake. *His* safety. But the lookouts were yards away, on the wings and out of earshot. "They can't hear us."

Their glances met, slid off. That tension was between them, as always. Smith suggested, "Shall we walk?" Talking might be easier then.

"Yes." She kept pace at his shoulder and did not hesitate now. "I want to – explain, about last night." Smith waited in silence, glanced at her as they turned at the rail. She had changed her clothes, wore a fresh dress that showed when her cloak flapped open on the wind. He remembered her carpetbag had come aboard with her last night. Her lips were painted again but she still looked young.

Elizabeth Ramsay wrapped the cloak around her and said, "You might understand if I begin at the beginning. My father was English but my mother was French. He was a restaurateur and my mother was a cook. He would buy a run-down place cheaply, work it up for two or three years then sell it at a profit and move on. We travelled all round the Baltic. A funny, gipsy sort of life, I suppose, but they liked it." She smiled faintly, remembering. "That's how I learned the languages, though I've been told I have a natural gift in that way – mimicry, maybe.

"I was fifteen when my mother died and I took her place in helping him with his work, though he employed a chef because I'm strictly a plain cook. Father taught me the running of the business and we went on as before, except that he left more and more in my hands. Early in 1914 he bought a place in Petrograd, but then the war came. He'd not expected that. He was a good man in business but took no interest in politics. He needed money to build up the place in Petrograd but virtually all his capital was invested or banked in Germany: he had always had a lot of respect for them as businessmen. He couldn't touch his money, he worried about the restaurant and me, then in that winter he caught pneumonia and died."

She looked quickly at Smith, then away. "That was the start of the bad times. I was twenty-two, with a big Petrograd restaurant that was barely making a profit and no one to turn to. He had never gone back to England and rarely talked of his family. I think there'd been a row because he was very bitter. Anyway, I didn't know any of them and they were a long way off so I had to make a go of the place on my own. I did. It wasn't easy, and one of the methods I resorted to was letting private rooms for intimate dinners. People would have a good meal and what went on behind closed doors was none of my business. But it got me a certain reputation."

Her mimicry showed now. She lifted her nose in the air and spoke in a refined British embassy accent: "That Mrs. Ramsay who runs a house of assignation!" She laughed then, but there was no amusement in it. "It was one means to an end but the end didn't come as I'd planned it. I took no more interest in Russian politics than my father had but I could see what was going on around me; strikes, unrest, talk of revolution. There was nothing I could do about it, nowhere I could run to. The revolution came and I lost the restaurant, everything I had."

For a minute or more she walked in silence, not looking at Smith but keeping pace, turning with him at the rail but always staring out at the sea that glittered with cold brilliance under the sun. Then: "So I had to go to the embassy. I had no choice. They knew about me, of course, or thought they did: 'That Mrs. Ramsay!' I suppose it was my own fault and I should have told them the whole story, but I didn't want to explain myself."

Smith said nothing.

She looked at him but he kept his eyes trained ahead, wary of meeting hers as she said, "You understand that?" He nodded, was conscious of her watching, uncertain for a moment, but then she made up her mind about him. "Don't get the wrong idea. I'm not trying to make out I am as pure as the driven snow. There have been men in my life – as there have been women in yours. There are a lot of things I'm sorry about but not many I'm ashamed of." That was neither defence nor defiance but a flat statement of fact: take it or leave it. She saw Smith nod endorsement.

Now she looked away. "So they knew about me at the embassy and it wasn't long before they asked me to contact a particular Russian officer, because he'd been a customer at my place, spent a lot. He was the leader of the plotters. You saw him at Kirkko; he was at the tiller of the *Anna*. He wasn't so much a devoted royalist as a dedicated capitalist. Later I met the whole group and they told me their price. I told them mine. I wanted one per cent, three thousand pounds. They agreed and it was a condition that I would return with the first instalment. That was *my* condition. I wanted to make sure I got that first thousand pounds, whatever else happened."

Now he stared at her. A thousand! That was more than three years' pay!

Elizabeth Ramsay saw that look though she did not meet it. "You think you understand now, why I was hell-bent on the scheme going through?" She shook her head. "I told you I had nothing, nobody. Only that label: 'the Russian Whore'. You've heard it and Ross knew of it. It showed in your eyes, all of you. It had started when I was visiting the Russian officers and I didn't deny it because it was a good cover – better than the Bolsheviks suspecting what I was really doing. And now I can't deny it because that plot is a state secret and will be when the war is over, and mud sticks. So now you know why the plot was important to me. It meant security: at least one thousand pounds, and three thousand if it succeeded. That would keep me for years, set me up in business again, maybe in America. It meant a new start."

She paused then, waiting for his reaction. He thought that at least he had the answer to a question that had plagued him all along: why did she have to go to the Russians with the gold? Now he knew they demanded it *at her insistence*.

He said, "It was dangerous."

The girl shrugged her shoulders inside her cloak. "It was that or destitution. I stand on my own feet. I have to."

"Does the Admiralty know?"

"About my share?" One corner of the wide, painted

mouth lifted in a wry smile. "No. They understand patriotism and duty but on the Board of Admiralty there are no penniless young women trying to make their way in the world. Well?" Now she was challenging. "Do you blame me?"

"I'm not sitting on a court."

"No, but I used some hard words last night and you're entitled to your say."

He might have wondered why his opinion mattered to her, but he did not. He asked, "Suppose the Russians had refused to agree to your having a share? Would you still have gone through with it?"

Elizabeth Ramsay was startled by the question but answered without hesitation. "There'd have been no need for me to go back to Russia. But you mean: would I have gone on with the plot while I was in Petrograd, acting as go-between? I was told it was vital the Russian Fleet did not fall into German hands. Of course I would have seen it through."

"Then I don't blame you."

The girl did not turn at the rail this time and he stood beside her. His eyes swept the horizon, as he had done a dozen times as they walked and talked. The sea was empty.

She asked, "You're going to try to escape from the Baltic?"

His orders ruled that it would be impossible once *Audacity*'s true identity was known, but: "By God, I am!"

His intensity surprised her but his answer did not. She said, "The men say you've sworn to take this ship back to Rosyth." And when he nodded: "What if the Germans catch up with you?"

He said, "My orders are that I can't dump the gold except in danger of capture. That means fighting a losing battle while we throw it over the side. And if we're taken afterwards then my men may be treated as spies."

Elizabeth Ramsay was in no doubt what fate would await her if she was captured. "I see. Then we're all in the same boat, in both senses."

"Yes."

"And I'm just a passenger."

"Not necessarily. McLeod says you're a better interpreter than he is. If I think you can be of use, I'll call on you." Not ask; he was the captain.

She took the point and nodded. "Of course." Then she climbed down the ladder and he turned back to his pacing. At the end there was still that current between them, as there had been all through their talking. An awareness and a memory of that moment at Kirkko, the pressure of his body on hers.

"Land off the port bow, sir!" The hail came from the lookout on that side of the flying bridge. Smith did not check in his pacing, nor did he when McLeod came running up the ladder.

The navigator said, "That should be the north end of Oland, sir."

Oland was a narrow island, sixty-five miles long and seven across at its widest point. It belonged to Sweden and ran southwards along the Swedish coast. A channel, the Kalmarsund, ran between Oland and the mainland. That channel was Swedish water and Smith would steer clear of it, taking *Audacity* south and to seaward of the island, outside the three-mile limit.

McLeod was stooped over the compass and now he straightened his thick body and said cheerfully, "Where it should be, sir, right on the bearing."

"Very good." The bearing was to the lighthouse on Storgrundet, an islet close off the northern tip of Oland.

"Smoke on the starboard beam, sir!" That call came from the lookout and now Smith halted, set the glasses to his eyes, focused them and found the smoke. The ship itself still lay over the horizon, as did the Swedish mainland. He thought it was probably a coaster running down to Kalmar, in Swedish territorial waters it had to be, but . . ."

"Watch her."

"Aye, aye, sir."

McLeod went down to the chart and Smith returned to his pacing and his planning. It was impossible to reach and pass through the Sound, more than two hundred miles away, this night. That passage had to be made in darkness throughout. So when they turned south they would steam slowly down off the coast of Oland, anchor out of sight of land before sunset and spend the night so. Tomorrow they could close the Sound – and before that he hoped to be rid of his prisoners. That was his intention but the reality might be different. He had tried to lay a false trail in order to draw off the main pursuit, but the closer he got to the Sound the more likely he was to meet the enemy. There could be destroyers coming out of Kiel, brought from the High Seas Fleet by way of the Kiel Canal –

"She's a coaster, sir. An' I think I can see the loom of the land beyond her."

Smith acknowledged the lookout's report: "Thank you." So he had been right.

McLeod was back on the flying bridge, to ask permission for the change of course. But now the port side lookout reported, "Smoke on the port beam, sir."

Smith crossed the bridge to stand at his shoulder, lifted his glasses and looked out, searching the arc of the horizon. The lookout muttered, "You should be just about on it now, sir." Smith was, seeing the black blip on the curving line where sea met sky: the smoke of a ship, or ships, below the horizon. Going away? No, because if it had crossed ahead of *Audacity* they would have seen the smoke long before now. So it was on a northerly course and closing them. Smith shifted uneasily. It might be a neutral merchantman – or several German warships.

He lowered the glasses. McLeod waited for the order to change course. Turn to port, towards that smoke? Or turn away and run north? There would be no running away from a destroyer with a ten-knot advantage in speed. Smith said, "Alter course to take us into the Kalmarsund, Mr. McLeod."

McLeod blinked, then, "Aye, aye, sir." He dropped down the ladder to the bridge and his chart again. Seconds later *Audacity*'s head edged slightly around to starboard and settled on the new course, still roughly at a right angle to the unknown threat.

Smith was aware that the placid domestic scene below had changed. The work went on but now the carpenter and his mates, the men grouped around the Camel, glanced out

163

every few minutes to that distant horizon, then up at Smith high on the flying bridge. They waited, and so did he. He wondered what kind of ship was steaming towards *Audacity* and went over his plans again, the options open to him. And eventually, inevitably, the gold intruded on his thoughts. Whenever he had a few moments of relative peace, not coping with shoals, ice, minefields, fog, whenever he was trying to plan what the *hell* to do next, thought of the bullion returned to plague him. Besides his ship and all aboard her, he had always to keep in mind the *bloody* gold.

He swore, and saw the starboard lookout's shoulders twitch as Smith turned in his striding only inches away. So the lookout knew the supposedly imperturbable Smith was in a foul temper over something. Was he? Or was this just a sign of unease, some instinct warning him of danger? The same instinct that prompted him to order the course for the Kalmarsund?

He paused by the port side lookout, raised his glasses again, stared out at the distant smoke and asked, "Can you make anything of that ship?"

"No, sir. She's still hull-down."

Nor could Smith. So aboard that ship too they would see only his smoke, not yet his ship. He let the glasses hang and swung on his heel to look out to starboard and the coaster. If you drew a line from the smoke to *Audacity* and then extended it, it would pass through the coaster as near as dammit. He faced forward. *Audacity* was closing the channel, the lighthouse on the northern end of Oland a bare mile away now. By the time that distant ship steamed up to this point, *Audacity* would be far down the Kalmarsund with the coaster just entering it. The lookouts on the ship to the south would have seen the coaster under her smoke for some time and might have no reason to suspect there had been two ships under that pall of smoke when they had first sighted it.

"Mr. Ross!"

"Sir!"

"Stand by to send away the motor-boat in ten minutes from now." Smith wanted to know what ship it was coming up from the south.

"Aye, aye, sir!"

So when *Audacity* rounded the northern end of Oland and was into the Kalmarsund, she stopped. The motor-boat was lowered, a petty officer in command, and headed back towards the lighthouse. The coaster was still some three or four miles north of the entrance to the Kalmarsund, but as *Audacity* steamed on down the channel at a lazy five knots the coaster slowly made up on her.

Smith watched the coaster. She would pass within a half-mile of *Audacity* and no doubt her master would spare a glance for this apparently German tramp, might even study her through glasses. Smith's gaze went to the deck forward of the bridge. The lid was off the box holding the Camel, the airmen still working on the machine, but the captain of the coaster would see the box only from the side, as a deck cargo of timber. The carpenter and his mates hammered and sawed away on the fo'c'sle now but that particular activity would seem innocent enough.

A lookout reported, "Motor-boat's coming after us, sir."

Smith nodded. *Audacity* was five miles into the Kalmarsund now and Hornsudde Point lay two miles ahead off the port bow, jutting out from a steep and wooded shore. There was no smoke to be seen past the coaster, astern of them to the north, but he picked out the white feathers of a bow-wave marking the motor-boat. She would be cracking on at her best speed, about seven or eight knots in this sheltered water. The third, mystery ship seemed to have gone on past the end of the channel.

He ordered, "Slow ahead." So *Audacity* dawdled while the coaster ploughed past her a half-mile away to starboard and the motor-boat gradually closed on her. *Audacity* stopped then, and recovered the boat before steaming on again, but now working up to eight knots.

The petty officer, Armstrong, short and thickset, young and quick, came to Smith on the flying bridge and reported, "We lay close under the lighthouse and made out we had a spot o' engine trouble, like you said, sir. The ship was a two-funnel destroyer, she crossed the channel entrance less'n a mile away and she was German, no doubt of that."

She looked to be one o' those big, new boats, S or V class. We couldn't make out her number an' she kept on to the north, making about twenty knots."

"Very good." He'd guessed right, thank God. Smith sent the man away. That destroyer might be out of Danzig, but more likely was from Kiel. Robertson had said the German destroyers in the Baltic were old ships, like those escorting the convoy in the Gulf of Riga, but this was a new boat. If she had been bound for Finland to support Von Goltz's troops there, her course would have taken her further eastward. There was only one reason why a destroyer might sweep up this Swedish coast: in search of *Audacity*. Now she had gone on to the north. If Smith had tried to run north then *Audacity* would have been finished. That new destroyer would have overhauled her in no time and shot her to pieces. But would she return?

Audacity kept station two miles or so astern of the coaster as they steamed south past Sandvik, then Borgholm, the channel nipped-in and narrow now, until Kalmar with its castle and cathedral showed off the starboard bow. The coaster pottering ahead turned to starboard, heading in towards Kalmar but *Audacity* held on, following the channel through the sound. Kalmar edged down the bow, came abeam, edged away down the starboard quarter until it was two miles astern and steadily receding. Another coaster was ahead, plodding up from the south, but apart from her *Audacity* was the only vessel in the channel and in another twenty miles they would be clear of it.

It would be almost dusk by then – Smith glanced up at the sky – because in this weather darkness would come early. There was a stiff breeze now, carrying *Audacity*'s smoke away to starboard, and clouds scudding on it, dark and heavy, thickening. It would be a usefully rough night, not a storm but weather bad enough to hide *Audacity*, steaming without lights.

"Boat on the starboard bow, sir!"

Smith turned at the lookout's hail. The coaster coming up towards Kalmar from the south was passing on the starboard side and a half-mile away. The Swedish mainland was a ruffled edging to the horizon beyond her while three miles to port lay the village of Degerham on Oland. Smith lifted his glasses to examine the boat just sighted. She was too distant to show any more than that she was small, too small for a ship, and making no smoke. A motor-boat? It could be a fisherman, or a wealthy Swede cruising for pleasure, but again Smith felt a stir of unease, his instinct warning him.

He climbed down from the flying bridge and found Ross waiting for him. Smith looked at the scene forward, Gallagher and his men working on the Camel, the carpenter and his mates, Elizabeth Ramsay in her chair. He told Ross, "Clear the deck. Complete disguise. Everyone below save the bare minimum."

Ross peered about him, wondering where the threat lay, then answered quickly, "Aye, aye, sir!"

At his bellow the scene changed. The two boxes were reassembled and the carpenter's work hidden in one, the Camel in the other. Bennett and his mates, the airmen under their petty officer, swept the deck clean and disappeared below. A seaman took away the girl's chair as she walked towards the bridge and her cabin. Smith turned on McLeod: "Be ready to do your act. And tell Mrs. Ramsay to be good enough to join me here."

He wondered if his instinct was false and he was making a fool of himself, but he forced a grin when McLeod returned with the girl and said, "There may be work for you soon, as an interpreter. I hope I'm wrong, but we'll see."

Elizabeth Ramsay smiled wryly. "You did warn me I might be called on, and I understand."

But Smith thought that none of them could understand the weight of responsibility he bore, for this ship and all aboard her, alone and hunted in the Baltic.

The lookout said, "She's flying Swedish colours, sir. Her crew, what I can see of them, are in uniform and there's an officer in her well. Leastways, there's something like gold braid. And she's turning to close us."

Smith used his own glasses and the motor-boat came up sharp and clear. She looked smart, no fisherman this, the yellow and blue Swedish ensign flying from the staff in her stern and the seaman standing in her bow was in naval uniform, his collar fluttering on the wind. And that was indeed an officer in the well, standing on a thwart and holding on to the cabin coaming with one hand. There was braid on his sleeve, the two rings of a lieutenant. This was a Swedish naval patrol-boat.

Smith lowered the glasses and turned on Elizabeth Ramsay. "If that officer challenges us in Swedish then Mr. McLeod can handle it, but as we're supposed to be a German ship he might choose to ask his questions in German. And Mr. McLeod says he isn't too hot at understanding that. So he will make the responses but you will be in the wheelhouse with me, interpreting so that I know what's going on and you are ready to prompt him if he needs it."

The girl nodded agreement. "I'm all right in German."

McLeod spoke frankly. "She talks it like a native, and thank the Lord we've got her. This Swede might keep his German simple like the guard-boat's skipper did, but on the other hand he might not." He stepped out to the wing of the bridge in his stained and greasy reefer jacket, his battered old cap set square on his head.

The patrol-boat turned in a smooth curve as the man at the tiller put it over, to close *Audacity* and run alongside within easy hailing distance. The lieutenant in the well of her shouted through a megaphone, "*Anna Schmidt! Ich : . .*" He continued in German.

Elizabeth Ramsay translated quickly. "I have just been talking with a countryman of yours!"

McLeod had understood that, answered, "*Ja?*"

The lieutenant continued, the girl whispering, "In the minesweeper – watching the mouth of the Kalmarsund."

Ross muttered under his breath, "*Hell!*"

Smith hissed at him, "*Shut up!*"

Elizabeth Ramsay was still translating. "You have not come from Kalmar!"

Smith said rapidly. "No. From Finland. Passing through the channel bound for Kiel with timber."

The girl translated instantly, calling softly to McLeod

who bellowed her words, phrase by phrase. But inevitably there had been a pause before he answered.

There was another now. Smith, peering from the wheel-house, breath held, could just see the lieutenant. He had lowered the megaphone and stood swaying to the motion of his boat, staring up at *Audacity*, head moving slowly as he surveyed her from stem to stern. It was a long pause, but then the lieutenant lifted the megaphone again. "I wish to come aboard, Captain."

Smith let out the held breath in a silent sigh. He was not the only one to act on his instinct today; the lieutenant had smelt a rat. Why? Smith cast one swift glance the length of *Audacity*. The German ensign, the deck cargo, the men on her, everything looked the part. There was no account-ing, however, for another man's instinct.

He could always run for it. *Audacity* would soon leave this little motor-boat astern and she carried no wireless, there were no tell-tale aerials strung from her stubby mast. It would take her two hours or more to get to Kalmar – but then the fat would be in the fire. The Swedes would be looking for *Anna Schmidt* and demanding an explanation from the German consul. Then the Germans too would be looking for her, and also putting two and two together as to her true identity.

"Tell him: 'Of course.'" He turned away and threw over his shoulder, "Stop her, Mr. Ross."

He went into his cabin, took from the cupboard his uniform jacket and cap and changed into them.

Out in the wheelhouse again, Ross shot a startled look at him. Smith said, "We've got to let him come aboard, and unless he's blind or a fool –" He did not finish, watched as the way came off *Audacity*, the Jacob's-ladder was dropped over the side and McLeod went down to the deck to meet the lieutenant as he came aboard.

He was not alone. Two tall seamen preceded him up the ladder. They carried carbines slung on their backs and when they reached *Audacity*'s deck they unslung the carbines and held them at the high port across their chests. Like them, the lieutenant was tall, and he wore a holstered pistol. He was a clean-shaven young man of about twenty-five. He saluted and looked around him, at McLeod, the faces of the seamen who had lowered the ladder, all of them seeming merchant hands in old clothes or overalls. He spoke harshly to McLeod, challenging, and Elizabeth Ramsay whispered, "He says the *Anna Schmidt* was here in December before the ice came. He knew her and her captain. This is not the *Anna Schmidt*."

Ross muttered savagely, "Of all the bloody rotten luck!"

The lieutenant stared at the 'deck cargo' and strode over to finger it, bang on it with his fist. He could see it was a box and turned on McLeod, his hand going to the holstered pistol.

Smith stepped out of the wheelhouse. He spoke in English. "Good day, Lieutenant." And as the Swede gaped at him, "This is a British ship, I am her captain and an officer of the Royal Navy." The lieutenant did not answer and Smith asked, "You speak English?"

"Yes, I speak it. Not so good as German but I speak it.'

"Good." Smith dropped down the ladders to the deck, saluted, and held out his hand to the lieutenant. "I am Commander Smith."

The Swede returned the salute, hesitated, then shook the hand once, released it. "Johanssen." Then: "This is a *British* ship? A ship of the Royal Navy?"

"That is correct."

Johanssen thumped the box again with his fist. "There is a gun in here?" He pointed at the other one forward: "In there?"

"No."

The Swede eyed Smith suspiciously. "Then what?"

"That is my business. But not guns, you have my word." The guns were elsewhere in the ship but that was not Johanssen's business either.

He accepted Smith's word with a nod, but: "You are a belligerent."

Smith smiled. "Of course."

"What are you doing here?"

"Passing through the Kalmarsund. You will understand I cannot tell you were I am bound."

The lieutenant nodded again but said stiffly, formally,

"These are Swedish waters, neutral waters. You are a belligerent and I must tell you that you may only shelter here for twenty-four hours. You entered the Kalmarsund this morning. You must leave tomorrow morning."

"That is understood. No doubt the same restrictions apply to German ships. You spoke of one at the mouth of the channel?"

Johanssen said, "A minesweeper."

"A warship, then?"

"She has a gun, yes."

"She is not in Swedish waters?"

"No. She patrols across the channel just *outside* Swedish waters. I am sure of that. I have been to her twice."

"Today, and . . . ?" Smith let the question hang.

Johanssen answered, "Yesterday. She has been here two days now. Her captain has orders to stop and interrogate every ship entering or leaving the Kalmarsund. He does so. In the day he lies at anchor with steam up and in the night he patrols with a big light – you know?"

Smith thought that he had been right not to try to run. He said, "A searchlight."

Johanssen went on, "He investigates every ship. When there is no ship he plays chess or writes to his wife in Hamburg."

Smith's eyebrows raised. "You know him well."

"Not well. I call on him. We drink coffee and talk, exchange views." He paused, then: "There was a report that a German ship was captured off Kirkko by a White Russian ship with a British captain." He looked question-ingly at Smith. "I think, maybe, he watches for you?"

Smith shrugged. "Who can tell?" Clearly that would be all Johanssen knew about *Audacity*. The story of the more recent action in the Gulf of Riga might have been wirelessed to the minesweeper, but her captain would not have told the Swede about that.

Johanssen asked, "What will you do?"

"I will anchor – for now."

"For now? And later?"

"That is my affair. What do *you* intend?"

Johanssen was silent. Smith could guess at his thoughts:

171

he should report the presence of this ship but the patrol-boat had no wireless. If he left her to go to Kalmar, twenty miles north, she might well sneak away, running close inside Swedish waters to evade the German minesweeper. He could not allow her to violate the laws of neutrality like that.

Johanssen made his decision. "I will stay with you."

"And see me safely clear of Swedish waters."

"That is so."

"I understand. In your position I would do the same." Probably. But in any case Smith wanted the patrol-boat here until the morning. That way at least *Audacity*'s presence here would not be public property before the next day. Smith turned towards the side and Johanssen took the hint, turned with him. Smith said, "Your English is very good."

Johanssen shrugged off the compliment. "You are kind. I think it is not bad. My German is better." And that reminded him of the minesweeper at the mouth of the Kalmarsund. "You will fight, Captain?"

Smith said honestly, "I don't know." He grinned. "Maybe our German friend will go away. The weather will be worse."

"But not so bad as that." Johanssen shook his head. "He will patrol, as always." He paused at the side, looked *Audacity* over again from stem to stern then said, "There is news today of a German raider. A telegram from Norway said a boat with survivors from a British ship had been found and they said the raider sank their ship just south of Trondheim. And another British ship was sunk off Bergen some days ago."

And yet another in the North Sea as *Audacity* started this voyage. Smith showed no change of expression, lifted his hand in salute. "Until tomorrow."

"Good day, Captain." Johanssen saluted in his turn and went down the ladder to his boat.

Smith told Ross, "We'll anchor." Ross bawled the order, then waited, expectantly. For Smith to reel off a plan already neatly prepared to meet this latest emergency? Smith snapped, "Normal routine, Mr. Ross. It's time the men were fed, or had you forgotten?"

He stalked away and climbed to the bridge, said shortly, "Mrs. Ramsay, Mr. McLeod. You both did well, thank you." He climbed again to the flying bridge, snapped at the lookouts there to get below and keep their watch from the bridge. He wanted this place to himself. They hurried away so he got the solitude he needed, and the torment that went with it. He paced alone as the sun slid slowly down the sky.

12

"We must take this ship!"

Smith stared out towards the distant entrance to the Kalmarsund. He could not even see the ship that bottled him in; but she was there, hull-down below the horizon, less than ten miles away. And there were doubtless other ships like her scattered around the Baltic, patrolling the approaches to ports and watching for *Audacity*. The minesweeper was sent here the day after *Königsberg* was taken and when *Audacity* was reported as headed westward for the Gulf of Bothnia. It might have seemed possible to the German Command that she could go on to the Swedish coast to attack German shipping there, maybe even into the Kalmarsund. She had entered Kirkko, after all. They'd had to do a lot of guessing as to where to place their ships and this time they'd picked a winner. He shuffled again through the alternatives open to him, re-examining each one, aware that Ross, McLeod, all of them below were waiting for him to get them out of this.

He could run north again through the Kalmarsund then back south down the long seaward side of Oland, so evading the minesweeper. But that was a diversion totalling a hundred and thirty miles, taking twelve hours or more, using his dwindling coal – and what if the destroyer that had passed the channel entrance was on her way south again? Alternatively, he could steam straight down on the sweeper and fight, and win, no doubt of that. Johanssen had said she had a gun. Just one gun meant she wasn't one of the big minesweepers built for the job but probably a trawler pressed into service with a crew of twenty or so. But she would have wireless. Before she was finished, therefore, she would get off a signal and the hunters would know where to seek *Audacity*.

Repeat the trick that had succeeded at Riga? But this German skipper sounded too much on his guard, and he'd only been here two days, not swinging around his anchor for weeks on end like the Riga guard-boat. And his searchlight meant that *Audacity* could not get near him without being seen.

Smith turned away in frustration and again began to pace the bridge, glaring at the Swedish patrol-boat that lay a cable's length to starboard. If he tried to slip out through the shallows and out of range of the German's searchlight, the Swede would follow. Johanssen had made that plain. The patrol-boat's navigation lights would attract the attention of the German and bring him down on *Audacity*. And Smith could hardly capture or sink the Swedish patrol-boat, a neutral in neutral waters, although it would be easy enough. She was unarmed, only slightly bigger than *Audacity*'s motor-boat, and –

He halted in his prowling, standing on the starboard wing and staring out, the pieces at last clicking into place in his mind.

He wanted to bellow but instead he called casually, "Mr. Ross!"

"Sir?" The first lieutenant's voice came from almost under Smith's feet where Ross stood, just outside the wheelhouse, his face upturned.

"Send the carpenter up here. And Fenwick."

"Aye, aye, sir."

"And, Mr. Ross!"

"Sir?"

"All officers in my cabin, in ten minutes. My compliments to Mrs. Ramsay and I'd be grateful if she would join us. And bring with you a list of every man under five foot six."

"Sir?" Ross gaped at that, then remembered he'd been given an order: "Aye, aye, sir!"

Smith grinned to himself when Ross had gone, bawling for the carpenter and sailmaker. Ross would find out all about it soon enough. He was too tall for the job and so were Gallagher and McLeod. Danby would be fine, though – if size was all that counted.

The carpenter and sailmaker came up the ladder, breathing heavily from running. Bennett had been at work forward, Fenwick in his mess right aft. The sun was low in the sky. There was possibly an hour of daylight left, and much to be accomplished.

Smith pointed at the Swedish patrol-boat, where she lay to her anchor, rocking gently. A thin drift of blue smoke came from a little funnel forward in the cabin that covered her for half of her length. She would have a head and a galley in there; a meal was cooking. The lieutenant sat in the well, a book on his knee. The blue and yellow ensign flapped from its staff in the stern by the tiller as the wind caught it.

Smith said, "Take a good look, and listen to what I want you to do."

The sun had set an hour ago. Smith stood outside the wheelhouse to port, by the motor-boat. It was chance that had dictated that the motor-boat was berthed on the side away from the Swede, but had it not been then Smith would have found some pretext to turn *Audacity* round. As it was, however, the wheelhouse, Smith's cabin, the two ventilator cowls and the funnel made a screen that hid the motor-boat from the Swede.

The boat's disguise was ready. She was only three-quarters the size of the patrol-boat and had been open along her length, but now a cabin was set between a short foredeck and a well right aft. The carpenter had knocked up both foredeck and cabin. It was quick, rough work, the ports in the cabin mere circular holes, and the door a rectangle, but they would look real in the night. Fenwick's hastily sewn Swedish ensign hung from a staff in the stern by the tiller.

Smith ordered, "Lower away." They let her down by hand, quietly. There was a light on *Audacity*'s poop and by Smith's order a crowd of thirty or more were bawling a ribald chorus to Wilberforce's concertina – to cover any noise made in lowering the boat.

Her crew climbed down into her: Buckley, a petty officer, Armstrong, and a dozen men, the Welsh second engineer, Price, and a stoker among them. Smith went last of all, preceded by Elizabeth Ramsay, her cloak wrapped around her. While she ducked into the little cabin where most of the men were huddled, he sat in the sternsheets by Buckley at the tiller. "Shove off!"

Danby, standing in the bow, and Buckley used boat-hooks to push the boat away from the ship's side. Four of the men who still sat in the well slid their oars into row-locks and began quietly pulling as Smith ordered, "Give way!"

Buckley eased the tiller over and the boat slid away from the ship, keeping *Audacity* between the boat and the Swede. So for a quarter-mile with Smith glancing over his shoulder at *Audacity*, then he ordered the oars in and the engine started. The sound would now be muted by distance, and covered by the cheerful chorus aboard *Audacity*.

There was a moderate swell in the sound between Oland and the mainland; outside it would be worse. The motor-boat made good time, punching through the rippling black water at nearly eight knots. Three of the four men who had pulled her thus far were now crowded inside the little cabin. Its roof was loose and had lifted then dropped again as they squeezed in. The fourth man, Tompkins, at five foot four the smallest man of *Audacity*'s company, sat in the sternsheets opposite Smith.

Buckley, at Smith's order, ran the boat along the Oland shore and a mile or so out until they passed Gronhagen, a fishing village on the Oland shore, pin-points of yellow light marking windows. The lighthouse showed at the southern tip of Oland and now they were feeling the weather. The swell was steeper and the wind gusting strongly as they pushed out of the sheltered water between Oland and the mainland. Spray flew inboard – or was that rain? Smith rubbed at it on his face. There was no moon nor star to lighten the darkness, the boat pitched and rolled. The men in her hung on and rolled with her.

Now Smith could see the minesweeper, or rather her searchlight, the sweeping finger of it showing over towards the mainland at first, then edging across the strait as the sweeper patrolled. Smith watched the source of that finger of light until: "Show the lights." Danby in the bow uncovered the lamps and now a green glow to starboard, a red to port, marked the boat. "Port your helm." Buckley eased the tiller over to port and that turned the boat's head to starboard. "Meet her . . . midships . . . steady." Now they were on a course to intercept the minesweeper.

Only minutes now. Smith wished Elizabeth Ramsay were not there but he needed her. At the briefing in Smith's cabin all his officers had volunteered to go on the raid, when he had not asked for volunteers. He told them: "I'm going myself." He gave no reason but it was partly because he felt responsible for getting them all into this trap and so it was up to him to get them out – if he could. It was also partly that he believed he was the best man for this job. "I want Mrs. Ramsay to come along for her German." Johanssen had said his German was better than his excellent English, so whoever hailed the minesweeper had to do so in utterly convincing German, and would need to understand and answer questions quickly. McLeod was not up to that and knew it. Besides, if this raid ended in total disaster and Ross was left to command *Audacity* then he would need McLeod, the navigator with a specialised knowledge of the Baltic.

Smith refused Gallagher because he was too big and anyway, if anything happened to him then the Camel would be useless. At first he had turned down Danby, even though he was small enough, because this would be work for seamen.

But Danby had said quietly, "I'm no stranger to a boat, sir. For two years before I came into the Service I spent all my spare time helping a chap who had a boat. He plied for hire, taking people out to their ships in the Pool of London. We didn't sink, and he didn't sack me."

And Smith had believed him.

Now Smith called, "Can you all hear me?"

"Aye, sir," from Danby.

"Aye, sir," from the cabin.

Smith's voice was harsh now, with a crack in it. His mouth was dry. "In two or three minutes we'll be alongside. You all know what you have to do. We must take this ship! Stop for nothing, nobody! Wounded must wait!"

Nobody answered him. In the cabin Elizabeth Ramsay had the hood of the cloak pulled up to cover her head but she shivered, sensing the pent-up tension in the men around her. They smelt of coal smoke, sweat, tobacco and gun oil. Every man carried a pistol in a holster. They would need their hands free when the time came, so Smith had decreed 'no rifles'. A detail, like the white armbands they wore knotted above their elbows so that they would not fire on their friends in the darkness. Details were important. This *had* to work.

The searchlight's beam swept towards the boat and Smith stood up in the well. So did Danby right forward in the bow and Tompkins aft. The beam slid over them, past, checked and returned, lit up the boat, the standing men and the ensign snapping from the staff in the stern. It held them for a second then resumed its sweeping.

They had passed the first test but there would be more. Smith swallowed. "Ready, Mrs. Ramsay?"

She was crouched at the door of the cabin a yard away: "Yes." He could see the pale oval of her face. He was asking a lot of this girl. He could not order her but he had set before her what he considered to be her duty and she had responded.

The motor-boat was closing the sweeper, coming in at an angle to her port side. The sweeper was the slower of the two, plodding along on her patrol at less than the eight knots of the boat and she was slowing now, stopping. Smith ordered, "Half ahead!"

The boat's speed fell away as she ran in towards the sweeper's side, in darkness now, below the beam of the searchlight that swept overhead. Smith saw the light was mounted atop the wheelhouse. What was that old saying? Always darkest under the light? After the searchlight's glare the night was pitch black, the sea with an oily glitter from the reflection of the beam, the rain driving silver on the wind. The night vision of the men aboard the sweeper would not be good and the motor-boat closing them was a passable replica of the Swedish patrol-boat, smaller but crewed with men to scale. The Swedish lieutenant and his crew were tall. Smith was not, nor Danby, nor Tompkins. And the hefty Buckley was seated at the tiller.

They were barely thirty yards from the sweeper now and Smith prompted: "Right, Mrs. Ramsay."

She pushed back the hood of the cape and he saw her pale face. Then she shouted, making her voice deep and hoarse, "*Guten Abend . . .*" They had rehearsed what she should say, so Smith did not bother to listen, would not anyway have understood. "I have some news for you! And this time I have brought the coffee!"

He muttered to Buckley, "Stop now! Lay us alongside abaft the minesweeper's wheelhouse!" He could see it, dim lit, the helmsman a silhouette at the wheel and another figure, bulky, beside him.

"Aye, aye, sir." Buckley put the tiller over. Danby and Tompkins stood ready with boathooks. Two men, moving black shadows, waited unsuspectingly at the side of the sweeper to take the lines when thrown. The motor-boat's engine was now silent as she slid in, the way coming off her, towards the minesweeper rolling sluggishly in the swell. The boat rubbed against her side, soared on a lifting wave and for a second the sweeper's deck hung level with Smith's eyes. Danby and Tompkins reached out with the boathooks, hooked on. They were alongside. And still the minesweeper's suspicions had not been aroused.

Smith shouted, "*Board!*" He leapt for the deck, threw himself at it, got arms and shoulders there, held on and swung up his legs. From the corner of his eye he saw the roof of the boat's cabin being lifted and tossed aside, the men rising to follow him. He got to his own feet running, like a sprinter from the start. There was a man ahead of him, the one who had been waiting to take a line from Danby. An open mouth yelling, a hand lifting, then Smith ran into him and knocked him aside, stumbled on.

The wheelhouse. He swung up the steps, one hand fumbling for the pistol, dragging it from the holster as he shoved in at the door. The helmsman was at the wheel, his face turned, gaping. Another man stood beyond him on the starboard side and two more at the back of the wheel-house, one with a rifle, loading it.

Smith shouted, voice cracking, "*Stand still!*" The man with the rifle carried on and worked the bolt. Smith thumbed off the safety-catch and fired over their heads. The muzzle-flash blinded them all for a second and the report in that confined, crowded space deafened them but it brought stillness. So Buckley entered into a frozen tableau: Smith pale and glaring, pistol trained at arm's length, four men motionless before him, one with a rifle pointed at the deck.

Buckley grabbed that gun first and tore it away, his own pistol thrust into the man's bearded face for emphasis. But emphasis was not needed. That one shot had had a paralysing effect on men taken completely by surprise. There was yelling and trampling overhead as Buckley herded the helmsman to the back of the wheelhouse with the others, lined them all up with their hands above their heads. The trampling overhead had ceased and now two seamen appeared at the door, their white armbands plain. They brandished pistols, breathless, on edge, and shoved another prisoner before them, a man bulky in sou'-wester, oilskins and sea-boots. One of them panted, "The feller working the searchlight, sir."

Armstrong, the petty officer, showed behind them, pushing in yet another prisoner. "The Sparks, sir. Never tapped his key. He shoved his head out of the door as we got to it, wondering what the row was about, I suppose." The German wireless officer was young, pale and shivering, yanked from his snug office into the night's bitter cold.

Smith told the seamen, "Put the pair of them with the others. Keep 'em here for now." And to Armstrong: "Carry on."

"Aye, aye, sir." He pulled back from the door and headed down the ladder and forward. Smith staggered as a bigger wave rolled the sweeper, leaned out of the open door and saw the motor-boat below, crashing against the ship's side while Danby and Tompkins strove to hold her there against the pounding, sucking sea. The girl sat in the open shell of the now roofless 'cabin', clinging to the side of it. He told one of the seamen, "Get a line to that boat and the people off it, then lead it aft for towing."

The man staggered away along the deck. There was an unconscious body sprawled where Smith had come aboard, and he thought Buckley must have been responsible for that. The flash and *crack* of a pistol came from forward. And again! His boarders? Or were the minesweeper's crew armed? He threw at the seaman left on the bridge, "Cover them now! Shoot if they move! Buckley!"

He jumped down from the wheelhouse and started forward, trying to run, the lift and slide of the deck under his feet setting him on a weaving trot. From the corner of his eye he saw Buckley at his side. A dark figure appeared before him but there were the white streaks on the arms.

Smith shouted the password: "*Audacity!* Captain here! Who's that?"

"Williams, sir! Armstrong sent me to tell you all secure forrard!"

"What was that firing?"

"Some of the Jerries jumped one of our blokes, sir, and tried to get the gun off him. It went off while they were fighting and one of them got hit in the leg. His mates are looking after him."

"Very good. Tell Armstrong to put a guard on them then carry on searching the ship. Reports to me in the wheelhouse. And for God's sake watch you don't shoot any of our own people."

"Aye, aye, sir."

Smith turned and started aft again, Buckley looming at his shoulder. Shooting a friend by mistake was always a possibility in a night action of this kind. White armbands or not, after the incident forward the men would be wary of anybody appearing close, ready to shoot first rather than be jumped on, hence Smith's warning.

He saw the boat was now empty of the girl and the men. They were aboard the sweeper and Tompkins and the other seaman were manoeuvring the pitching boat along the ship's side, hauling it aft with the lines, fending it off with boathooks.

The wheelhouse and a man at the door: but again the white slashes identifying him. His voice came: "Captain, sir?"

"Yes!"

"All under guard aft and a couple o' the lads are going through to see if anybody's skulking in a corner."

"Very good." Then Smith pushed past him into the wheelhouse as a whistle came from the voice-pipe in there. He answered, "Bridge."

"Engine room. I've got one engineer and one stoker sitting on the plates down here. Is that you, sir?" It was the quick, high Welsh voice of Price, the second engineer.

"Yes. Can you give me half ahead?"

"Half ahead, sir."

Smith told Buckley, "Take the wheel." And to the seaman guarding the prisoners: "I'll watch them. You go aloft and work that light. You remember the signal I told you in the briefing before we left *Audacity?*"

"Up at the sky then dip it. Six times, sir." He staggered out of the door as the sweeper rolled.

Smith grabbed one-handed at the door-frame to steady himself, the other levelling his pistol at the prisoners. "Mrs. Ramsay, please! Mr. Danby!"

The girl came in answer to his shout, Danby at her back, both of them shifting from handhold to handhold like climbers as they strove to keep their feet against the rolling and pitching of the ship. As they entered the wheelhouse the deck began to tremble beneath their feet with a steady vibration. The minesweeper was under way again. Outside Smith saw the beam of the searchlight slide down the night to touch the sea then rise again.

Buckley reported, "She's answering the helm, sir."

A tactful reminder to Smith that a course was needed. He answered, "Steer sou-sou-west!" He had laid off that course on the chart in *Audacity*. Aboard her now they would see that distant finger of light, rising and falling; *Audacity* also would be getting under way.

"Mr. Danby! Make your way through the ship from bow to stern. I want a report on exactly how many prisoners we've got, where they are, the condition of any man injured and if he can be moved. Every time you meet someone identify yourself by the password – loudly. Be ready to shoot anyone without armbands. Understood?"

"Aye, aye, sir."

Danby, small but capable, swung out of the wheelhouse and Smith glanced at Elizabeth Ramsay. "Are you all right?"

She was not. She felt sick and was still frightened from the boarding, the ugliness, the violence. His voice, harsh and urgent as always at times like this, and the cold glare from his pale blue eyes, unsettled her still further. But she answered, "I'm fine."

He said, "Ask who is their captain. Tell him he and his men are prisoners. They will be treated correctly if they behave correctly. If they do not – they will be shot." He heard the catch of her breath at that. She believed him.

She spoke to the prisoners in German and one of them, bearded, older than the others, acknowledged that he was the captain. Their eyes moved from the girl to Smith as she went on. They saw no more feeling in his eyes than in the barrel of the pistol he aimed at them. She finished and there was silence. Then the captain muttered something.

The girl said, "He has agreed. He says you must remember the Geneva Convention."

"Tell him I am aware of the Geneva Convention, and that there's nothing for him to agree to. I've told him the alternatives."

Elizabeth Ramsay spoke again in German, briefly, copying Smith's curt tone. She waited as the German captain looked from her to Smith and the pistol again. Then he answered, grudgingly, and the girl translated: "He understands. He will see that his men understand."

Smith said grimly, "He'd better."

Danby appeared, Armstrong and two men behind him. "All secure, sir." He jerked his head at the P.O. "Armstrong's got 'em all in the fo'c'sle under guard. Eighteen all told and that includes the two from the engine room. Only one injured, shot in the leg and he's got a dressing on it for now."

There was cause for relief. "Armstrong, put these forrard with the others." Smith pointed: "But *he* is the captain so lock him up somewhere on his own. With a guard."

"Aye, aye, sir." Armstrong and his two men hustled the prisoners away.

Smith conned the minesweeper out of the entrance of the Kalmarsund into deeper water and there he stopped her, dropping two anchors and lying head to wind and sea, lifting and falling to it. He took a succession of bearings to the lights he could see ashore and confirmed that the anchors were holding. So far, so good. The searchlight's beam was dipped down to the sea astern, a mark for *Audacity* – and now there she was. Not steaming up the cone of light but skirting the edge of it. Ross brought her up and stopped her to lie a cable's length away, waiting for Smith's signal.

She was not alone. Danby's voice lifted above the wind, "Boat coming up astern, sir! Looks like the Swede!"

Smith thought it would be. Johanssen had made it clear he would escort *Audacity* and he had done so. She had left him some way behind, *Audacity* having the edge in speed, but now he was coming up as fast as he could in this sea. He would certainly have betrayed *Audacity*'s presence if she'd been trying to slip out unseen. But by now he would have a rough idea of what had happened and Smith could guess at his state of mind.

The Swedish patrol-boat came pitching up astern of the sweeper, seeking what little lee was there. As the boat ran in through the dipped beam of the searchlight Smith saw Johanssen standing in the well, both hands clamped on the coaming of the cabin to keep his balance. He was too far away for his expression to be seen and when the boat closed the minesweeper's side it was out of the beam of the light and in near darkness. But he could not fail to notice *Audacity*'s motor-boat pitching astern of the sweeper, still with its disguise, its improvised but now roofless cabin. There was no need to see the lieutenant's face; his anger vibrated in his voice as he bawled, "I'm coming aboard!"

Smith answered, "I'm ready to take your lines!" Buckley and a little party waited on the port quarter, watching the boat as it swept in towards them. Smith told them, seeing their startled faces, "Have your pistols ready. As soon as she's secured alongside –"

He stopped, then made a funnel of his hands to bellow at the approaching boat: "Hold off!" He was too late. The

Swede, anger blunting the edge of his concentration, was making his approach too quickly. Luck and the rope fenders hung over the sweeper's side might have saved him even then, but a big sea was sweeping in. Smith heard the lieutenant shout some order but his boat was already driving in broadside to the minesweeper and lifting to the sea that almost swept the Swedish boat inboard. It struck with a force that shook the squat, solid ship under Smith's feet, its timbers smashing as the impact stove in its side. He saw it holed for a quarter of its length as it fell away again and he shouted, "Get lines to her! Get those men off her!"

Already lines were flying out to the wreck of the Swedish boat. As it wallowed close alongside, Smith saw the men aboard it clinging on. The lieutenant was shouting again and two more men came stumbling from the boat's cabin, hauled out by him. They snatched at lines, roped them around their chests under the arms and plunged into the sea as the lieutenant urged them, pointing the way with one hand, shoving them with the other. Then as the last of them went over the side Johanssen lost his balance and fell backwards, smashed against the cabin's coaming and bounced off to be thrown into the sea.

Buckley pulled off his boots and dived in. He disappeared from sight, then his head came up and he struck out for the boat. Smith shot a glance at the rest of his party, dragging aboard the men from the boat. He shouted, "One good swimmer on a line!"

Then he saw Danby knotting a rope across his chest, a broad seaman coiling the slack. Danby dived, disappeared like Buckley and then was swimming strongly. He reached Buckley who had turned on his back and clutched the Swedish lieutenant. The two of them laboured back to the ship with the unconscious man, Smith toiling at the line with the seamen to heave them in. Buckley and Danby clung to the fenders and between them got a line around the lieutenant. Smith and the others pulled him aboard, then his rescuers.

Smith shouted, "Get them into the waist then rig all the fenders you can find. *Audacity* will be coming alongside, port side to!"

He retraced his steps along the pitching deck to the wheelhouse, found the signalling lamp there and flashed a short and a long, saw it acknowledged from *Audacity*'s bridge. She crept down on them, her side festooned with fenders, and Ross brought her alongside as gingerly as if there were eggs between the two ships. They still ground as they worked together under the pressure of the sea. Lines flew across and were secured, boarding nets were unrolled down *Audacity*'s side, the whole scene lit now by the lowered beam of the searchlight.

Smith made out Ross at the door of the wheelhouse, McLeod and Gallagher on the deck with the men lining the side. He used the sweeper's megaphone to bellow up at McLeod, "I want those last two scuttling charges! And there are twenty-three prisoners coming across, one of 'em with a gunshot wound! Tell the S.B.A.!"

McLeod's arm lifted in acknowledgment; any shouted answer without a megaphone would have been lost on the wind. Smith turned forward. There the prisoners were being herded out of the fo'c'sle. "Get 'em aboard!" He lowered the megaphone and told Danby, "You and Buckley get Johanssen and the crew of that Swedish boat across. You'd better see that every one of them goes up on a line. Their dip in the sea will have taken it out of them."

Danby took the megaphone Smith pushed at him. He hesitated when he saw only Gallagher on the rail above him; McLeod had gone for the charges. But then he lifted the megaphone and called up for lines for the Swedish crew.

Smith glanced at Elizabeth Ramsay, holding on to the side of the wheelhouse as the sweeper rose and fell. "I think you'd better have a line, too."

Her gaze went to the net hanging down *Audacity*'s side, bellying out as the ships rolled, smacking back against the rust-streaked steel as they recovered. She agreed: "Yes."

He saw her climb with the others, on a line but struggling like them with the net's swaying and sagging, and like them she boarded *Audacity* safely. Smith was last to leave the minesweeper, immediately after McLeod who had come over and set the charges below. They made the climb in darkness with the wind howling about them; the searchlight had been extinguished.

An hour later *Audacity* was running south west by south at ten knots, a darkened ship. The minesweeper lay far astern, sunk in nearly twenty fathoms.

Ross came on to the bridge and Smith asked him, "Got 'em all stowed away?" He meant the prisoners.

Ross said ruefully, "All secure, sir, but they're getting to be more than a nuisance."

"A bit crowded."

"We're bulging at the seams, sir."

Audacity was designed to carry a crew of seventy-four, in conditions bearable but not palatial. She had sailed without the bomb-throwers' crews but now, besides the twenty airmen, she had fifty-one prisoners – and the seven Swedes – crammed into her. Smith thought he had an answer to that but would not commit himself. "I'll bear it in mind. How is that Swedish lieutenant?"

"Dried out, fully conscious, and hopping mad, sir. He asked to see you. I told him he'd have to wait and to shut his row."

"Bring him to my cabin. And tell Wilberforce I want three large whiskies."

Smith was leaning against his desk when Ross tapped at the open door, stepped into the cabin and said, "Lieutenant Johanssen, sir."

The Swede entered scowling, tight-lipped. Smith said quietly, "Please be seated." He pointed to the leather-covered bench: "You too, Mr. Ross." He wanted a witness at this interview. "The sun isn't up, yet alone over the yard-arm, but I thought in the circumstances we deserved a drink."

Wilberforce knocked and entered, handed out the three whiskies from his tray, and left.

Smith raised his glass to Johanssen. "Your health. I'm glad my seaman was able to save you." He was determined to nail that down. Buckley had risked his life for Johanssen and Smith would not have that discounted.

Johanssen had to swallow his temper for the moment.

He muttered, "I am grateful for that. I might have died."
He responded to the toast with a sip of the whisky.

Now Smith smiled and gave him his opening: "You asked to see me. I would have invited you before but my duties prevented me. You will understand that, of course."

"I understand." Johanssen was a fellow naval officer, but then he said, "I must protest. Your actions tonight were a flagrant breach of neutrality. You used Swedish waters as a base for your operations."

Smith looked surprised. "Oh, come now! This ship had taken shelter in the Kalmarsund, as we had every right to do. We were under notice to leave inside twenty-four hours and did so. The fact that I went first in the motor-boat is neither here nor there."

That silenced Johanssen for a moment, then he snapped, "You mounted a warlike operation!"

"Against an enemy ship which was *outside* neutral waters, remember. As *we* were when you came up with us."

Johanssen digested that then shrugged. "I must report to my superiors. They will decide what protests diplomatic should be made. You will return my crew and myself to Sweden, please."

Smith shook his head. "I can't do that."

Johanssen gaped, then burst out, "You cannot keep us prisoners! We are neutrals! You must understand my position!"

"You must understand mine!" Smith barked that, at last showing temper. "This ship is alone in the Baltic and hunted by God knows how many of the enemy! If I return you to Sweden or permit you to use my wireless then the position of this ship will be known to them. I have a duty to you, but first I have a duty to my ship and my men!" He paused, glaring, then finished more quietly, "You are not prisoners but survivors, and will be treated accordingly. I will return you when that will not endanger the safety of this ship. I make no promises, but I think it may be soon."

Johanssen was silent, thoughtful, probably trying to imagine how he would feel if he commanded this ship and flinching at the prospect.

Smith drained his glass and pushed away from the desk, signalling the end of the interview. "Mr. Ross, will you conduct Lieutenant Johanssen to his quarters then come back here." Ross stood and Johanssen slowly followed suit, turned to the door. Smith said, "One more thing. You mentioned reporting to your superiors. I must report to mine. It will be to the effect that in the zealous and gallant pursuit of your duty, in hazardous conditions, you were unfortunate to lose your patrol-boat but in my opinion no blame attaches to yourself."

Johanssen took that in and realised it meant the saving of his career. "Thank you, sir."

"Good night, Lieutenant."

Left alone, Smith sat at his desk to scribble a rough first draft of his report while the details were fresh in his memory. A minute or two later there was a tap at the door and Ross entered. "Sir?"

Smith looked up, paused in his writing. "I want your report of that conversation, because it may well be needed as evidence before a court. Immediately, please."

"Aye, aye, sir." Ross hesitated, then: "Can I ask a question, sir?"

"Yes?"

"As it's turned out, sir, we've got clear away without anyone being the wiser. But we knew the Swede would follow us out. Suppose the patrol-boat hadn't been wrecked and Johanssen could have gone back under his own steam and reported our position?"

Smith broke in flatly, "He wouldn't have gone back."

"Sir?"

"You've had the answer to your question, Mr. Ross. Understood?"

Ross stared, then comprehended and took a breath. "Yes, sir." But outside the cabin again he blew out the breath in a low whistle and muttered to himself, "If not a survivor, then a prisoner . . . The court-martial would have murdered him."

Smith knew that very well and it gave him pause as he bent over the desk again, pen poised. He had banked on Johanssen following *Audacity* to sea, had never intended allowing him to go back and report; one way or another he and his crew would have stayed aboard *Audacity*.

While the Swedish patrol-boat lay in the neutral waters of the Kalmarsund Smith could not attack and capture her to ensure her silence. But here at sea it was another matter. Neutrals were frequently stopped and searched on the high seas by both sides in this war, and if their cargo was contraband it was seized. That was not the same thing as capturing a neutral naval vessel but it might be argued that information could be contraband and the Swedish boat was carrying it: *Audacity*'s position. It would have caused a major diplomatic row and Smith would have borne the whole blame. But to save *Audacity* and her crew he would have done it.

He had not saved them yet. There was tomorrow – today; it would be light soon.

He went back to his report.

13

The Camel

Gallagher lifted on one elbow to peer across at Danby. His watch told him it was morning but the deadlights were clamped over the scuttles, blacking out the day, so that it was by the dim glow from one small bulb that he made out Danby's sleeping form in its cocoon of blankets. The glow also showed the stark interior of the cabin, an eight-foot-square box of steel that ran with condensation. Gallagher thought, Home, sweet bloody home! But Danby slept quietly, did not twitch or whimper, untroubled by conscience or thoughts of the day ahead. Or of last night; Gallagher had to admit Danby had done well in that desperate action. So maybe he had a good point or two. But . . .

Gallagher slowly eased back on to his bunk, stared up at the deckhead and wondered what had woken him. A bad dream? There were plenty of those but he could not remember any tail-end of a nightmare at his waking. He would sleep again in a few minutes because he needed to be in perfect physical pitch later. Smith said the Zeppelin flew most days but had only started these patrols since the end of the winter. By that he simply meant the break-up of the ice in the Baltic; it would still be bloody cold in an airplane cockpit. Anyway, maybe the Zepp would not fly today after all and Gallagher could spend it reading or lazing about.

He doubted that. The news of *Audacity*'s actions would have been wirelessed the length of the Baltic so the Zeppelin would surely be on station. Maybe not seriously expecting them, because of Smith's false trail back to Russia, but it would be there just in case. And Smith would expect him, Gallagher, to deal with it. Smith was hard as nails. He saw his objective clearly, went after it and God help anybody who got in his way.

Like Gallagher himself, the famous ace? He grimaced at that: conceited sod. He was a survivor, that's all. Lucky. But still the man who flew the Triplanes, Pups and Camels, and steadily notched up the kills. And who knew about flying off from ships.

He lay thinking, working out how to do it, remembering how it was with the Pups and calculating the changes he must make because this time it would be a Camel. The Pup was docile but the Camel was a dangerous beast and a pilot had to keep it under control every second. One careless move could kill. Well, he was a pilot. He would do the job. He had to because there was nobody else who could, no Johnny Vincent.

He was satisfied he had the technique right in his head by the time he heard the thudding of boots overhead as the watch changed. When it was quiet again he drifted into sleep, his mind at peace now.

McLeod was on watch and he called Smith from his cabin in the forenoon when they came on the fog. "It's banked right across ahead of us, sir."

Smith said, "Coming," and: "Send for some coffee."

As McLeod returned to the wheelhouse he answered over his shoulder, "I've done that, sir."

Smith climbed stiffly from his bunk, hauled on his over-coat and went out to the bridge. The sight was only too familiar after these last days, a dark grey sea running into a lighter grey of mist, a wall that was insubstantial but deep. As they pushed into it, steadily the visibility fell and he ordered a reduction in speed, sucked at coffee as the mist enclosed them.

McLeod murmured, "We've had worse, anyhow. We can still see a good half-mile, I reckon." He called to the lookouts, "Keep your eyes skinned!"

Smith asked, "Position?"

"I looked at the chart just before I called you, sir. We should sight Tat any time now." He added under his breath, Smith just hearing it, "Bloody easy to miss it in

193

this, though." Tat was one island in a little group of four, none much more than a quarter-mile in length, mere pin-points on the chart.

McLeod called the anchor-party and they gathered in the bow, the petty officer in charge with his face turned towards the bridge. Bennett, the carpenter, was still working up there on the fo'c'sle with his mates amid stacks of sawn timber, but keeping well clear of the anchor-party. Below the bridge the lid on the box holding the Camel was pushed back, the fitters and riggers inside working on the aircraft. There was no sign of Gallagher or Danby. They would be in their bunks, Danby in particular catching up on his sleep after last night's attack on the sweeper.

McLeod sighted the island before the lookouts: "There it is." He used his glasses, then, more doubtfully: "Can't be anything else."

Smith, through his own glasses, saw only a darker shape in the grey murk ahead but as *Audacity* closed it took on sharper definition.

Now McLeod said firmly, "Tat." It was just a rock in the sea, almost featureless, two cables long and half as wide, but he added, "Seen it before, sir."

Audacity crept in towards the island, a man at the lead once more, and anchored barely a cable's length away. McLeod, glasses at his eyes again, said, "I think I can see the loom of Graesholm" – that was the next island in the group – "but Frederiksholm and Christianso are too far away in this fog."

Smith ordered, "Double the lookouts, close up the guns and call Mr. Ross."

That last was not necessary because the engine's stopping and the rumble of the anchor cable running out brought Ross up from his bunk, rubbing his eyes. "Good morning, sir." He squinted at Tat and muttered, "What a bloody benighted place!"

Smith agreed, but: "It will serve. Bring up the prisoners aft of the bridge and call away the boats' crews. I'll be down to talk to the masters, and that Swedish lieutenant, in ten minutes. Ask Mrs. Ramsay if she will join me there to interpret."

In his cabin he shaved carefully and dressed in his uniform. The mirror showed his thin face to be even thinner, his pale eyes staring out of dark sockets, but he did not notice. His mind was busy. He heard the men moving about in the housing of the four-inch gun just twenty feet aft. The guns were manned because while *Audacity* lay here there was always a chance one of her hunters might come suddenly out of the mist. Smith thought there were long odds against that but only a fool would fail to take the precaution.

Ross waited with Elizabeth Ramsay at the foot of the ladder abaft the bridge. He had woken her by hammering on her door. She had slept for only a few hours but dragged herself from the bunk as the first lieutenant's voice boomed outside: ". . . in nine minutes!" That meant she was to be ready for Smith in eight minutes at most. She had learnt that aboard *Audacity* no one kept the captain waiting. So she dressed quickly with fumbling fingers, splashed icy water on her face and brushed her hair. Ross was checking the time by his watch as she picked her way carefully but rapidly down the ladder.

Less than a minute later Smith ran down the ladder and looked about him. All the prisoners were crowded on the deck aft of the bridge, crammed around or sitting on top of the boxes. Armed sentries watched them from the poop and the after superstructure. The three German captains formed a muttering group and Johanssen stood aloof a yard away, his crew behind him. The muttering ceased as Smith appeared and they stared at him in his uniform, neat but shabby, the gold on the cuffs, the peak of the cap shadowing his eyes, the thin face smiling.

He saluted. "Good morning, ma'am, gentlemen." They returned the salute and he went on, "I am about to set you free."

Elizabeth Ramsay translated into German and the officers exchanged glances. A murmur ran through the crowd and faces lightened. He continued, "This ship now returns to Russia and this lady to her home. I don't wish to take you there. We haven't the quarters aboard and we may yet be in action when you would be at risk." He looked at

Johanssen. "Your neutrality would not shield you."

The Swede nodded stiffly. Smith waited until the girl finished translating, then he pointed: "There is the island of Tat. It is uninhabited, as is the next island of Graesholm. Christianso beyond has a small population. I'm putting you ashore on Tat with provisions and water, tarpaulins, paraffin and coal for fires. You will have to spend the night there but as sailormen you will be able to make yourselves comfortable. Tomorrow, when the fog lifts, they will see you from Christianso and take you off. My best wishes, gentlemen."

He waited again until Elizabeth Ramsay translated, then he saluted and left with the girl. He would not be involved in discussion or argument, would hear no complaint or protest. They had to leave this ship, for *Audacity*'s sake and for their own.

The girl halted at the door to the lobby that led to the wardroom and thence her cabin. "I ought to congratulate you on last night's work. It was a nightmare to me but I understand you performed a minor miracle in getting us safely out of the Kalmarsund."

Smith said uncomfortably, "I don't know about that."

Elizabeth Ramsay nodded, a smile twitching the corners of her mouth. "I have also heard you don't like back-slapping."

That sounded like Ross and Smith wondered if she was laughing at him but she watched him seriously now. He answered, "We didn't lose a man."

"That's important, of course."

"I sleep easier."

"You think a lot of them."

"There are none better." Then he grinned. "But your own crew are always the best."

She laughed at that and went on to her cabin. Smith climbed the ladder to the bridge thinking that for once they had talked with some ease. Then the future crowded in again as he saw Gallagher standing on the bridge-wing, leaning on the rail and looking down at the work going on in the box right below him. Smith paused at his side. The riggers were bolting the wings on to the Camel and, as planned, there was just room for them to do it inside the twenty-eight-foot width of the box. Smith asked, "She's nearly ready?"

Gallagher nodded. "Another couple of hours or less. They've just got to true her up."

"What?"

Gallagher grinned. "Make sure the wings are on dead-right and not cock-eyed, that there's the right tension on all the wires. Otherwise . . ." He drew a finger across his throat then pushed back from the rail. "Which reminds me, I slept through breakfast and my stomach thinks my throat's cut. I'll see if Wilberforce can fix me up with some lunch."

He sauntered easily aft to the ladder and dropped down it on his way to the wardroom. Smith went to his cabin and changed back into the ancient clothes of his disguise. He watched from the bridge as *Audacity*'s boats plied back and forth between ship and shore, the motor-boat packed with stores and towing the other boat filled with prisoners. It was an uneasy time for *Audacity*'s crew. She had steam up and a party on the fo'c'sle ready to knock off the clip and jettison the anchor if an enemy burst out of the mist, but they knew she would still take time to get under way, would lose her boats and the men in them. And if her attacker was a ship of any force, then *Audacity* would be battered to pieces.

Smith was unperturbed. He had made his decision, taken his calculated risk. He had to be rid of the prisoners. Nevertheless, the net was closing around *Audacity*. The new destroyer seen yesterday off Oland would not be the only one to come out of Kiel after making the passage of the canal from the North Sea. There would be others. Also, before this day was over the Swedes would be wondering about their missing patrol-boat and the Germans about the minesweeper. They would search, and though both vessels had sunk there would be tell-tale flotsam. At another time the Germans might have assumed an accident, an explosion aboard the sweeper or that she'd hit a mine. Not now: they had lost too many ships in the last few days and their thoughts would inevitably turn to

Audacity. Tomorrow the prisoners from Tat would reach Bornholm, ten miles away, where there was wireless. They would tell their story of the raider heading back to Russia, but that tale had to be wearing thin now. Smith reckoned that sinking the sweeper and stopping her broadcasting *Audacity*'s position had given him just twenty-four hours' grace. *Audacity* could survive that long in this western end of the Baltic, possibly for a second day, but no longer.

He thought of the German raider in the North Sea and wondered if she also was skulking in fog now. He had no cause for envy there because her captain had his own problems; British destroyers would be hunting him as the Germans sought *Audacity*.

The last of the prisoners landed on the island, the boats returned to the ship and were hoisted inboard. On Tat tarpaulins mushroomed into shelters and fires burned, the coal doused with paraffin to start them. The coal put ashore, ample for the prisoners' needs, would not have moved *Audacity* a mile.

Bennett's mates were sweeping up the litter of shavings and sawdust on the fo'c'sle as the carpenter came to the bridge. "We've finished, sir. It's all ready now and we can set up that platform quick as you like when you give the word."

"Thank you." Smith sent him away. "Have something to eat and get your head down for an hour or so."

Ross reported with relief, "Ready to proceed, sir."

"Very good."

Audacity weighed anchor and headed eastward away from Tat, on a course for Russia, but when the island was lost astern in the fog she came around to port on to a bearing of almost due west. Ross said, looking out at the fog then down at the Camel, "We may not need it if this lot holds right up to the Sound."

Smith answered, "I hope we don't." If fog covered their approach to the Sound and the Camel did not need to fly then they would have wasted a lot of effort bringing it this far. But they could not have relied on fog covering them, might have waited days for it, and *Audacity* did not have that much time.

An hour later, in fact, the mist shredded and soon they ran out of it, *Audacity* steaming over a quiet sea. There was cloud cover but it was high, white fluffy cumulus that picked up and reflected shafts of light from the pale sun sinking towards the west. Gallagher came up to stand on the wing of the bridge outside the wheelhouse. He had no flying clothes so instead was dressed in so many layers of sweaters and trousers that he walked with a wide-legged gait, all topped by a greatcoat that strained at its buttons. A scarf was coiled loosely around his neck and a balaclava pulled over his head. He carried a pair of goggles and gloves and stared out over the bow. Smith wondered where he had got the goggles.

He ordered Ross, "Tell Bennett to rig that platform now." Then he turned to Gallagher. "You're ready, I see."

The pilot shrugged. "Any time. Bring on the Zepp." That was not bragging, just an easy confidence. This was his job and he knew he could do it; he'd done it before.

Bennett appeared on the deck forward of the mast, his gang of men with him. The box between mast and fo'c'sle was struck down. The frames and supports hidden inside it, that the carpenter and his mates had constructed in every available minute, were taken out and set up. The top and sides of the box itself would form part of the completed platform.

Smith watched the work as *Audacity* steamed steadily westward. The sections of the platform were hammered into place one by one, fitting like the pieces of the plan he had formed that day they fought the old destroyer off Kurgala, when he believed *Audacity*'s identity was no longer a secret. He knew then that to get out of the Baltic he had to evade the patrols at either end of the Sound and traverse the length of it in one night. There would be just enough time if he made the approach in daylight, as now, but then *Audacity* would be seen by the Zeppelin. So he had wanted the Camel and Gallagher, and *Königsberg* for her timber, both as a disguise and for the platform. And he had needed to get them all here, and now.

He had done it.

The Camel and the platform might still not be necessary, this might be one of the days the Zeppelin did not fly, but he dared not have relied on that any more than on fog. *Audacity* could not wait to pick her time.

The platform was complete for half its length, Bennett and his gang working now on the last twenty feet that extended out over the fo'c'sle. Smith warned, "Keep a sharp lookout overhead. We might see her soon." They were four hours away from the Sound and there were still three hours of daylight left. He lifted his glasses from where they hung against his chest and slowly swept the horizon ahead. The sky was empty.

"Sir!" There was excitement in McLeod's voice as he approached.

Smith glanced around at him. "Yes?"

"From Sparks, sir. I've just decoded it." He held out the flimsy and added as Smith took it, "He says reception is very good today." As always when *Audacity* was out of sight of land or other shipping, her wireless aerial was rigged and the operator keeping a listening watch.

Smith read the signal, looked up and saw Ross waiting curiously and told him, "One of our destroyers reporting to Admiralty that she's in pursuit of a German raider."

The signal gave a position and McLeod anticipated the next question. "I plotted it, sir. About a hundred miles north-west of Bergen."

There were grins all around the bridge and Ross said delightedly, "She's bound to catch the bastard! Marvellous!"

"She should." Smith handed the signal back to McLeod. "My thanks to Sparks and tell him to keep listening."

He saw that only Gallagher was not smiling, did not seem to have heard and was staring absently ahead.

Danby had met him on his way up to the bridge and said, "I meant to give you these before but it slipped my mind. We've all been pretty busy." He dug into a pocket of the damn silly jacket that was three sizes too big for him, produced the goggles and held them out. "They were Johnny's. I thought you'd want them so I hung on to them. They were all that was left . . ." His voice tailed off into embarrassed, nervous silence.

Then one of the armourers shouted from the box where he was working on the Camel, "Mr. Danby, sir!"

"Coming!" Danby almost ran away and Gallagher glared after him . . .

Petrograd had been an awful place. The Russian Empire was falling apart and mobs roved the streets. The Flight was resting after some costly operations and Gallagher went to Petrograd with Johnny. They were both a bit low because they'd lost Miller and Young, two good pilots, on the same day. They needed something to set them up again but they didn't find it in that cold, strife-torn city. Only Russian vodka. Then just two days after they'd got back to the Flight, Johnny was shot down and taken off to the hospital. And when he came back . . .

"There she is, twenty on the starboard bow."

Ross said it quietly but they were all silent on the bridge now. Smith trained his glasses, searched the sky and found the far-off speck.

McLeod said, "She's heading south – and about twenty miles away?"

He discussed the matter with Ross and used his sextant to measure the vertical angle between the distant horizon and the Zeppelin edging slowly across the sky just below the cloud ceiling. Gallagher irritably broke in, "She's making fifty to sixty knots at ten thousand feet."

McLeod looked up from his calculations and blinked. "I work it out to that."

Smith judged that the Zeppelin was now on the southbound leg of her patrol. Her captain must have seen *Audacity*'s smoke but would not turn towards it: he knew he'd be over this ship when he returned on the northbound leg in an hour or so. Then he would be able to see what kind of vessel it was and where it was headed – south to Kiel or west to the Sound – and report to the destroyer. Or destroyers; after *Audacity*'s rampaging there might be more than one waiting off the Sound.

He ordered, "Slow ahead," and to Ross, "Transfer the Camel."

Audacity's speed dropped until she just had steerage way.

Ross supervised the plane's transfer, using the derricks fore and aft of the mast to lift the Camel, swing it up from the box and out over the sea then inboard again to its new resting place on the rear end of the platform just forward of the mast. Smith saw it settled, then called for: "Half ahead." Soon it would be full ahead. He glanced across at Gallagher who still stood at the rail, his eyes on the Camel, and wondered what the pilot was thinking.

Russia had been bad from the start and those last weeks it got worse until the last day, and that was the worst of all. He'd flown the first patrol with Griffiths, knowing he'd have to fly the second with Danby and not looking forward to that. The Russians were falling back and the Camels being used for low-level attacks on German troops and transport. Nobody liked that job. They still had four machines but only himself and the other two pilots to fly them. Danby was very raw. Griffiths had loads of experience but had become very shaky lately and said he couldn't sleep.

So Gallagher planned to take each one with him in turn and if that meant he flew all day, well, he was the flight commander and the bloody ace, wasn't he? But that first patrol with Griffiths had been disastrous. They took off loaded with four twenty-five-pound bombs each, found a column and bombed it, then swept along it with the twin Vickers blazing, but there were all kinds of stuff coming up at them from machine-gun fire to the shells from field pieces. Gallagher thought it was one of those shells that hit Griffiths but all he saw was the machine blown apart in mid-air and the bits of it falling along the road among the burning transport and dead infantry.

Gallagher was in trouble, anyway. His Camel was shot full of holes and he was hit; he didn't know how badly but he felt sick and sleepy so he had to squint to focus. He nursed the Camel back to the field at Kunda Bay and slapped it down on that apology for a runway. The ground-crew started pulling him out and that hurt so he yelled, but they yelled back that a flight of German Albatroses had trailed him back to the field and he had to be out of it before the attack came in. Then he saw Johnny, back from hospital, and he knew it was going to be all right. Johnny stood by the cockpit, watching the men lifting Gallagher out. He looked changed, thinner, and older. Gallagher asked him, "When did you get back?"

"Half an hour ago." Johnny's voice had changed, too; it was hoarse, the words blurred.

But Gallagher's mind was on other things. "You and Danby get those two Camels into the air before Jerry attacks."

Johnny asked slowly, "You want me to fly now?"

What the hell was he on about? "Of course I want you to fly! You've got to! Somebody has to look after that squirt, so no heroics or fancy stuff. Those two Camels are all we have left, Johnny, and we don't want them shot up. Get them off the ground and out of the way."

Johnny nodded. "If you say so."

"I'm bloody glad to see you. You're the only one I can rely on."

"All right."

Then they lifted the stretcher and trotted with it across the field to the ambulance. They loaded him into it, he heard the engines of the Camels running up and then the surge of power as they ran away along the field.

And then the smash.

And then they told him the Camels had collided on take-off and Mr. Vincent was dead. And the German planes never attacked. They turned back, for some reason, just short of the airfield.

The Camel was waiting on the platform.

Gallagher turned and walked aft past the wheelhouse, then Smith's cabin, towards the ladder. Danby came up it quickly and asked, "Anything I can do?"

"No."

"I could run her up for a minute or so while you –"

Gallagher had pushed past him. Now he turned. "You heard what I said! Keep out of my way. Don't you realise, every bloody time I look at you I remember Johnny?"

Danby flinched. "That was an accident."

"More like murder! He was one of the best pilots I ever saw and you killed him!"

"No!"

"What d'you mean: 'No'? You said you didn't know what happened. You said the pair of you were taking off and you collided. *Collided!* Johnny never made a damnfool mistake like that in his life – and remember, you'd already crashed one Camel on that field."

Danby swallowed, said, "He was ahead of me and well to the left but then as we lifted off he swung over in front of me. I tried to haul clear but –"

"Are you saying it was *his* fault?"

Danby looked away. "I'm only saying –"

"The truth is you were too busy shitting yourself to see straight. Or perhaps you'd primed yourself with Dutch courage? Was that it? A good slug of issue rum to hold the stomach down?"

"No! It was Johnny who –" Danby stopped.

Gallagher whispered, "*What?*"

"Nothing."

"You were going to say *he* was drunk!" Memories flashed into his mind of Johnny's enthusiasm for Russian vodka, and the sprees they'd had. He suppressed them. "You lying little bastard!"

Danby met his gaze. "It's true –"

Gallagher swung, a boxer's right hand, but the constricting layers of clothing made the movement awkward and slow. Danby stepped back so that it only mashed his lips against his teeth. It hurt and there was blood salty in his mouth. His back slammed against the side of Smith's cabin and he bounced off it, lashing out with his own fist. He was not a boxer and the blow was unskilful, a wild reaction, but it landed high on Gallagher's chest with all Danby's forward-moving weight behind it. This time it was Gallagher who was forced to take a step back to keep his balance. But there was no deck behind him, only space. He fell backwards down the ladder, turned over once in the ten-foot drop, and landed heavily with his legs tangled under him.

The messenger came to Smith on the bridge. "Mr. Danby says to tell you, sir, that Mr. Gallagher's broken his leg."

There was shocked silence for a moment, then Ross said, "That's torn it."

Smith went down to the wardroom. The men Danby had got together to carry Gallagher were just coming out. Smith paused in the door, hearing voices raised in anger, and saw Gallagher stretched on the table, Danby standing beside it. Gallagher grimaced with pain, but jerked up at him, "I don't believe you. The groundcrew would have known if that was true."

Danby said, "I told them to keep their mouths shut. He deserved better than that sort of talk, and so did you. He was your friend."

Smith stepped forward into the wardroom and asked, "What happened?"

Gallagher frowned, was silent for a moment. Then said, "I slipped and fell down the ladder."

Smith knew that was a lie. There was blood on Danby's mouth and on Gallagher's knuckles. But that was unimportant. Smith demanded brutally, "Can you fly?"

Gallagher's head moved slowly. "No." And: "Sorry."

Smith thought that the whole plan, so painfully put together, had failed now – and through bloody stupidity. But it might have failed earlier for the same or any other reason. War was a chancy business. So they simply had to start again, seek another way. If there was another way . . .

He looked at Danby. "What about you flying the Camel?"

Gallagher shook his head. "He's Administration."

Smith said slowly, "So you told me. And none of your airmen has said he could fly but we know they hold their tongues. He's young to be an Admin. officer, those jobs usually go to older men with a lot of experience of the right procedures – or wangles. He had some experience in boats so why didn't he just go to sea? And wouldn't a replacement be more likely to be a pilot, where you take your casualties, rather than an Admin. officer?" He waited, then pressed, "Well?"

Gallagher admitted reluctantly, "He's a pilot, but I grounded him after he crashed his second Camel."

Danby broke in angrily, "I just explained –"

"All right." Gallagher closed his eyes, remembering Johnny Vincent saying slowly, the words blurred, "You want me to fly now?" And his own reply: "Of course." He sighed. "All right. We'll agree that one wasn't your fault. But –"

Smith said, "You could always unground him."

Gallagher shook his head again. "He's only done fifteen hours and then only on Pups."

"They're not the same as Camels, are they?"

"No," said Gallagher shortly, "they bloody well aren't."

Smith asked Danby, "What do you think?"

Danby looked from Smith's cool stare to Gallagher's scowl. "Well" – he hesitated – "as I understand it, if this Zeppelin reports us, then sooner or later we're sunk." Smith thought, Sooner rather than later. Danby went on, eyeing Gallagher stubbornly, "That second time I took off right. I think I could do this. You could tell me how."

Smith glanced at his watch. The Zeppelin would be turning to head north soon. There were seventy-odd souls aboard *Audacity*. God help him for what he was about to do. He asked Gallagher, "Could you coach him?"

"I'm not letting him try to –"

"No," Smith cut in, voice harsh, "I'm ordering him to!"

Gallagher thought, Hard as nails. Sees his objective and goes after it. He scowled at Danby. This was no Johnny Vincent, no easy grin nor years of experience. This poor little bugger didn't know what he was letting himself in for. If this boy – if any of them – were to survive, Gallagher would have to pump into him the know-how, and then the confidence that came with it. But Johnny had always been ready to try anything, right from the beginning.

Gallagher said, "In that case I'd better do what I can."

There was a tap at the door and the S.B.A. entered. "They tell me there's a suspected broken leg in here, sir."

Smith told him, "Yes, come on."

Pearson felt carefully along the leg, then winced. "Yes, sir, it's broken. I'll have to set it." He studied the leg, chewing his lip. "I've done one before but I'd want to look at the book first, to refresh my memory, like."

Gallagher said, "Setting will hurt, won't it?"

"Well –" It would hurt like hell, Pearson remembered that much.

"Leave it for a bit. First I've got a flying lesson to give." Gallagher glanced at Smith.

Who said, "Carry on, Mr. Gallagher."

The flight commander turned on Danby. "You'll have to get some extra trousers and socks, bigger boots. And you'll have to *listen!*"

Smith left them to it and returned to the bridge. Ross turned and asked, "How is he, sir? Is it broken?"

"It's broken, so Danby is flying instead."

"Danby!"

"He's a pilot." Of some sort or other. Fifteen hours on the docile Pup and two Camels wrecked. But there was no point in sharing his fear with the others so he spoke easily, as if the change was just routine.

Ross said, "I didn't know." But then, reassured, "That's all right, then."

Smith said, "The Zeppelin hasn't showed up again yet." Not a question; he would be told the instant it was sighted.

"Not yet, sir."

Danby must be in the air well before it came. There might be just enough time because the wind was out of the north and the Zeppelin would be butting into it. There was only a moderate sea and that was a blessing, *Audacity* hammering through it at fifteen knots or better. "Starboard five." He turned her until she was headed into the wind, her funnel smoke rolling down along the white track of her wake. Then he went quickly down to the wardroom, met Danby already on his way out and told him, "The wind is ten knots and we're making fifteen."

Danby was now squat in layers of clothing, long woollen underwear, two pairs of trousers and of socks, and a fitter's boots a size bigger than his own, with Gallagher's overcoat on top and reaching almost to his ankles. He wore Gallagher's balaclava and scarf with Johnny Vincent's goggles pushed up on his forehead. His face glistened with grease to combat frostbite. He answered, "Gallagher said they used to fly off at thirty but he thinks twenty-five or so should be enough with this length of platform." He shivered and pulled on his gloves. He was only eighteen years old and looked it. "No point in hanging about. It's bloody cold." He clumped forward to the ladder and climbed down to the deck.

Gallagher called from inside the wardroom, "Sir! The S.B.A.'s collecting some men to carry me up to the bridge. I – ought to be there. Is that all right?"

"Yes." Smith went back to the bridge. Out on the starboard wing he looked down and saw Elizabeth Ramsay with a group of airmen gathered aft of the platform. Her face was turned up to him, pale and anxious. Danby stood directly below him at the foot of the ladder, sizing up the Camel.

It was a short-bodied biplane and looked what it was: a fighting machine, a killer. It thickened quickly up from the tail to the hump of the housing covering the breeches of the twin Vickers machine-guns. That hump gave it the name: Camel. Engine, guns and cockpit were all crammed into the front seven feet of the body. Its grey-green paint was mottled after the repairs but the red, white and blue roundels on wings and fuselage were clear. There was an extra white circle painted around each one, the mark of the Royal Naval Air Service. Danby wondered if that was correct now that they were Royal Air Force?

Gallagher had started: "Now, listen! I'll run through it all, though you've heard most of it before, just to get you *thinking* it. And remember, this is just another aeroplane. It has its own idiosyncrasies you've got to learn, but it's *just another aeroplane*. And flying off from a platform is just one more stunt."

Danby waddled across the deck and climbed laboriously on to the platform. It would be cold up there, in spite of all his clothes. He was cold now, the sweat running chill against his skin. His head ached and he felt sick. The wind froze his face: twenty-five knots. Should be just enough, Gallagher said.

Should be?

There was a trestle at the back of the platform holding a slotted steel tube six feet long. The Camel's tail was lifted and the tail-skid entered in the tube's slot so that the Camel stood in a flying attitude. A ball on the tip of the skid ran in the tube and could only come out at the end. That kept the machine straight for the first six feet of its run. At present the Camel was locked to the platform by a quick-release clamp on the undercarriage. A wire led from the quick-release to the back of the platform and was held by a rigger.

They were waiting for him. A fitter and a rigger stood by the machine but the rest had cleared off out of the way and stood behind the platform. He saw Mrs. Ramsay there and she smiled at him. The seas were not big but *Audacity*'s speed through them gave her a rocking-horse motion and her deck bucked steadily under his oversize boots. He shoved the toe of the left one into the step cut in the fuselage just behind the lower wing and pulled himself up to sit on top and just aft of the cockpit. He swung his legs in, one either side of the stick, then slid down into the seat. His boots scraped on the rough wooden planking of the floor then settled on the rudder-bar. He took the stick with its spade-grip top and worked it cautiously, moved the rudder-bar with his feet. Everything was working all right. On top of the triangular spade-grip was the engine switch and inside the triangle were the triggers of the twin Vickers.

Looking forward over the guns and under the top wing he had a view of the timber platform stretching away to end sharply at the bow. Was that forty feet? It looked so short! There was the line of the edge of the platform cut against the sky like a false horizon, then – nothing. That false horizon soared and plunged as *Audacity* crashed on at full speed and the spray burst inboard, driving into his grease-slicked face like rain. If he pancaked over the end then the ship's bow would grind him and the Camel under –

A voice. "Switches off!" He tore his eyes away from the emptiness over the bow and looked down, saw the fitter and the rigger staring up at him, faces blue-white and pinched with cold, realised the fitter had twice called up to him.

209

His gaze flicked inside the cockpit, checked the two magneto switches were off and the petrol fine adjustment lever was shut. He turned on the petrol tap, felt for the handpump and worked up the fuel pressure. A wind-driven pump would do it once he was airborne.

If . . .

He pushed the petrol fine adjustment lever half-open and called, "Switches off!"

"Petrol on!" The fitter reached up to the propeller.

Danby answered, "Petrol on!" As the fitter pulled the propeller round slowly, Danby lowered his gloved left hand to the long lever of the throttle valve and edged it forward, heard the suck and gurgle of the mixture of petrol and air. He pulled the straps of the Sutton harness tight over his thighs and fastened them with a conical pin thrust through holes in the straps. He held them on the pin with one hand as he brought each shoulder strap down over his chest and on to the pin. Then he locked all four straps with a spring clip pushed through a hole in the narrow end of the conical pin. Pulling out that spring clip would release all four straps at once, sliding off the pin, but now he was belted in to fly. He pulled his scarf up over his mouth and nose so that only his eyes showed between scarf and balaclava.

The fitter ceased his steady turning of the propeller and held it with arms at full stretch above his head. He bawled, "Contact!" The rigger moved in behind him and locked one hand in the back of the fitter's belt.

Danby flicked the switches on, the petrol fine adjustment back and the throttle half-open. "Contact!" It came out a whisper he hardly heard through the muffling scarf. The fitter waited, fingers twitching on the propeller, nervous. Danby thought, Christ! *You're* all right down there!

Gallagher had told him: "Look, you can do this. The first smash was bad luck, we all have them. The second – I didn't know about Johnny, I'm sorry."

He'd looked wretched, but he meant it. Gallagher didn't lie.

Danby shouted squeakily, *"Contact!"*

The fitter yanked the propeller down, a quick snatch,

and the rigger's hand in his belt jerked him back clear of the spinning propeller as the engine fired. Danby ran it up until the indicator showed the revs were right and it *sounded* right, then pulled down his goggles with one hand, keeping the other on the stick. Gallagher had said, "She's sensitive. Hold the stick forward until you feel the pressure then let it come back. *Don't* pull the thing!"

Johnny's goggles. He remembered Johnny's Camel suddenly, inexplicably sliding across in front of him, then the crash. They smashed in from only a few feet at the end of the field. He got out of his own Camel before anyone could come up and tried to pull Johnny clear of the flames. But he could not reach the belt's locking-pin, only got his hands on Johnny's head, lolling as the goggles came away, dangled from his fingers, the fire beating him back.

He licked his lips, tasted blood on them still from Gallagher's blow, sucked in air through the folds of the scarf. He kept his eyes on the short strip of rough timber decking. The Camel was vibrating, held on the leash. He lifted one hand, signalling, brought it quickly back to join the other on the stick, felt the kick as the rigger at the back of the platform pulled on the wire and the anchoring quick-release on the undercarriage snapped free. The Camel shot forward, the platform sliding fast under the wing. He yielded to pressure on the stick, let it come back – and there was no platform. A foam-flecked, cold green sea lay below him but the Camel was flying.

Gallagher's voice in his head: "Don't try to turn when you first take off. The torque effect of the engine can be murderous. If you bank left she'll try to climb and she'll stall; turn right and you'll bang her nose-first in the drink. So ease the stick forward again and keep her level. You'll soon reach a hundred knots and *then* you can climb."

Danby held it forward, one eye on the airspeed dial, one on sea and sky. Now. He let the stick come back an inch, then another and the nose lifted. He was climbing steadily.

Pearson and his party had brought up Gallagher, injured leg splinted temporarily by boards, and sat him in a chair lashed to the starboard wing of the bridge. With Smith he watched in silence until Danby took off and began to climb. Then he said quietly, "Thank God!" The aircrew on the deck below were cheering.

Smith ordered, "Port ten." He brought *Audacity* around on to a course of south-west, steering as if for Kiel and Germany. The Zeppelin was still not in sight. He told Ross, "I want to talk to Mr. Gallagher." And when Ross had gone away into the wheelhouse: "You owe me an explanation."

Gallagher answered absently, head turned and eyes still fixed on the shrinking, climbing Camel. "I had a friend once . . ." He turned back to Smith. "He'd flown too many patrols. I should have thought of it, seen it happening because I'd seen pilots crack up before. But Johnny was – well, special. It just never entered my head that it could happen to him. He was always steady as a rock. We saw a lot of service, shared a lot of life. Then we went to Russia." He told Smith the whole bitter story as *Audacity* hurried south-westward.

Danby could hardly believe he had flown off the Camel and he sat tense, but his gloved fingers were cautiously gentle on the stick. His eyes searched the sky to the south though he knew he should not see the Zeppelin yet. He became aware of the freezing cold. At a thousand feet he levelled off then made a careful, slow turn to the left so he was flying south-westward. He let the stick come back again and recommenced the steady climb, now slanting towards the sinking sun.

At twelve thousand feet he eased the stick forward and levelled off, cocked the twin Vickers then set his thumbs on the triggers and fired a short burst, testing. He'd done exactly as Gallagher told him. The idea was to meet the Zeppelin on its northward run and out of sight of land. Gallagher estimated it was flying at ten thousand feet and between fifty and sixty knots. Danby's fifteen minutes of climbing should have taken him to the west of the Zeppelin's course so he would be up-sun.

He ought to see it soon.

Would he? He had never flown a combat flight, let alone

hunted a Zeppelin. He'd been told that inexperienced pilots often flew their first patrols without seeing any of the distant enemy aircraft that older hands picked out in one sweeping all-round glance. And he was flying through confusingly scattered banks of cloud now, cautiously turning this way then that to skirt them, peering through the breaks.

He *had* to see it!

"There it is!" McLeod snapped it out, glasses at his eyes. "Fine on the port bow!"

A silver splinter above the horizon, the Zeppelin was all of twenty miles away but closing *Audacity* at their combined speeds of around seventy knots. In a few minutes they could make out the cigar shape, foreshortened because it was flying more or less towards them. Then it foreshortened further still as the Zeppelin turned and headed directly for the ship.

Gallagher burst out, "For Christ's sake! Where's Danby?"

The sky was laced with strung cloud through which the sun blinked out of the west so that they had to squint their eyes against it. There was no Camel.

Danby leaned to starboard, looked out and down, wondered if the Zeppelin had taken a more westerly course and was sailing past while he searched the sky to the east. He could see nothing but the wisping cloud and the gunmetal sea far below. He looked up and winced, momentarily blinded as the sun blazed into his eyes. He turned away from that glare and searched to port again. It had to be there. He must see it. This cloud was a *bastard*! It was like peering down through holes in a fence that you were sliding past very quickly. For a second you saw the sea below then lost it. Now you see it, now you don't.

Gallagher had said to stay at twelve thousand feet: "You'll need that height to hit him from above." Danby had obeyed but up here he could see nothing. He told himself: Use your common sense. If you can't see, go down and have a look.

He banked the Camel gently but with growing confidence now, then with the sun at his back he eased the stick forward and took the plane down into a gap in the clouds. As he passed through he was aware of his widening arc of vision, the sea spreading out and out. That had to be *Audacity*, a lone toy ship at the end of a long track of white water that was her wake, the trailing feather of her smoke bent round to the south on the wind like a quill laid on the sea. Then his eyes changed focus and he caught his breath. The Zeppelin was a thousand feet below, almost between him and *Audacity* so that he had in fact looked past it, missed it as he peered at the ship. He did not understand how he could have done that. The long silver sheath of it sliding slowly below was big enough, for God's sake.

He turned again, slightly, to port so that he was on the same course as the airship. Gallagher had said, "Go at him from above and behind. They used to have a machine-gun mounted in an observation bay on the top but our chaps operating in the North Sea say the Hun gave up manning it a while ago."

Danby inched the stick forward and the nose tipped down, pointed at the Zeppelin. He was watching it over the Aldis sight as he descended in a shallow dive. It swam along like a great silver fish, eerily silent because the whirring clatter of the Camel's Clerget engine blotted out all other sound. A slow fish, growing bigger and coming closer with every second. His eyes flicked to the airspeed dial and he read 140 knots, saw the needle still climbing. His gaze jerked back to the Zeppelin and it was huge, monstrous, rushing up at him. A glance along the top of the Aldis sight showed him the guns would not bear because he was slightly to the left of the Zeppelin so he edged to the right. He was coming down out of the sun as Gallagher had said, so aboard the Zeppelin they wouldn't see him until he was right on top –

He was too close!

He remembered just in time not to snatch at the stick and nursed it back, felt the gravitational pull as the Camel came out of the dive, the nose lifting to sweep along the length of the Zeppelin from stern to bow and about thirty feet above it. As the finned tail of the airship slid towards him he saw the pale wink of flame amidships, and for a split second did not realise what it was. Then he did: the machine-gun *was* manned.

It raced towards him as he planed over the top of the silver monster, the two tiny figures behind the gun growing with terrifying speed. In those first seconds he did not think of firing back, did not think at all but sat with his thumbs idly on the triggers. He felt the shock of the bullets striking the Camel but didn't realise he was flying straight down the German's cone of fire. Then something tore along the side of his head and he flinched, cried out at the pain of it. That flinching swung the Camel out of the cone of fire, banking to port away from the Zeppelin and climbing. *"Watch she doesn't stall when you turn to port!"* Gallagher's voice again. Danby kept pressure on the stick and the climb gentle. Smoke from burning castor-oil poured from the engine and streamed past his face.

Gallagher said heavily, "He's hit."

The Camel curled away from the Zeppelin, turning on one wing, then climbed, smoke trailing from it. The turn became smoother, the climb shallower. On the bridge they waited for the little whirring machine up there to falter, the sun bringing tears to their eyes.

The pain and smoke acted on Danby like icy water. He shuddered and found he had a sudden clarity of vision. The Camel's speed had taken him soaring out ahead of the Zeppelin, turning to port and climbing. He was in a wide, banking circle that would bring him round to lie astern and above the Zeppelin again. He had thrown his best chance away, wasted that huge advantage of surprise, the Zeppelin never expecting an attack by an aircraft here at all, let alone out of the sun. He had not even fired but had simply flown the Camel in like a game-bird to be shot at.

The Clerget was running erratically now and it set the airframe vibrating. He thought he could see black tendrils whipping from the fuselage just abaft the engine, and that meant fire. He remembered how Johnny Vincent looked when they had finally put the fire out and cut him from the wreckage. He pulled down the scarf, leaned over the side of the cockpit and vomited.

He wiped his mouth on the scarf, thinking: You went in too fast. He felt empty, weak, and his head hurt. He eased the Camel out of the turn and put its nose down again just enough for him to see the Zeppelin in the gap between the twin Vickers and the upper wing. He checked his airspeed and this time it was just a hundred knots. He saw the pin-pricks of stabbing flame from the gun on top of the Zeppelin and set the Camel swinging in text book style from side to side of its mean course so that the gunner had to chase his target and missed. The smoke streamed across Danby's face each time he turned, blinded him briefly and made him cough, but he ignored it. Gallagher had said, "Come in nice and steady, give him a long burst."

When he reckoned he was forty feet above the Zeppelin he levelled off behind its tail and laid the Aldis sight on the long silver body. He pressed the triggers and saw the tracer flying; the guns were loaded one round of explosive ammunition to one of tracer. The bursts ran ahead of the Camel like a knife slitting the silver envelope. The flame from the gun on top of the envelope ceased and there was a ball of flame of another kind. He stopped firing and turned away as the Camel passed the bow of the airship, craned his head around to look back and saw the fireball blow itself up into another sun, swallowing the middle of the Zeppelin. The ends of it fell away crumpled and flaming, the fabric flesh stripped from the bones of the frame in seconds as the hydrogen burned.

He hung his head over the side as his stomach heaved again at the sight but only sour bile came up. His engine died. There were flames from the vents at the bottom of the cowling and the underside of the fuselage was smouldering. He looked for *Audacity*.

Gallagher shouted exultantly, "He's got it!" Then he was suddenly silent. The second burst of cheering from the deck also died away. He watched the Camel slide steeply down the sky, its nose turning to point at the ship. The wreckage of the Zeppelin hit the sea but passed unnoticed.

Smith ordered, "Call away the sea-boat's crew!"

The boat was lowered and hung from its davits a foot above the water with a fender to hold it off from the side. All eyes were turned forward to watch the Camel at the leading end of its long streamer of smoke. Gallagher's lips moved soundlessly, as if in prayer. The Camel's nose lifted at the bottom of the dive and it ripped along the surface of the sea, the wheels spurting feathers of white spray to join the brown and yellow smoke. Then the spray thickened for a second before the wheels dug in and the Camel ditched on its nose.

Smith said, "Stop her! Send away the boat!"

The crew were into the boat before *Audacity* stopped, slipped and pulled away as the last of the way came off her. The Camel had smashed into the sea not far off *Audacity*'s bow and the boat was soon alongside the waterlogged remains.

Danby saw the boat coming. When the Camel had stood on its nose the Sutton harness had held him in his seat. It had hurt, but he was not thrown out or injured. Now he pulled the spring clip out of the conical pin, the straps of the harness fell away and he slithered out of the cockpit into the sea. The cold shock of it left him gasping, but the boat's crew quickly found him, clinging to the fuselage, goggles pushed up to show white sockets in a face coated with grease, spattered with castor-oil and grimed by smoke. His teeth chattered so that he could not speak. They hauled him in like a wet sack and took him back to *Audacity*.

Smith watched from aft of the wheelhouse, standing on top of the four-inch gun's housing and close by the funnel, feeling the warmth from it. He saw the petty officer in the boat raise a hand, signalling success, and was thankful.

Elizabeth Ramsay, outside the wardroom on the deck below him, saw the relief on his face and called, "He's safe, then?"

Smith glanced down at her. "Yes."

She harked back to their earlier conversation: "You'll sleep easier."

Smith said, "I sent him up there, but only because I had to. I'm very glad that he's OK."

On his orders they left the Camel to sink and *Audacity* turned on to a course for the Sound. Minutes later McLeod reported, "Sparks picked up a transmission about the time Danby attacked the Zeppelin. He took it down and it was in clear, not coded, but short and garbled. I looked at it with Mrs. Ramsay and we make it something like" – he consulted a signal flimsy – "'Attacked by fighter' – and then a row of figures, their position. Some of that's guesswork but it's the best we could do."

Smith grinned. Getting Danby back on board was like a huge weight lifted from his shoulders and he said cheerfully, "That sounds like the Zeppelin. If she did send a report of us, before that signal, it could only be that we were on a course for Germany. As we were when she was close enough to see."

So *Audacity* approached the Sound unheralded. In the dusk they sighted a destroyer steaming eastward from the Sound. The sun had set and she stood out against the red afterglow like a black paper silhouette, but *Audacity* lay in darkness safely to the south-east of her.

Ross said, "She's steaming full speed. Going to look for survivors from that Zeppelin?"

Smith nodded, hoping that maybe she was leaving the gate unguarded.

They passed through the Sound as they had come, steaming its length at twelve knots, creeping through the shallows of the southern entrance and northern exit with a man at the lead or the motor-boat probing the depth ahead. The night was dark but clear; there was no fog. If they were seen from the Swedish or Danish shores they must have been deemed innocent because no one tried to stop them. The next night they passed the minefield at the mouth of the Kattegat in the same way. It was tense, eye-straining, nerve-stretching, exhausting work and they came out of it hollow-eyed and staring, weary. But *Audacity* was free of the Baltic.

Then that morning Ross heaved a sigh of relief and said, "Compared with going in, that was just too easy."

That jarred on Smith. They were not home yet.

14

Audacity

Audacity made a good twelve knots after clearing the shallows off Göteborg and she was ten miles away when the sun rose astern. McLeod kept the morning watch and Ross had the forenoon. Smith had spent the night on the bridge and now snatched a few hours of restless sleep. When he went out to the wheelhouse shortly before noon he found Ross there.

"What's our position?" Smith hunched his shoulders and dug his hands into his pockets. He felt chilled. It was a fine day with a clear sky and there was even some warmth in the sunlight streaming in through the windows of the wheelhouse. But the cold was in his guts, an illogical apprehension. He stood by Ross at the chart table as the first lieutenant laid the pencil's point on the line of the ship's track that McLeod had drawn. Smith saw they were passing between Denmark and Norway, out of the Skagerrak into the North Sea.

Ross moved the pencil on along the track to rest on a neat, small cross. "Where we meet the escorts, sir. A little over forty miles ahead, less than four hours' steaming."

Smith nodded. The destroyers would be on station now, had patrolled since first light, waiting for *Audacity* as they had every day since she entered the Skagerrak. "Thank you." He was aware of an air of anticipation in the ship as her company shed the tension that had ridden them these last ten days. Wilberforce had been cheerful when he brought Smith's tea: "Everybody's looking forward to gettin' home, sir." Even Ross, gaunt and hollow-eyed, somehow looked more relaxed this morning. Thinking of his young wife? Smith would wait his time to celebrate.

He stood at the front of the bridge. The launching

platform was gone from forward, as were the two boxes from aft, all of them dismantled and jettisoned with the rest of the disguise of the *Anna Schmidt*. The Swedish ensign now flew at the stern while the blue and gold boards hung against the sides below the bridge. This was once again the Swedish *Lulea* and that name was on bow and stern. Wilberforce's concertina wheezed away, jerkily and jauntily, from the steward's pantry below the wheelhouse. Smith wondered if Wilberforce had set out the two deck-chairs below the break of the fo'c'sle. Or maybe it was Danby because he sat in one of them, none the worse for wear now, two days after his crash. Elizabeth Ramsay had the other. They would be sheltered from the wind in the lee of the fo'c'sle, sitting in a sun-trap. The girl wore her cloak but it was thrown open. She was laughing at some remark made by Danby.

Smith asked, "Anything from Sparks?" There had been no signal addressed directly to *Audacity* because he would have known of that at once.

Ross answered, "He's hearing a lot of wireless traffic but you can expect that here." Besides merchant shipping there were the stations ashore in Denmark and Norway, the German Navy at Kiel and Wilhelmshaven, British and German patrols in the North Sea. He grumbled, "Nothing more on that raider." There had been one signal, received the night before last as they passed through the Sound, the destroyer reporting she had lost the raider in the night. Ross muttered, "She gave them the slip in the dark – and there might have been fog, too. So she's still out there, sinking ships; different hunting-ground, that's all."

Smith nodded. The raider would seek fresh fields after being chased by that destroyer. Out into the Atlantic? The Western Approaches? She would have several previously arranged rendezvous with colliers so she could coal from them and keep the sea for weeks on end. Her cruise had barely started. She might head for the South Atlantic . . .

Audacity's voyage was almost done and he would soon exchange the problems of the sea for those of the land. For the first time since that forenoon outside Kirkko, when he thought he would soon be in England, he remembered he had a home, or at any rate a house. That and its mortgage would ensure he stayed a poor man. And there was enough gold in his cabin to solve his money problems ten times over. The bloody gold! It had left a trail of death. The destroyer off Kurgala, the convoy in the Gulf of Riga . . .

Ross glanced at his captain from the corner of his eye, saw the set face and thought, Keep out of his way this morning.

Smith watched them on the deck below the bridge. Danby was making patterns in the air with his hands held flat but turning at the wrists. Smith had seen other pilots use their hands like that to show how they had flown. Elizabeth Ramsay listened intently, a half-smile widening her red mouth, but then her eyes lifted to the bridge and found Smith for a long second before turning away.

Smith's scowl faded and he said, "I'll take a turn around the deck." He left a relieved Ross, dropped down the ladders to the deck aft of the superstructure but then changed his mind and descended further still, to the austere little cabin shared by Gallagher and Danby. The door was hooked back and Smith stepped in, nodded at Gallagher where he lay in his bunk with the blankets humped over the splinted leg. "How is it?"

Gallagher let the book he was reading drop on his chest. "Not bad, so long as I don't move." Pearson had set the broken leg as *Audacity* passed through the Sound, and Gallagher had had a bad time.

Smith chatted with him for a minute or two, thinking that one reason why the flight commander and Danby got on better now was perhaps that Danby had slashed the gap of experience dividing them: they were both Camel pilots now, a breed apart.

He continued his tour of inspection. He was looking at the men and again he saw their relaxation, a looking-forward. He passed under the superstructure and walked the length of the foredeck towards the two deckchairs with Elizabeth Ramsay's eyes on him, turned the corner of the forward hatch and was in the lee of the fo'c'sle, out of the wind and feeling the warmth of the sun.

Danby jumped to his feet as his captain arrived and Smith

waved him down again. "No, don't get up."

But Danby said, "I'm just leaving, sir. I thought I'd look in on Malc and see if he'd like a drink before lunch."

'Malc' would be Malcolm Gallagher. Smith said, "Tell him they're on me."

"Thank you, sir."

Smith watched the young pilot stride away aft and unthinkingly sat down in the chair he had left. Elizabeth Ramsay said, "He's a nice young man. He was telling me that when they get back he's going to Gallagher's place to spend some of his leave. And Gallagher told me he thought he could fix Danby up with a girl." She was laughing.

Smith grinned, "Good luck to him." They would all be making their plans for when they got ashore.

"That boy worships you." The girl was still smiling, but serious. "They all do. They say nobody else could have got them out of the Baltic and safely home."

"Rubbish!" He'd been lucky. And they weren't home yet. He felt that stir of apprehension again. Was it simply due to reaction and overstrung nerves? Or was it because he was tired? He was bloody tired. He took off his cap and ran his fingers through his hair.

Elizabeth Ramsay asked lightly, "What happens to you when we get back?"

Smith shrugged, "There'll be fresh orders for me."

"But not at once." She watched him for a moment as he sat blinking tiredly, gratefully in the sunlight, looking younger now without the cap, but still too thin to be handsome. She said quietly, "I understand you have no family."

Smith frowned. Somebody had been talking. Ross? No, Buckley, who knew a lot more of Smith's private life than anyone else aboard, who made up his own mind in whom he should trust or confide. And who had always been right. Smith's frown cleared. He answered, "That's so."

"I'll have some time on my hands." The girl was off-hand now, clearly hoping, but she would not beg. "I want to go somewhere quiet after this, where I can think, but I don't want to be alone. Do you?"

This was an invitation, and certainly the house in Norfolk was quiet enough. He was used to being on his own but loneliness was a state of mind and he knew he would be lonely there without her. There was an easiness between Elizabeth Ramsay and himself now, the glances no longer sliding away but holding. They were closer. He looked at the woman, her cloak thrown back, the lines of her body unmistakable under the dress. He wanted her but lust was not enough: hers had not been that kind of invitation. She wanted that but a lot more as well.

Did he?

He heard the hail faintly, coming down against the wind from the starboard lookout high on the flying bridge: "Smoke green four-oh!"

Smith stood and said, "Excuse me."

"Of course." She smiled, but as he walked quickly away her smile faded.

McLeod poked his head out of the wheelhouse as Smith reached the bridge. "Too soon to be our escort, sir, unless they're a long way off station."

Ross muttered, "Could be a patrol. Ours – or theirs?"

Smith snatched his glasses from the wheelhouse, ran up the ladder to the flying bridge and joined the starboard lookout. "What d'you make of her?"

The man said, "Can't tell yet, sir, she's just coming hull-up under the smoke, but in a minute or two –"

Nor could Smith see what kind of ship this was so they waited, watched. Ross appeared on the wing of the bridge below and McLeod climbed up to join Smith, standing a pace away. And after a time it was the navigator who said with relief, "She's a merchantman. Looks as if we'll cross her bow a mile ahead of her."

There was reason for his relief. When *Audacity* steamed through the Skagerrak on her way to the Baltic her seeming neutrality was some protection: a German patrol was unlikely to stop her, knowing she could only be bound for a German or neutral port. But now she was headed out into the North Sea and if the ship ahead had been a German destroyer she would certainly have stopped this supposedly Swedish tramp because her cargo could be contraband destined for a British port.

McLeod leaned over the rail to call down cheerfully: "You can start breathing again, old son!"

Ross grinned up at him.

Smith said nothing and kept his face expressionless as he watched the other ship. Seen now with the naked eye, she was just a black break on the horizon under her smoke. He waited for her to come closer, so he could be sure, one way or the other.

McLeod glanced sideways at him, puzzled, then lifted his glasses again.

So did Smith. The ship was a merchantman as McLeod said, like hundreds of others, but there was something about the look of her, the flush-deck, the derricks set low on her masts – no single feature betrayed her but the whole picture called up another stamped indelibly on the mind.

The lookout started, "Sir –" Then he hesitated, not sure.

Ross was. His voice came up. "She's that raider we saw nearly two weeks ago! And under the same Norwegian flag!"

The lookout said, "That's what I thought, sir."

McLeod muttered endorsement: "It looks like her."

Smith let the glasses hang against his chest. "Yes. Send a signal to our escorts: Enemy raider – course, speed, my position."

"Aye, aye, sir." McLeod dropped down the ladder to take the position from his chart.

The destroyers would arrive in an hour but that would be too late for *Audacity*.

The raider's six-inch guns would sink her.

Smith jammed his hands into his pockets and stared out at the ship, thinking. The raider had last been reported north-west of Bergen, about forty-eight hours ago. There had been ample time for her, after slipping the pursuing destroyer in the night, to steam down the coast of Norway and be here now. But why was she? There had been no report of her before she was first sighted by *Audacity* off Kristiansand, when they saw her sink the British tramp, so presumably that had been the beginning of her raiding cruise. Normally such a cruise would last for weeks but here she was, already on a course for home. Why was she returning so soon? Had she suffered damage at the hands of the destroyer? Or developed some fault in her engines that only a dockyard could repair? Either was possible and there could be other reasons, but whatever these were lack of success was *not* one of them. In the Baltic several reports had reached Smith of ships she had sunk and there could well be others he had not heard of.

Ross called, "She's not altering course!"

McLeod was back now from passing Smith's signal to the wireless office and his voice answered gloomily, "She don't need to. We'll pass her close enough."

Which was true if *Audacity* stayed on this course. Alternatively, Smith could turn her south, crack on full speed, and might just reach the sanctuary of Danish territorial waters before the raider could get near her – provided those big six-inch guns did not disable her first. His orders had prevented him reporting the raider's presence that day off Kristiansand, or going to the aid of the tramp. How many men had died since then? How many more would die if she returned to Germany, to cruise again and sink more ships?

He saw McLeod and the others waiting, Buckley up on the flying bridge now with him, Ross on the bridge below, his face upturned. "Mr. Ross! Sound action stations and get the chief on the pipe for me."

"Aye, aye, sir!" Ross vanished into the wheelhouse and Smith dropped down the ladder to the bridge. The alarms buzzed throughout the ship and he heard the clatter of running feet as the crew of the four-inch doubled through the passage from their mess to the gun housing.

As he swung into the wheelhouse Ross said, "The chief's at the pipe, sir."

"Be ready to hoist every ensign we've got. Ours mind; no funny ones this time. And tell the 'panic party' to stand by below the bridge."

"Aye, aye, sir."

Smith stooped over the voice-pipe to the engine room. The raider would call on *Audacity* to stop and show a gun to prove she could enforce the demand, so she would be able to get in the first blow. Smith could open fire first, before the other ship signalled or uncovered her gun, but that would mean a straight fight at comparatively long range and he dared not risk that with the weight of armament so heavily against *Audacity*. The raider mounted four big six-inch guns forward, another gun aft. So: the 'panic party'. He was going to use a variation of an old Q-ship tactic.

"Chief! That German raider we saw off Kristiansand just over a week ago is ahead of us now. We'll be in action soon. Be ready for some rapid changes in revolutions. And I want a drum of oily waste, old cleaning rags – anything that will make a lot of smoke when it burns – forward of the bridge. You've got two minutes."

"Aye, aye, sir."

"Good luck, Chief." Smith shut the lid on the voice-pipe and wondered what the engineers and stokers were thinking now, down below the waterline. Only the thin metal plates of the hull protected them. Shells would rip through it as if it were paper. They were surrounded by boilers and pipes carrying high-pressure steam that could flay the skin from their bodies. The off-watch engineers and stokers were not down there so they might be lucky. Only 'might', because some were on damage-control and the rest in the 'panic party'.

He glanced quickly around the bridge, checking that all was as it should be. McLeod was there, the coxswain at the wheel, Buckley standing at the back – and Elizabeth Ramsay waited by the door.

She asked, "What can I do?"

Where could he send her? Her cabin offered no protection from the shells but that could be said of any part of the ship. And what *could* she do? He asked, "Have you done any nursing?"

"Only when my father was ill."

That was not relevant but never mind. He asked, "Will you go to the sickbay? Pearson, the S.B.A., may need help." That was an understatement with *Audacity* about to fight for her life.

Elizabeth Ramsay bit her lip then said, "I have no experience of wounds."

"The S.B.A. has." Smith would show her no mercy. "And there may be badly wounded or dying men who will need your help, somebody to talk to them, or to hear them."

The girl nodded. "I'll do what I can." She turned and left the bridge.

Smith faced forward. No place in this ship was safe but the sickbay was probably a little less dangerous than many others. This bridge, for one. Ross had seen Smith's orders carried out and gone aft to direct the fire of the twelve-pounder on the poop and to lead the damage-control party when needed, and it would be. He would also command the ship if the bridge took a direct hit.

Smith's mind shied away from that possibility and his duty claimed all his attention. He stepped out of the wheel-house and stood on the bridge. The ship was quiet now. There were men moving around in leisurely fashion on fo'c'sle and poop, as if at work but in fact standing by to man the twelve-pounders. Danby was one of those on the fo'c'sle, face turned towards the bridge. He was ready to relay orders from the voice-pipe to the gun and direct fire if necessary, if the orders did not come because the pipe was severed or the bridge obliterated. The 'panic party', over a score of them, the off-watch black gang augmented by some of the airmen, waited squatting on the deck, hidden below the bulwarks. The raider steamed off the starboard bow and only some two miles distant now. It would not be long before she ordered *Audacity* to stop. He wondered what these men of his thought of him now. He had sworn to take this ship home and they had come very close to returning safe and sound. Would they die cursing him? He had seen the bloody debris of battles and could picture this ship after such a fight. He had seen too much of war. He believed the cause was just but the results sickened him.

He turned to stare at Buckley, standing at ease but watchful at the back of the wheelhouse. Buckley's face was grim as their eyes met and Smith thought, He knows what it's like; he's seen it.

Two of the chief's stokers appeared on the deck forward

228

of the bridge, rolling an oildrum on its rim. Smith could see the oily waste and rags stuffed inside it, the holes punched around the bottom to make it a crude brazier, could sniff the reek of paraffin. He ordered, "Put it by the mast and set it alight. Then stand by with a hose to put it out when I tell you."

One of them lifted a hand to show he'd heard and Smith told McLeod, "Stand by with the lamp." He looked over the rail at the 'panic party', their faces turned up to him. "Remember you're trying to get away from a sinking ship – and *panic!* But make sure the boats are lowered all right." Q-ships had sometimes sent such a party away in the boats after being attacked, in order to make it look as if the ship was abandoned and so persuade the U-boat it was safe to surface. Smith would not wait for a shell or torpedo to hit *Audacity*. The oildrum would serve instead.

It was burning and the smoke swirled aft on the wind, around the bridge and the men gathered below it. One of them swore and some coughed. Smith shouted above it, "Who's in command?"

"I am, sir." A stoker petty officer stood at the front of the group.

Smith told him, "Don't start the motor-boat's engine to begin with. Use the oars. Get away on the port side and steer on south towards Denmark if we don't pick you up. Once the action starts you can use the motor-boat's engine. All clear?"

"Aye, aye, sir."

Smoke was trailing astern now, thick and oily, rolling across the sea. Smith ordered, "Stop her!" The bridge telegraphs jangled and the steady beating beneath Smith's feet slowed and stopped. *Audacity* lay still. Smith looked out at the raider, now less than a mile away and said, "Send, in Swedish, mind: On fire. Need assistance."

McLeod worked the shutter of the lamp, blinking out the signal. Smith waved at the stoker P.O., "Off you go!" Then to Buckley: "I want Lewis guns up here on the bridge, the poop and fo'c'sle head."

"– sir!" Buckley hurried aft but had to wait until the last of the 'panic party' had stumbled up the ladder before he could descend. Smith watched the men mill around the boats carried abaft the wheelhouse, waving their arms. The few airmen among them were novices at this, ignorant of boat work, fumbling and awkward anyway without need to put on an act. The stokers shoved them out of the way, simulated a botch-up of lowering one boat, letting it go with a run and bow first. But they checked it short of the surface of the sea, levelled it, got it into the water.

McLeod reported, "She's acknowledged, sir, and turned towards."

The raider's bow pointed at *Audacity* now. She was a half-mile away and closing at ten or twelve knots, would be alongside *Audacity* in minutes. The boat was pulling away from *Audacity*'s starboard side, leaving the falls dangling from the davits so that the ship had an unkempt, abandoned look. The smoke still billowed from the drum standing by the mast. The two stokers, standing ready with the hose to put out the fire, had cannily stationed themselves upwind out of the choking stench of it. Smith crossed the front of the bridge and saw the motor-boat crabbing away with oars out, the P.O. in the stern looking back for the boat from the starboard side – that rounded the bow now. Both boats headed slowly south, away from the ship.

Smith turned forward and shouted down to the two holding the hose, "Play it on the deck!" The raider would see them soon and they should look as if they were fighting the fire.

He watched the raider come on. She was half as big again as *Audacity*, maybe faster, certainly more heavily armed. It was a fine clear day, a beautiful day. There was neither darkness nor fog to hide *Audacity*. She had to fight this unequal contest in the open. Smith knew he had only one card to play, and that was surprise.

His ruse was working. The raider was slowing, stopping less than a cable's length away, little more than a hundred yards, still not showing a gun.

One man with a Lewis now crouched out of sight on *Audacity*'s bridge-wing, still panting from his run up the ladders. Another lay in hiding on the fo'c'sle head, a third on the poop. The lookouts had gone down from the bridge and now there were only the coxswain, McLeod and Buckley in the wheelhouse, Smith standing outside its door. He looked across at the raider, saw nearly a dozen men on her bridge and the wink of light on the glasses being used by one or two of them. They would see nothing to alarm them, only a tramp stopped and on fire with most of her crew pulling away in the boats. They had seen sights like that often these last two weeks, had been the cause of them. The forward half of *Audacity* was now covered in smoke, the fo'c'sle standing out of it like an island, the men there flat on the deck and so hidden from the sight of those watching from the raider.

Smith thought that now was the time. The raider would not remain stopped indefinitely, nor come closer because she would be wary of the fire spreading to her.

He said quietly, but clearly, "Half ahead. Starboard twenty." To get way on *Audacity* so as to be able to manoeuvre.

McLeod answered from the wheelhouse: "Half ahead. Starboard twenty, sir."

"Guns to concentrate forward of her bridge. All guns commence." Said in that conversational tone still. He heard McLeod repeat that and then bawled at the smoke below, "Put that fire out!"

There was a yelled acknowledgment and the smoke swirled, was cut off from its source as the stokers played the hose on the flaming drum.

The machine-gunner was on his feet and mounting the Lewis on the post on the bridge-wing. Smith shouted at him, "Sweep her bridge!"

"– sir!"

The housing around the four-inch fell apart as if knocked down by a hammer, the barrel of the gun swung out to point at the raider and the breech clashed shut behind the round. The twelve-pounders forward and aft were upright on their mountings and likewise trained out to starboard. There was a second's pause as the gunlayers gave the last quarter-turn to their wheels to bring the sights on. In the near silence he heard the machine-gunner cock the Lewis, saw commotion on the raider's bridge and the bobbing heads of men showing above the high false bulwarks as they ran along her deck. Then the storm broke.

The guns fired a split second apart so the three reports blended in one long, rolling explosion that drowned the chattering of the Lewis. The three shells burst almost as one in the well forward of the raider's bridge in a long yellow flash that filled the well. As the breeches clanged open he felt the slow beat of the engines through the gratings beneath his feet: *Audacity* was moving. He watched from the wing of the bridge as the guns fired again, a second apart this time, each shell bursting in flame in the other ship's well. There was smoke and the dirty orange glare of a fire there; that would be the ready-use charges stored close by the six-inch guns, a few kept there so the guns could be brought into action quickly in an emergency without waiting for ammunition to come up from the magazines. No one stood on her bridge now. The Lewis gunner still fired but in short bursts, changing his target each time, looking for it.

There was white water at *Audacity*'s blunt bow now and a spreading wake astern of her. The White Ensign flew from the jack on the poop, and those on each mast flapped out on the breeze as she got under way. The guns were having to train around as she slipped steadily astern of the raider, and she was turning to swing slowly around that stern. Great holes were smashed in the high bulwarks still in position forward of the German's bridge and through them her big guns could just be seen in the smoke and flames there, still trained forward and aft.

Audacity fired again, two shells bursting again in the well forward of the bridge, the third below the bridge itself. The bulwarks aft of it collapsed now, belatedly yanked down by men unseen behind them. The raider carried a single gun there, mounted on the centre-line and abaft the mast. It looked to be a four-inch and its barrel was training around towards *Audacity*.

Smith bawled into the wheelhouse at McLeod, "Shift target! Gun abaft her bridge!" He had to bawl to be heard above the din of the hammering Lewis guns. Also they were all deafened by the firing and the cotton wool plugged in their ears against that firing.

"– sir!" McLeod's acknowledgment came faintly.

"Ease to ten!"

"Ease to ten, sir!"

To make the turn less tight. The range was opening as *Audacity* steadily edged around to pass astern of the raider. There was white water churning at the raider's stern. She was getting under way and someone was in command of her. Maybe her captain had survived the machine-gunning of his bridge or another officer had come from aft to take over. The Norwegian colours had gone now and she flew the German ensign with its spread eagle.

The flash of the gun aboard the raider came as *Audacity*'s guns fired, so Smith felt their jar in successive shivers through the frame of the ship, then another shudder and a yellow flash right under the fo'c'sle as *Audacity* was hit. The crew of the twelve-pounder sprawled about the fo'c'sle, thrown down by the blast. He saw shells burst aboard the German but the four-inch there still stood and winked flame again. He thought the range had opened to a quarter-mile now, but in gunnery terms that was still point-blank. The shell passed over *Audacity*'s bridge with a ripping shriek. He crouched, too late and uselessly anyway, but instinctively, then straightened and saw McLeod doing the same in the wheelhouse.

He stepped to the rail and looked forward. The deck was empty now, the drum standing in a pool of water and wisping smoke, the two stokers gone to seek some shelter. That hit below the fo'c'sle must have burst in the deserted mess of the twelve-pounder's crew. If a few yards further aft it would have found the gun's magazine and there would have been little left of the fo'c'sle, the gun or its crew. They were in action again, the twelve-pounder firing, recoiling. A damage-control party appeared on the deck below him, Ross at the head of a dozen men, off-watch stokers and airmen who had not gone with the boats. They ran forward to the fo'c'sle. The twelve-pounder aft on the poop was now commanded, in Ross's absence, by the leading-seaman-gunner, who knew his business very well.

233

Smith turned, seeking the raider. *Audacity* was passing astern of her now and her single gun aft was hidden by her poop and so unable to fire. He thought: Four big guns forward, a smaller one aft. It made control easy, maybe suited the trim of the ship. More than enough, anyway, for her job of sinking merchantmen, more than enough to finish *Audacity* if only they could all be brought into action.

The four-inch slammed behind him, then the twelve-pounders. *Audacity* was still in the slow turn, had passed across the raider's stern and now was opening her port side. That single gun aft was in sight again, just, and in action: there was the flame of it. The layer must have fired the instant *Audacity* moved into his sights. Was the raider turning? He felt the shudder and saw the flash as *Audacity* was hit again, this time between superstructure and poop. The bomb-throwers' messes were there. He saw Ross and his damage-control party running aft again, so there was clearly no danger now from the hit below the fo'c'sle.

The raider *was* turning to port, so she would be broadside to *Audacity*. There was still smoke forward of her bridge but streaming away to starboard on the wind now she was under way. The bulwarks were down at last, exposing the two six-inch guns on this port side, one of them leaning at a drunken angle, surely from a direct hit. But the other was manned and through his glasses he saw the barrel trained out to point at *Audacity*. Then it fired, the muzzle licking out a long red tongue and a second later the shell roared over *Audacity* with a sound like a train.

McLeod, straightening from a crouch again, bellowed at Smith: "That was a big 'un!"

It was, and just one hit from one of those guns would – He ordered, "Full ahead! Hard astarboard!"

"Full ahead, hard astarboard, sir!" McLeod's face, turned to him, was grimy from the smoke blown into the wheel-house, shouting mouth showing pink. Smith knew his own face would be as filthy. He could taste the burnt oil on his lips as he could smell the burnt cordite from the guns. They were still firing, the breeches clanging open then slamming shut on the round with the regularity of a

234

trip-hammer. The enemy had been hit at least a score of times already, while *Audacity* –

"Sir!" It was a messenger come running to the bridge, coated with dirt, oil and soot, face black with it but Smith knew him: one of the stokers who ran aft with Ross a minute ago.

"Yes?"

"First Lieutenant says that hit forrard started a fire in the lamp room an' paint store but it's out now." He added, "Made a right mess o' the gunners' mess an' all – if ye see what I mean, sir."

Lamp room and paint store were right forward in the bow and the gunners bunked just aft of them. Smith said, "I can believe it. Very good."

The stoker trotted away to rejoin Ross and his party, now hidden below deck and seeking the damage from the hit taken aft. Smith thought that the gunners' mess under the fo'c'sle head would be inches deep in water after the hosing and hard lying for them tonight.

God knew where they would be tonight.

The coxswain had the wheel hard over and *Audacity* was beginning to turn but too late, she was still starboard side to the raider. Smith saw a long finger of flame poke out again as the six-inch fired. He had time to suck in a breath and tense. Then the blast hurled him against the rail and almost toppled him over it to fall on the deck below. He shoved himself away from the rail, holding his middle where it had cut into him, blinked eyes filled with tears from the pain and peered to see where *Audacity* was hit. Not the four-inch, that was still in action and fired as his head turned towards it. But there was a huge hole torn in the side of his cabin –

McLeod appeared at the door of the wheelhouse. "It burst on the other side, sir, but no fire."

So there would be hard lying for Smith, too – if he was lucky. He turned towards the raider again, looked at her over *Audacity*'s bow that was now swinging rapidly in a tight turn and he could feel the quickening pulse of the engines as they began to work up to full speed. Only the twelve-pounder on the fo'c'sle would bear and was in action, the others masked by the superstructure and funnel. The burst of its shell was just one brief, brighter flame against a background of smoke and fire. The raider was burning in a dozen places and she was off *Audacity*'s port bow now as that bow continued to swing to starboard.

Another shell from the six-inch crashed into the sea off the port side, too far away to do damage but in the engine room they would be deafened by the clanging shock of it on the hull. The raider was now off the port beam and sliding away astern. "Midships!"

"Midships, sir!"

To cross the wake of the other ship and take *Audacity* out of the field of fire of that murderous six-inch gun. It had not fired again although its layer would still have *Audacity* in his telescope sight. Some of its crew could be wounded, maybe the layer himself, or ammunition not reaching the gun from the magazine. It would be a chaos of smoke, flame and din, dead and wounded, aboard the German now.

Audacity was almost astern of her when the single gun abaft her bridge fired and hit again between *Audacity*'s bridge and poop. Smith was on the port side of the wheelhouse, hanging out of its door by one hand and he saw the raider was on fire aft as well as forward, raising a yellow and brown curtain that almost hid the gun behind it.

Then she blew up, the blaze erupting in a fountain of wreckage that soared higher than the masts and fell around her in the sea. Her stern sagged, she stopped and across the half-mile of sea came the whistling roar as she blew off steam.

McLeod stood at Smith's shoulder and said, "My God!" And, "She's lowering boats."

She was. One was in the sea already and men clambering down into it while another was swung out and hung in the davits. Smith ordered, "Cease fire!"

McLeod demurred, "She hasn't struck, sir."

Smith glared at him. *"Cease firing!"*

"Sir!" McLeod jerked back from that cold glower and stooped over the voice-pipe to the guns: "Check! Check! Check!"

236

There was an ear-ringing silence. Smith was aware that the German ensign still flew from the raider's mast. That might mean defiance or fouled halyards or just that no one had been ordered to strike it. The raider fired no gun, her crew were leaving her and she was sinking. Smith would not continue to fire into her.

He asked, "Where are our boats?"

"About a mile south of us, sir."

"Starboard twenty." To run down to them. Minutes later he saw them heading to meet the ship, the motor-boat with her engine running and towing the other boat. He had scarcely expected to see them again; they had not expected to see *Audacity*. He had thought she might survive and still escape but dared not envisage the damage she would suffer, outgunned as she was. Devising a plan based on surprise to neutralise that enemy advantage was one thing; making it work was another.

Audacity recovered her boats and started to work up to twelve knots. The lookouts reported smoke to the west and McLeod said, "That must be our escort, sir." Smith looked out to starboard where the raider still lay, a mile away. She had settled, was decidedly lower in the water. Some of her boats were still alongside but others had pulled clear of her. The Danish coastline was not far. The raider still flew her ensign but she was sinking, no doubt of it. Smith was glad he had stopped firing into her.

He turned and went into his cabin, morbidly curious to see what damage had been done by that one big six-inch shell. He stood by the door and looked from the hole in the starboard side where the shell had entered, the edges of the steel plate ragged and bent as if hacked by a giant tin-opener, to the bigger hole to port. There the shell had burst and all that side of his cabin had disappeared. His bunk had gone and the gold with it, blasted into the sea, cut out of his ship like a cancer.

He heard Ross behind him in the wheelhouse: "I thought you'd like to know, sir, that we haven't lost a man. Pearson says there's not even a bad wound."

"Thank you."

That was the main thing. There would be an inquiry into the loss of the gold but it would have to be secret and he could not be held guilty. The verdict would be 'loss by enemy action'. To hell with it. He was taking his ship and his crew home safe.

He heard Ross's voice faintly, passing on the news to McLeod, the pair of them out on the wing of the bridge. Then McLeod's voice loud, startled: "Here! She's fired a gun!"

Smith turned quickly back into the wheelhouse. He heard no roar like an express train, knew nothing.

He lay in the corner of the wheelhouse, right under the screen. Ross was saying, "Don't move him! Find where he's bleeding! *Careful!*"

McLeod: "All right. Where's Pearson? Get Pearson up here on the double!"

Ross answered, "I've sent for him. What's that bloody Hun doing?"

"Nothing. She's laid over on her side. She got that one round off then rolled. She'll fire no more. Just that one."

Smith could see them now, blank-faced with shock, kneeling either side of him. Two yards away to the right stood the coxswain at the wheel, legs planted solidly against the lift and fall as *Audacity* steamed westward. The door of his cabin hung sagging on its hinges. He thought the shell must have burst in there, lightning striking twice in the same place. Not supposed to happen.

He was bleeding, could taste it where it ran down his face and into his mouth, could feel it under his hands where they rested limp on the gratings, saw it around his feet. He was cold. All this cruise it had been cold. Ice, fog, shoals. He was tired.

Pearson shoved in at the wheelhouse door, his satchel of dressings swinging from one hand, Elizabeth Ramsay following and Buckley bringing up the rear. Ross and McLeod scrambled to their feet out of the way, Pearson and the girl took their places. Buckley crouched at Smith's feet.

The girl asked, "Can't you take him down?"

"Got to take a look at him first, ma'am." Pearson's fingers were already busy.

Smith spoke to Elizabeth Ramsay: "Listen. I have a house. Use it. Buckley, you hear that? Ross?" He paused for their muttered answers, then: "You're witnesses." He was tired and closed his eyes.

Pearson's voice said, "Right. Where's that stretcher?"

"Here." That was McLeod.

Smith said, "Buckley? I made a right balls of it this time. Look after her, for God's sake."

Ross searched for the lamp. The two destroyers, in line ahead, were closing rapidly with sterns tucked down and big white bow-waves. He framed the signal in his head: 'Request doctor for serious wounded . . .' while his mind grappled with the realisation that he commanded *Audacity* now. He found the lamp and went out to the bridge-wing.

David Cochrane Smith was not passed fit for duty until late in October of that year and was at the house in Norfolk at the time of the Armistice. Early in 1919 he was requested to leave the Navy and did so with the rank of captain. In April he sailed for Yokohama to take up new employment in Japan. Elizabeth, his wife for almost a year, did not go with him. She was expecting their first child.

If you have enjoyed this book and would like to receive details of other Walker Adventure titles, please write to:

Adventure Editor
Walker and Company
720 Fifth Avenue
New York, NY 10019